All The Courage We Have Found

BOOKS BY CARLY SCHABOWSKI

The Ringmaster's Daughter

The Watchmaker of Dachau

The Rainbow

The Note

CARLY SCHABOWSKI

All The Courage We Have Found

bookouture

Published by Bookouture in 2022

An imprint of Storyfire Ltd.
Carmelite House
50 Victoria Embankment
London EC4Y 0DZ

www.bookouture.com

ISBN: 978-1-80314-624-9
eBook ISBN: 978-1-80314-623-2

This book is a work of fiction. Whilst some characters and circumstances
portrayed by the author are based on real people and historical fact, references
to real people, events, establishments, organizations or locales are intended
only to provide a sense of authenticity and are used fictitiously. All other
characters and all incidents and dialogue are drawn from the author's
imagination and are not to be construed as real.

To Natasha, whose kindness and thoughtfulness makes me proud to call you my sister.

PROLOGUE

He had arrived too late. The bells of Saint Jerome rang mournfully as he sprinted up the staircase and flung open the door to find her lying on the bed, her eyelids half-closed, the eyes underneath seeing nothing.

The child's bed she lay on had been empty for days, weeks now, its linens washed and stored away as if they would be used again when both she and Hugo knew they would not. Yet, she had come here to rest, clasping the small teddy bear to her breast.

He knelt beside her and whispered a prayer, not knowing whether he still believed in God any more, released the bear from her grasp and left, knowing that he would never return.

PART ONE

1942

ONE

HUGO

Vannes, France, October 1942

Cécile had left early, and Hugo rolled onto his side to find her. The sheet was still warm where her plump behind had rested, and he placed his hand flat on the mattress so his palm could feel the spot until the sheet cooled once more.

Hugo wondered why she had left – none of the others did. Usually, they stayed – stayed too long until he had to ask them to leave, to make some excuse: 'I'm moving to England,' he would say to their crying faces; he would wipe away their tears. 'I shall remember you fondly, with all the love in my heart.' The crying girls would nod, smile and finally leave.

He did not stay in bed too long – it was already midday and he needed to tend to his writing that lay in unhappy and messy heaps around the house.

He found his cigarettes on the floor next to the bed, lit one and walked into his office still naked and stood in front of the windows, ignoring the curling pages of his latest attempt at an essay and watched as the waning autumnal sun streamed light upon his olive and lemon groves.

Why had she left? He would have liked her to have stayed a little while longer, to check those curves on her body once more. He tapped his foot impatiently on the tiled floor.

Making up his mind, he stalked away from the window and dressed hurriedly in trousers and a white shirt that was splattered still with dirt from the previous day's activities in the vineyards. He did not bother with shoes – never did, what was the point? – and quickly walked out of his house and climbed onto his bicycle. He had to find Cécile. His work with her was not yet finished.

The small commune of Vannes nestled itself along the north-western coast of France, and Hugo's faded white-bricked stuccoed house looked out onto the Gulf of Morbihan that brought a daily salty breeze which cooled him as he cycled. He looked out over the sea and imagined what lay further; beyond the Gulf led to the Celtic Sea, and then to English shores. He had visited London once or twice and had enjoyed his time there, although the English women were always timid, so difficult, a challenge. Hugo smiled to himself as he cycled; he had always enjoyed a challenge.

He skirted past the rocky steps which led to the small beach, and the town rose up before him like Poseidon breaking through the white crashing waves, standing full in all his glory. He rode quickly around the walls of the Bastille, ignoring the few scattered German soldiers that sat, bored and smoking, barely noticing him as he rode on.

He left his bike propped up against the church and then remembered his bare feet just as a woman shrouded in black, a French widow with bowed legs, noticed them. She clicked her tongue at him in disapproval as she passed.

Unusually for him, he smoothed down his wrinkled shirt before he began his short walk to the bakery where Cécile worked alongside her father, who was not much older than Hugo himself.

He stood tall as he walked and could feel the looks of the townsfolk and imagine their thoughts: *There goes the mad writer, no shoes, do you see? Ah, he's no harm, though, no harm. Doesn't go to church, mind. He tithes, though. Gives money to anyone who needs it. Leave him.*

He smiled and nodded at the local chief of the gendarmerie, Pierre, who stood with his arms folded. Hugo had always thought of Pierre as a decent sort until the Germans had arrived, but now he took his new role under the regime a little too seriously – always watching, always noting things down in his notepad as if Hitler himself would be interested in what was happening here.

'*Bonjour*, Monsieur Hugo.' Pierre stopped him. 'You realise you have no shoes again.'

Hugo smiled. 'I do. They won't be interested, you know,' he jibed.

'Who won't?' Pierre scrunched up his eyes into little slits. 'Interested in what?'

Hugo shook his head and laughed.

'You should dress better,' Pierre said. 'People think you're mad.'

'Maybe I am.'

'You know what they do with mad people? Same as Jews. Take you away.'

'You wouldn't do that to me, would you, Pierre? After all, I've wine that needs to be drunk and who else will do it?'

A thin smile crept onto Pierre's face. 'I'll pick up a few bottles tomorrow. Test them. See if they are good enough.'

Hugo continued his walk to the bakery and waited in line with the three women who stood in front, all with wicker baskets; all with a chattering air of gossip. Cécile caught his eye once, then she ignored him and tended to her customers alongside her father, Henri, whose ruddy face never cooled after so many years in front of the stoves. Finally, it was his turn, and he smoothed his shirt once more.

'What can I get the famous writer?' Henri cried, his face getting redder as he grinned. 'You have come late, you know. I barely have anything left.' He spread his arms wide to indicate the empty shelves.

'I'm not so famous any more,' Hugo replied.

'Pah!' Henri spat the word. 'We think you are.'

'You're too kind. But I've had nothing published for years.'

'You'll always be famous to me,' Henri said, then looked distractedly at a German soldier who had stopped outside the bakery, casually smoking a cigarette.

Hugo followed his gaze and watched the soldier who seemed interested in Cécile, who had started to sweep the floor.

'Cécile,' Hugo beckoned her.

She turned to face him and smiled. 'You came to find me,' she said.

'You did not stay.'

'And why would I?' She laughed at him, then flounced away, her skirts dancing as she walked.

He stood for a moment, flustered then annoyed. Then, he straightened up and walked out of the bakery – he knew she would be back; he was sure of it.

He followed the cobbled street to the doctor's surgery, noticing how quiet it was even though many refugees had come to the town from Paris, wedging themselves into any available space – barns, hotels, empty bedrooms. His friend, old Dr Maurice, had taken in a young mother and child and had implored Hugo to allow someone to stay in his home too, which he had so far resisted.

He thought of this as he walked, and a gnawing of guilt scratched at his belly. He should do more, he knew, but also he was afraid to. He had lived alone for ten or more years now, and the solitude calmed him – he was unsure of who he would become if he had no sanctuary.

He stopped outside the surgery and walked inside to an empty waiting room and a closed office door.

'Maurice!' he sang out. 'It is I, your one and only friend!'

He heard a creak of floorboards as Maurice gently padded to the door, opened it and without a word of greeting retreated to his desk.

'I have other friends, you know,' Maurice replied dryly, as Hugo entered.

Hugo sat on the chaise longue. 'None as good as me.'

He watched as Maurice shuffled through some papers on his desk, his brush of a moustache covering his top lip as groomed and straight as the bristles in a blue whale's mouth. Hugo wondered if Maurice's moustache was there for a reason; just like the whale that caught krill between those slivery whiskers, did Maurice too use it to catch crumbs of food?

Maurice finally looked at him and, raising one bushy eyebrow, asked, 'You think very highly of yourself today – it seems you're in an exuberant mood, no?'

'I am, I am indeed.'

'Let me guess,' Maurice said, and placed his fingertips together under his chin as he thought. 'A girl. Yes. A girl. But not just any girl... *Cécile!*' Maurice snapped his fingers. 'It is, isn't it? You've finally got what you wanted.'

Hugo smirked at him.

'You're a scoundrel, you know.' Maurice's tone quickly changed. 'Running about with anything that moves. Look at the state of you – no shoes again, dirty clothes. Why do you care so little for yourself?'

'I care plenty enough, Maurice.'

Maurice harumphed as he began to pack his pipe with tobacco. 'You can at least care more for others.'

'Ah, this again,' Hugo said. 'Just because I take no interest in this war, in politics, you think I don't care for others? That just isn't so. Guess what arrived last night?'

This question stopped Maurice, who finally smiled. 'The supplies.'

'Indeed yes. The gauze you asked for and the medication. I care for you, you see. You asked me to get you a few things, *et voilà*,' Hugo raised his arms in a flourish, 'they appear as if by magic.'

'It is a magic trick, yes, I agree.' Maurice lit his pipe and sucked hard at it until puffs of smoke billowed out. 'You enjoy the sleight of hand, I think. On the one hand, your father was German, so you curry favour with our occupiers, offering them wine, making friends with them so that they don't see what the other hand is doing. *Et voilà*, your Frenchness comes to the fore and you show that indeed you care about this war.'

'You are trying to draw me into a discussion, Maurice,' Hugo said. 'A discussion that will end with us quarrelling again. I care for you and myself, that's all.'

'I see the goodness in you, Hugo.' Maurice grinned, the pipe between his teeth. 'I don't know why you want to keep it so hidden, or maybe I do—'

'And now I shall take my leave of you.' Hugo stood, then his hand shot out and grabbed a manila folder.

'Gah!' Maurice stood quickly and tried to reach across to grab the folder back. 'Patient files, Hugo. Confidential and you know it!'

Hugo quickly flicked through the papers. 'Madame Claudette has piles again. I would treat them with a poultice, I think.'

'So you're a doctor now.' Maurice finally managed to snatch the file back.

'I am – well, I was.'

'You were a Doctor of Philosophy as far as I can remember. That does not translate to medicine.'

Hugo shrugged. 'Who's to say? What is medicine but learning and remembering ailments and treatments?'

'Ah look, the philosopher has returned!' Maurice cried. 'Why do you not go and do something useful and write your thoughts down – finally finish that book? You do nothing all day but annoy me, drink and sleep.'

'Monsieur?' A voice interrupted them.

Hugo turned to see Madame Claudette hovering in the doorway, her cardigan pulled close to her body even though the temperature outside was unusually warm for this time of year.

'Ah, please, please.' Maurice indicated for Madame Claudette to enter and with a small nod of the head made it clear that Hugo should leave.

'Tonight?' Hugo quickly asked Maurice.

Maurice nodded his agreement and closed the door on Hugo, the chatter from Claudette suddenly rushing forth now she had the full attention of the doctor.

Hugo lay on his chaise longue, listening to the upbeat jazz of Raymond Legrand and his orchestra whilst he smoked and stared at the ceiling. He could feel the bottle of red he had already drunk coursing through his veins, making his face warm and his thoughts numb. He liked it when his thoughts felt this way – as if they were on a fluffy cloud somewhere, in the light, not giving in to the dark. He sat up and three photographs fell to the floor. He stared at them for a moment, forgetting that he had earlier looked at them, then placed them on his chest. Now, he gathered them up and put them back in the bookcase drawer where they belonged.

A knock at the door, three quick raps, indicated that Maurice had arrived, and he padded to open it for his friend.

'You're late,' Hugo said, as he opened the door.

'And you're drunk,' Maurice replied, closing the door carefully behind him.

Hugo tripped over a discarded bottle that languidly rolled on its side, then disappeared under the couch. He flopped down on the sofa, raising his right leg and balancing his left on it, watching as Maurice eyed the scattered mess of papers and books that had found homes on the floor and side tables.

'You need a cleaner,' Maurice said, and removed a sheaf of papers from the armchair and set them on the dusty floor.

'I had one – Cécile,' Hugo replied. 'I left you a drink on the side table there – see? Red. A vintage year.'

'And why is your house still a pigsty if Cécile was cleaning for you?' Maurice asked.

Hugo rolled his eyes, then laughed. 'What can I say?' He raised his arms up in question.

'You're barbaric,' Maurice said.

'Drink your drink, then I'll get you the supplies.'

'Who brought them this time?' Maurice asked.

'A dear friend from Marseilles. A pleasant chap. Someone I once knew from a poker game.'

'And you trust him?' Maurice asked.

'Sure, why not?' Hugo answered.

'I worry, you know. I worry you're not being careful enough.'

'Ah, Maurice! It is the black market. Of course I'm being careful. But you have to take risks, no? Although I tell you it is not so much a risk as it is simply being robbed of most of my money for things that you and I need. A thinning of the old wallet, so to speak.'

'Indeed, indeed.' Maurice's eyebrows were knitted together as he looked at the wine in his glass.

'What is it, Maurice?' Hugo asked.

'I need your help, Hugo,' he said quietly. 'It is apt that you talk of taking risks. I need you to do something for me, but you have to promise you will be careful with this.'

'More gauze? Some wine perhaps?' he asked, then laughed.

'No. Not wine. I need your help – seriously.'

'Then I shall seriously help you,' Hugo said.

'Can you be sensible for one moment of your life? Sit up, look at me.' Maurice's voice had taken on an edge that Hugo had not heard before, and despite himself, he raised himself to a seated position and listened.

'What is it?'

Hugo watched as Maurice leaned back in his chair and stroked his thick greying moustache. 'I need you to let someone stay here. Just for one night.'

'Who?'

Maurice did not answer and lifted the glass to his lips where his brush of a moustache seemed to take a thick gulp of the red.

'A friend, sort of.'

'A friend? A lady friend?'

Maurice shook his head. 'It's nothing like that. I've wanted to confide in you for some time, Hugo, and it is not that I did not trust you, but you know how you can be when you have had a few too many.' He paused.

Hugo felt his face flame but said nothing.

'The thing is, I've done more than just allow a few refugees from Paris to stay in my home. A little more than that—' He stopped as the record began to scratch against the needle, and Hugo jumped up to rescue it and put it back on course.

'You are talking of the resistance, aren't you, Maurice?' Hugo asked him softly.

'I am.'

'And you want someone to stay here?'

'I do.'

Hugo kept watching the record spin and spin. 'I can't.'

'And why's that? It's one night. That's all, Hugo. One

damned night! Can you not, for once in this thing you call a life, raise a hand to help out when it is needed the most?' Maurice suddenly yelled at him.

Hugo turned away like a petulant, scolded child and sat back on the sofa.

'Come now, Hugo.' Maurice's tone was gentler now. 'I know you want to pretend the war isn't happening – no, not just the war, life. I see you, day in day out, living in a fantasy world, escaping from it, but you can't escape forever, you must begin to live again—'

Hugo raised a hand to cut him off. 'I do just fine.'

'But you care for nothing and no one. You can do this one thing. You sit passively whilst a war is literally raging around you and you do nothing.'

'And what would you have me do, Maurice? Fight? I have a bad leg and a weak heart, so you'd have me do what? Why should I care if the Germans come, or if they win? In fact, I welcome them, they can shoot me, and I won't have to continue in this futile existence as you have so plainly described it to me.'

Exasperated, Maurice stood. 'Do something!' he shouted. 'Just something. You have the gendarmes and soldiers in your pocket and the local mayor and politicians. You're a half-breed of German and French – the perfect combination. You believe yourself to be French, yet through your father you're able to pretend to side with them – you're immune.'

'My father was a pacifist,' Hugo said, as he held a cigarette between his teeth, then lit it with a quick flash of a gold lighter.

'So? And are you a pacifist too, O great philosopher?'

Hugo shrugged. 'Does it matter?'

'Yes.'

'Why?'

'I'm not going to have one of our debates now, Hugo. This is not the time.'

'I would have thought it was the perfect time.'

'Look. You are more intelligent than me, by half, and I'm sure you can argue a way out of answering a question directly, or hide yourself away behind the big words and theories you have digested over the years. But I don't want to hear it, Hugo. You weren't always like this – as a boy—'

'As a boy I was foolish,' Hugo said. 'Full of stupid dreams and ambition, and look where it got me.'

Maurice walked up to him, and, for a moment, Hugo thought the old man was going to slap him, but Maurice simply sat by his side and placed his hand on Hugo's knee.

'Hugo,' he said, his voice quiet, calm. 'I need you, as a friend, to do this one thing for me. It can be your way of helping, of being active in the fight that we face. Please. I ask you this one thing. It is one person who will be here one night and then they will leave, across the shores to England and you shall be done with it, and you can go back to eating, drinking and making merry with whichever woman of this town you have not yet claimed. You can go back and live in your half-world reality where you don't care if you live or die.'

Hugo looked into the eyes of his friend and knew that this time Maurice would have to win.

'Fine,' he said. 'One night. That's all.'

TWO

KASIA

Poland, October 1942

A light rain fell as Kasia walked along the pavement, her small heels click-clacking, her hands deep inside the pockets of her long overcoat. Underneath, the two sweaters she wore bulked and stretched at the buttons of her coat. She stopped briefly under a streetlamp and awkwardly tried to smooth the fastenings.

A man walked past her and dipped his hat, to which she replied with a quick smile and a nod, then continued to walk through the rain-slicked streets of Warsaw.

A convoy of German jeeps rumbled past, and she raised her head to look at them briefly, feeling a knot in her stomach at the insignia of the Reich that glared at her as the vehicles moved on.

All around her the city was a wasteland of half-bombed buildings, crumbling into the nightly shadows. A skinny dog emerged from a pile of bricks that had once been a magnificent milliner's, and in the early days of living in Warsaw, she had gone with Maja many a time to try on exotic-looking hats with plumes of ostrich feathers or adorned with giant bows. The dog looked sullenly at her, and she wished she had something to offer him.

Soon the wall of the ghetto emerged, the razor wire that topped it almost glistening under the streetlamps. 'Enticing,' she once told Marta. 'Like you can't help but want to know what it feels like on your fingertips...'

Marta had laughed at her – that quick burst of a laugh that she gave when she was impatient. 'Don't ever find out, Kasia,' she had told her. 'Otherwise, you'll be back working at a desk. Don't make me regret this.'

That conversation had been six months ago now, Kasia recalled. Six months of nightly visits to the ghetto, sometimes her, sometimes Marta or one of the other women. All of them with goods hidden about their person – medical supplies, food, guns. It had been exhilarating at first for Kasia. She had been released from her desk, from radio operating duties, under-standing codes, ciphers, and relaying messages to the others in the organisation to being in the field herself. Not that it had come about in an agreeable way: there had been many losses, women caught and killed, or injured, and Marta had had to take a risk on Kasia, 'the bookworm' as she called her.

It wasn't exhilarating any more, though. On nights like this, when the moon hung so low and hid itself behind clouds, when the rain soaked through to your underwear and when every sound made the small hairs on your neck stand to attention, it made Kasia wish for her desk.

Suddenly, she shook her head at the selfish thought. *I wish for my desk? These people wish for their lives.*

Soon, she reached the gates on the south-east of Chłodna Street, and felt her heart begin to race – where was he?

She looked once more at the two guards who stood at the entrance – she didn't know them.

She should not stop, she knew, but she had already slowed her pace. If she carried on walking now, it would look more suspicious, so she stood still and smiled – the smile that Marta had always said could win a thousand men's hearts in a second.

The two faces of the guards she did not know were impassive – one young – too young, the other in his twenties with a thin moustache that looked as though someone had drawn it on.

'*Dobry wieczór,*' the guard with the thin moustache said, as she approached. His accent was wrong – German, she assumed, trying out the mother tongue of her people.

'I'm looking for Hans,' she replied in German.

'One of his women, heh?' the man with the moustache replied. 'He said you would be coming. Nice, too. Look at you – perfect – green eyes I think?' He leaned close to her, so close she could smell his stale breath and see the bloodshot veins in his eyes.

'Want to be one of my women?' He grinned.

She stepped back and realised she had made a mistake. Always stand your ground. Always be confident. She took a silver cigarette case from her pocket and with a wide smile offered one to both guards. The younger one did not smoke, the moustachioed guard told her.

'More for us then.' She twinkled at him.

He laughed and lit her cigarette for her and then his own.

'Tell me, where can I meet women like you? Hans says he met you in a bar, yes? Which bar is this? Can you introduce me to some of your friends?'

'Why, a man such as you shouldn't be frequenting the kinds of bars that Hans does,' she said, then blew out a plume of smoke. 'Hans likes his beer, a fight now and then, but you,' she took a step nearer closer to him, 'I can tell that you're far more sophisticated.'

He seemed to like the compliment and leaned against the wall, his eyes scanning her from head to toe.

'You'd better not be resting,' a voice came from the dark, then into the light came Hans.

Hans. Thank God.

Hans grinned as soon as he saw her, and she allowed him to kiss her gently on her cheek, even though her hands itched to wipe it away.

'You must be quick,' he told her. 'Half an hour and no more.'

'What's this then?' The man with the moustache leaned in to listen.

'Nothing that will trouble you,' Hans replied, and led Kasia through the gate into the darkened quiet streets.

'You have something for me,' he said, as soon as they were a few feet away.

She dug into her pocket and pulled out an envelope thick with money, which he grabbed from her and placed into his own coat. The transaction complete, she made her way quickly to number 126, a three-storey house that Kasia could imagine had looked quite grand in its prime but now was shrouded in darkness, litter in the gutters and fallen leaves that had stuck to the wet pavement, squelching underfoot.

She climbed the few steps to the front door and knocked, once, then a rap of three, then two more. A shadowy figure appeared behind the frosted glass and opened the door a few inches.

'It's Kasia,' she whispered.

The figure did not respond but opened the door wide enough for Kasia to enter, then quicky closed it behind her. She could see that the figure was Janusz, a man in his seventies that she had met a handful of times. He always spoke little, and his face seemed to be always etched with pain.

A small bulb lit the hallway, the other light fittings bare, and Kasia followed the shuffling figure down the narrow hallway to the small kitchen at the rear. Before Janusz opened the door, he extinguished the one bulb.

'Eight o'clock,' he said. 'No more after eight.'

At the table four women sat, stumps of candles melted onto the wooden top.

'Kasia,' the elder woman of sixty or so stood, and enveloped her in an embrace.

'Lena,' Kasia greeted her, then kissed her papery thin cheek. She could smell an odour coming from Lena, musky, almost soil-like, and without meaning to, moved her head a fraction away from the old woman's neck.

'I know, I smell,' Lena said simply. 'So many of us here now, we cannot bathe as much.'

Kasia looked to the other women, none of whom she had met before and quickly greeted each one, hugging them to her, feeling their thin frames relax into her warmth. Once all the women had been introduced to her, she quickly undid her over-coat and removed the two bulky sweaters she wore and handed them to Lena.

Next, from the lining of her coat where extra deep pockets had been sewn, she removed bread, cheese, and porridge oats, again ferried away by Lena who would distribute them evenly throughout the house.

'It's not much this evening,' Kasia said. 'Marta will come tomorrow with more.'

'And the weapons?' Janusz asked in a hoarse voice.

'Again tomorrow,' Kasia said. 'But it will be the doctor who brings them.'

Janusz nodded, then sat at the kitchen table and stared at his hands as if something would magically appear.

'I'm sorry,' Kasia said helplessly. 'I wish it were more. It was hard to get in the past few nights.'

'You got a new one?' Lena asked.

Kasia nodded. 'Hans.'

'Bet he couldn't believe his luck, eh?' Lena let out a raspy laugh, and the other women, who had up to that point been warily looking at Kasia, now laughed along with her. 'She's good with them is our Kasia.' Lena looked to the other women. 'A few bribes, a few dates, and here she is, our angel from outside.'

Lena suddenly held out her hand, and Kasia knew what she wanted.

'I almost forgot,' she said, then drew out the last gift for Lena and the others – cigarettes.

Lena lit a cigarette and Kasia watched her as she smoked. The old woman suddenly seemed lost in the moment, savouring the small pleasure.

'I hope this kills me soon,' Lena said. 'My chest is bad, you know. This will help it along.'

'Lena,' her husband said sharply. 'Don't say such things.'

'So you'd rather they kill you?' Lena asked.

Janusz did not answer and resumed looking at his hands.

'I need you to do something for me,' Lena said.

'Of course,' Kasia replied. 'What do you need?'

'Get someone out.' Lena dragged heavily on her cigarette.

'It can be arranged, you know it can, but it's dangerous, Lena. They need to understand that.'

Lena shook her head. 'They can't understand that, and we can't wait. You have to get them out now. Tonight.'

Kasia almost laughed, then checked herself. 'Impossible.'

'You, my dear, can do anything you put your mind to. And I need you to do this for me. You said that this Hans likes you, yes? He likes you on his arm at the bar. He likes the money you're giving him, so he lets you come and go?'

Kasia nodded.

'Well then. He'll let you go with them.'

'What? You think I am to simply walk out with someone? It can't be done, Lena.'

'It can and it must. Come.'

Lena placed her palm flat on the table and raised herself with a grimace, then peeled away one of the stubs of candle, holding it carefully in her hand as she shuffled from the room.

Kasia followed her down the dark hallway, then into what was once, she supposed, a living room, but now housed around six people, some asleep on thin mattresses on the floor, some sat on chairs that were huddled around a small fire that burned in the grate.

'These came yesterday,' Lena said. 'We have the kitchen and the dining room, they have the living room, then upstairs four more families. Every time someone new comes, I say to Janusz that we can't possibly fit any more in, but still they come.'

A woman from the kitchen pushed past them and went to a mattress in the corner where a small bundle sat.

'That's Sarah, the two sat at the fireplace her husband and son. The younger ones are already asleep.' Lena nodded at the sleeping bodies.

'Then there's this little mite.'

Sarah had shifted the bundle on the mattress and woken a small girl who stood and held Sarah's hand, rubbing her tired eyes with her free hand.

Kasia crouched down as the child approached her. 'And what's your name?' she asked.

'Don't bother. She won't answer.'

Kasia looked to Lena. 'She can't speak?'

'Can't, or won't, we don't know. We don't know her name even.'

'Where are her parents?' Kasia asked.

Sarah stepped forward and turned Kasia away from the child. 'We found her. When we were taken from our homes, there were others on the streets who had resisted – you know?' Sarah stopped.

Kasia nodded. She knew. She knew that those who had resisted would have been shot, or at best beaten.

'She stood over two bodies, her parents I think.' Sarah shrugged. 'I just grabbed her hand and pretended she was with me. No one said anything, no one asked.'

'And she hasn't spoken?' Kasia asked.

'Not a word. We tried, you know. Tried to play a game with her to get her to tell us her name, or anything about her, but she just stares at you. No crying, no nothing.' Sarah quickly looked over her shoulder at the child who was indeed staring at them, displaying no emotion on her pale face.

'How old?'

'I'd say eight, maybe ten at a push, I'm not sure. She could be small for her age. My boy, David, over there,' Sarah nodded, 'he's eleven, but he's tiny, so you know, it's hard to say.'

Kasia stepped towards the girl, who hadn't moved an inch. 'Hello,' she said to her, and placed her hand on her head, feeling the silky hair underneath. Then, she crouched down once more, and Lena brought the candle close so Kasia could see her face.

Suddenly, it was as though the air had been sucked out of the room and out of Kasia's lungs. The child had one brown eye and one green.

'It's unusual,' Lena said. 'The eyes.'

'Makes you nervous I'd say,' Sarah added.

'She's beautiful,' Kasia whispered, feeling the tug of the past as she looked at the eyes that she had known all her life – and yet, it was not possible.

'We found this.' Sarah handed Kasia a piece of paper. 'It was in her dress pocket.'

Kasia read the words – an address in America, California.

'Family, we think,' Lena said. 'You have to take her. Get her to safety. Get her to her family in America.'

Kasia stood then and began to button her overcoat. She had

been here too long. 'I can't. It's not safe. But let me speak to Marta, she will come up with a way to do this.'

'It has to be now,' Lena hissed. 'They haven't noticed her yet. Haven't noticed that her papers are not the same as Sarah's. When they do, and trust me they will, they will take her away and put her with the orphans. She'll become lost in a sea of abandoned children. She can't speak. She has no one. Please, Kasia.' Lena held onto her arm tightly. 'We can't get her to eat, to drink. She won't survive here. Please.'

Kasia looked at the girl once more. At the eyes that tugged at her heart with long-ago memories buried away.

'All right,' Kasia said. 'I'll do it.'

THREE

KASIA

Kasia helped the girl button her navy-blue woollen coat and fixed a small red hat on her head that was a little too large for her.

'She has nothing else,' Sarah said. 'We had to find her a coat and shoes. When she was taken, she was standing in nothing but her bare feet and a dress.'

Kasia shook her head. 'Don't worry, we'll find her some things.'

They left the house quickly, the girl gripping Kasia's hand like a tiny vice. 'It'll be all right now,' Kasia said. 'I promise everything will be fine.' She waited a moment in case the girl replied, but she remained silent, her little legs almost skipping to keep up with Kasia's pace. Kasia could see Hans waiting, looking left, then right. She had been too long and now she had to convince him to let her leave with the girl.

Hans spotted them and for a second did not move, then ran over to them, his voice low. 'What the hell, Kasia?' He tapped at his wristwatch, then looked at the girl.

'I need to know your price,' she said.

He shook his head. 'You're mad, you know that?'

'Please, Hans.'

'I can't. The others will see, and then what? Wait until daylight and maybe you can get her out with some of the workers like last time.'

'It'll be too late, Hans. Please. Just this once. Name your price.'

Hans did not answer but looked to the little girl. Kasia could feel her heart thumping against her chest and was sure that Hans could hear it too. A lone dog howled somewhere in the distance, and Kasia concentrated on it, holding her nerve.

'It will be a lot,' he finally said. 'I have to pay the other two, you understand?'

Finally, Kasia felt herself relax. 'Give me a number and the money will be with you tomorrow.'

'Don't ask me for anything else,' Hans said, the little muscle in his jaw jumping with the tension in his face.

'Agreed.'

She watched as Hans walked towards the other guards and after a brief conversation waved her over. The girl's hand was sweaty in her own, and Kasia let go for a second to wipe her palm at which the girl grabbed her arm.

'It's all right.' Kasia quickly bent down. 'It is going to be fine. I won't let you go.'

The girl held her hand out for Kasia to take it, and together they walked out through the gates, Hans pressing a piece of paper into her pocket as she left. The price. What would Marta say?

They reached the safe house in record time, Kasia making the girl half run alongside her and burst through the door to see Tosia and Irena sat on the couch, both exhausted and holding thick tumblers of whisky. Marta sat in her armchair, her throne as she called it, discussing the evening's events with them.

'Kasia.' Marta looked up as they entered. 'What's that?' She pointed one of her long fingers at the girl.

'A child,' Tosia exclaimed, and clapped her hands excitedly. 'I love children! Come here, little one.' She held her arms out to her. 'What's your name?'

The girl would not move from Kasia's side, so Tosia went to her and picked her up.

'She doesn't speak,' Kasia said. 'Lena asked me to take her.'

Kasia relayed the story of the child to Marta as Tosia and Irena fussed at the girl and tried to get her to smile.

'This is insane, Kasia.' Marta looked at her furiously once Kasia had explained it all. 'You've put us all in jeopardy.'

'Hans won't tell. We just need to give him more money. He won't say a thing.'

'You'd better hope not. You'd better hope that he loses his damned voice too.'

Tosia and Irena unbuttoned the child's coat, sat her next to them on the sofa and tried to ply her with sweet milk. The girl would not drink and looked to Kasia who stood in the middle of the room as Marta paced it like a caged animal.

'It's all right, you can drink it,' Kasia told her, and the girl obeyed and drank the milk back in quick gulps.

'I have to think.' Marta stopped pacing and reached into her pocket for her cigarettes, lit one and resumed, waving the cigarette in the air as she walked and spoke. 'You,' she pointed at Kasia, 'I was going to tell you the good news, but now I don't know if you can go.'

Kasia felt her heart leap in anticipation. 'Go where?'

'France. The Special Operations Executive have a resistance group, and they think you will be useful. It's where you wanted to go, yes?'

'I did. I do,' Kasia said, then looked at the girl. 'I have to go.'

'I've arranged it all. It took a while to get you somewhere to stay near your contact, but it's happening.'

'When?'

'Tomorrow.' Marta stopped and walked up to her. 'But now we have the girl, and she seems to have latched on to you.'

'I can leave her,' Kasia said, her voice wavering slightly.

'Can you?' Marta raised an eyebrow at her, then laughed lightly. 'I know you. I see why you agreed to take her – those eyes. It was foolish, you know that? We could have got her out in a day or two. But I see it, Kasia, really, I do.' Her voice was softer now. 'We'll get her somewhere safe to stay.'

'So I'm going?' Kasia asked.

'You are.' Marta grinned. 'Make us proud. You're the smartest of us all, and they are expecting great things from you.'

Marta slung herself into a tatty armchair and draped her legs over the side. 'We'll take care of her and get her a family tomorrow. Somewhere in the countryside. She'll be fine.'

Just then, Kasia felt a tug on her arm. She looked down to see the girl who cried silently and took Kasia's hand in hers and squeezed it tight.

Don't do it, Kasia, don't do it, she told herself. Yet, despite herself, the words jumped out of her mouth.

'I'll take her with me.'

Marta didn't move, and Kasia was unsure whether she had heard her.

'I'll take her,' Kasia said again.

Marta slowly started to unfurl herself and sit up straight.

'Think about it,' Kasia rushed the words out before Marta had a chance to open her mouth. 'Me travelling all that way alone could be suspicious, despite my papers. But with a child? I'd say she'd be an asset to get me there safely.'

'And when you're there?' Marta asked.

'I'll find a way to get her to America. To the address that was in her dress pocket.'

'That will take time,' Marta said.

'I know. But, again, a woman and a child being together is less suspicious than a woman alone.'

Marta slowly nodded. 'I suppose there will always be someone to take care of her regardless.'

'What do you mean?' Kasia asked.

Marta waved her hand as if swatting at a fly. 'I just mean it's a small village. There'll be people who can help.'

'Her papers,' Kasia said. 'We'll need them tonight.'

'Tosia!' Marta yelled even though she was just a few feet away. 'Your job is not yet done for the evening.'

Kasia looked to Tosia, a young woman in her early twenties who swore endlessly and seemed scared of very little in life. Tosia rolled her eyes, then stood, 'If it weren't for the child, I wouldn't do it, you know. I need my sleep.'

Kasia kissed her on the cheek. 'Thank you.'

'You can thank me with a bottle of whisky,' Tosia threw over her shoulder, as she walked out of the room. 'Or bring me back a nice French man, I've always quite fancied a French husband! Or better yet, get one for yourself before you end up an old maid!'

FOUR

HUGO

Vannes, November 1942

They arrived on the tail winds of the mistral that had shaken Hugo's house, rattling at shutters and whistling through gaps in the window frames. He stood at the window and watched as three figures ducked their heads against the wind whilst dust bellowed around their feet. Three people. One he knew was Maurice, the other it looked to be a woman, and the third – a child?

As they drew closer, he went to open the door for them, his heart beating nervously in his chest – a child? A woman? Maurice had made a mistake, surely?

He did not wait for them to knock but opened the door, which jumped out of his grasp from a gust of wind that knocked it into the wall. Maurice bustled in first, his hat askew on his head. Followed by the woman and the child.

'Close that damned door,' Maurice grumbled as he removed his jacket. 'Dust in the eyes, the ears, my moustache, even!'

The woman laughed lightly as Maurice spoke, but the child that held tightly onto her hand showed no emotion – she simply stared at Hugo, making the hairs on his neck stand to attention.

'Come, come.' Maurice fussed over the pair and led them into the living room, and Hugo found himself alone in the hallway wondering what on earth was going on.

'Hugo.' Maurice popped his head around the door. 'Get us some drinks, will you? They've had a hell of a journey.'

'Maurice...' Hugo began.

'Later.' Maurice held his hand up to stop him. 'I'll explain later. Drinks first and food if you have any in this hovel.'

Despite his gnawing frustration and unease, Hugo did as his friend commanded and went to the kitchen to pour wine in four glasses. Then, realising a child could not drink wine, he picked up the glass full of red and knocked it back, feeling the warmth spread itself down his throat and into his chest.

'Food. Food is what he wants for them, and who are they?' he hissed under his breath, as he bashed about smacking plates down on the countertop and sawing into day-old bread that had more than a little staleness about it.

He found some ham and a runny chunk of camembert that he had been planning to eat the following day when it was at that exact moment of pure ripeness before becoming spoiled. A glass of water was filled for the child, and with a fully laden tray, he walked carefully into the sitting room where Maurice was talking to the woman in hushed tones.

'Here, this is all I have.' Hugo clumsily set the tray on a low table, the wine spilling a little.

'Thank you,' the woman said, her French almost perfect, but still betraying an accent that Hugo could not place.

He fell into his armchair across from the girl and the woman who were comfortable on the sofa, Maurice perched on the chaise longue.

'Hugo, meet Kasia,' Maurice said, and raised a glass in the direction of the woman.

'And this is?' Hugo asked, pointing at the child.

'She isn't mine,' Kasia said.

'Hugo,' Maurice interrupted. 'I may have deceived you slightly.'

'Slightly?' Hugo shouted.

The girl with no name flinched as he yelled, and Maurice grabbed Hugo's arm. 'Perhaps this is better done in private?'

Maurice stood and walked into Hugo's messy office, and Hugo followed suit, eyeing Kasia who smiled at him in such a way that he felt as though she were mocking him.

Once in the office, Hugo slammed the door closed. 'What the hell, Maurice? You said one man, one night!'

Maurice settled himself behind Hugo's desk, his moustache twitching with a smile hidden underneath.

'You think this is funny?' Hugo asked.

'Not so, not so, my friend. And I did not say one *man*. If you remember, I did not specify male nor female.'

'Maurice.' Hugo placed his palms flat on the desk and leaned into his friend. 'Enough. What is going on?'

'I admit I should have told you a little more. But I thought if I did, you would never agree. The woman out there is Polish. She has been working with the resistance there for years and is somewhat of a genius by all accounts. Speaks six languages fluently, can crack codes, risks her life for others. She is fearless, Hugo! Utterly fearless and an absolute find, if I do say so myself!'

'And what, pray tell, is she doing in my house?'

'Well. The British government have been in touch with a small resistance group in the area, of which you now know I'm a part. We needed a radio operator and through our network we came upon Kasia: a woman who incidentally wanted – no, needed – to get to France. Why, I don't know, nor do I care. The

British were happy to accept her into the organisation as she was known to them as far back as three years ago, when she assisted with a few codes that no one could break. But she did it, Hugo! She did! An absolute find.'

Hugo watched as Maurice drank his wine, his cheeks glowing red from the warmth of the alcohol, his eyes almost dreamy with his find of the woman.

'Yet, once again, I ask you, what is she doing in my home with that child that apparently has yet to be given a name?'

'This is the good bit, Hugo. She is to stay for a while and work with me as my nurse. She will be able to travel around with me and use the radio – which will be arriving in just a few days' time – to help us in our fight! Isn't it brilliant? She will help end this war, mark my words.'

'But again, Maurice, you have yet to tell me what I have to do with this? Why is she not at your house?'

'Too risky, my friend. Far too risky. I will relay any messages from the group to her and she will relay them back. She can't meet the others – it would not be safe. But here's the genius part: she is to be your cousin – a distant cousin with a small child that will live with you for a while. I admit, the child was not originally a part of it, but it makes it safer for us all. Who would think a woman with a child would be working for the resistance? No one, that's who, and you with your contacts and your friendships with our occupiers, why, they'll never bat an eyelid!'

Hugo watched his friend who had become more and more animated as he spoke, his eyes bright and hands waving about in the air.

'And you did not think to ask me if I would agree to this?'

'I knew you would refuse,' Maurice said simply.

'Do I not have a right to refuse?' Hugo stomped over to a bookcase and, unsure of why he was there, turned back to Maurice. 'This is my home. Mine. Do I not have a right to decide who should live in it? And a child too, Maurice? You did not even think that would be a problem for me?'

Maurice stood and placed his hands on Hugo's shoulders. 'For my deception I'm sorry. I am. But she won't be here too long. She has to move about. The child will not be here for long either – I hear she has family in America, and we will arrange for her to go there. It won't be long, Hugo, please. I know how you feel. I understand why you're angry. But this war is not going away anytime soon. Listen to what Kasia will tell you about what's happening in Poland, and not just in Poland – everywhere! It's evil of the first order, Hugo; women, children all forced to starve, stripped of their belongings, their homes. So many dead, Hugo. And don't think, just because not much has changed in our lives so far, that it will not find us eventually. We are all at risk. I beseech you as your friend to do this for me. It will not be for long.'

As if exhausted by his speech, Maurice slumped back into the chair behind the desk and stroked at his moustache.

Hugo wasn't sure of himself – of what to think and feel. For years now, his life had become a routine of drinking, playing at writing a new book and chasing women. He had created a world for himself that kept his thoughts and the past at bay. But now, Maurice was slowly breaking through that cleverly crafted shell, asking Hugo to do more, to be more – to essentially become the person he had once been; but he was unsure whether that Hugo even existed any more.

'The war...' Hugo began, his voice low, his head muddled, trying to choose his words carefully. 'It isn't that I don't care, that I don't worry. You think I've deafened myself to the news of what's happening all around us, but that's not so. I feel like it does not matter what I do – what could I do that would really help? Yes, I get you supplies, but that, to me, is perhaps more of a game, or so you have rightly said before. It is easier for me,

Maurice, not to feel, not to think. I thought you understood that?'

'I do, Hugo. By God I do. But I didn't think that this melancholy would affect you for so long. Each day I wonder when I will see the old Hugo again.'

'He's gone.'

'He has not. He is stood in front of me. He is here, you just have to trust that he is.'

'I'm not sure, Maurice...' Hugo shook his head. He was tired, confused. *A child.*

As if sensing Hugo's resistance beginning to break, Maurice stood and took Hugo in an embrace, then gently led him back to the sitting room where his guests waited.

FIVE

HUGO

The girl's eyes followed him as he walked into the room. He sat once more across from them and stared back at the child, willing her to look away first.

'She needs a name,' Maurice said, and delved into his pocket and drew out a small boiled sweet wrapped in red foil and handed it to her.

The child took it eagerly but did not smile or unwrap the candy. She simply stared at it in her palm.

'What's your name?' Maurice crouched in front of her. 'Can you whisper it to me?'

'She won't understand you,' Kasia said. 'She's Polish. I very much doubt that her parents spoke French,' she ended with a little laugh, and Hugo wasn't sure whether it irritated him or if he actually wanted to hear her laugh again.

Maurice stood and smoothed his moustache down even though not one bristle had dared to move. Suddenly, the girl smiled as she watched Maurice.

'Is it funny?' Maurice laughed and twitched his top lip so that the moustache seemed to dance and wiggle.

'See, she likes it, she likes me, don't you!' The doctor patted her on the head, and the girl's smile disappeared.

'We gave her a name, on her documents.' Kasia rustled around in a small leather handbag and drew out a sheaf. 'We called her Elodie Garnier. And I, to all intents and purposes, am Delphine, although I don't expect you to call me that around the home, but you need to get used to calling me Delphine in public.' She looked at Hugo. 'Remember, I'm your cousin now, my husband died and I've come to live with family.'

'And if they check? As far as I'm aware I have no cousin listed anywhere by the name of Delphine Garnier,' Hugo belligerently asked.

Kasia did not answer for a moment but looked at him through narrowed eyes, then a smile appeared on her lips. Hugo felt goosebumps as she regarded him and wondered why he suddenly felt like a mouse that was being eyed by a hungry cat.

'They won't,' she said confidently. 'You'll have to trust that I know what I'm doing.'

Hugo leaned forward, ready to argue with her – her naivety, her misplaced confidence! Who did she think she was?

'Here, eat.' Maurice gave Hugo a sharp look, one that he saved for when Hugo was being particularly irritating, and began to tear at the bread and handed some to the girl. 'And here,' he proffered the cheese and ham.

'She can't eat that,' Kasia nodded at the meat. 'Jewish.'

'And you? Are you?' Hugo asked her.

Kasia picked up a piece of ham and popped it into her mouth. 'Not really. I am and I am not. My mother was Polish catholic, my father Jewish but never conservative. We ate whatever was given to us, pig, cow, didn't matter. But then we had little choice, little money to be fussy.'

Kasia yawned, then reached for her glass of wine and drank it back in one go.

'That's a vintage year. You're supposed to savour it,' Hugo said bluntly.

He watched as she licked her lips and looked inside the empty glass. 'Well, silly me!' she said. 'How rude of me.' Then she laughed and, once more, Hugo couldn't tell if she was genuine or joking with him.

'You must be tired,' Maurice said. 'Hugo, get the rooms for our guests ready.'

'No need.' Kasia stood, then held out her hand to the little girl and said something in Polish. The girl stood and took Kasia's hand.

'We'll see to it ourselves, up the stairs?' Kasia asked, looking at the staircase.

'First room on the left for the child,' Hugo said. 'It needs a clean, but it will do for now. And the other room at the end of the hallway. Don't touch anything. I will sort it myself tomorrow.'

'Understood,' Kasia replied.

'And tell her too.' Hugo pointed at the child he was to call Elodie. 'Tell her not to touch anything that's not hers.'

Kasia gave a sharp nod of the head. 'I don't suppose you have fresh linens?' she asked.

He shrugged.

'We'll get you some fresh linen tomorrow, won't we, Hugo?' Maurice cajoled.

'I suppose we will,' Hugo mumbled.

'Well then, we bid you a goodnight, gentlemen, and our thanks once more for your help.'

Hugo watched as the pair left the room, then heard them climb the stairs, Kasia muttering to the child, never receiving a reply.

'Could you be more petulant?' Maurice asked.

'I could, I think.'

Maurice stood and readied himself against the wind that

still blustered outside, buttoning his coat and pulling his hat low over his eyes.

'I'll be here in the morning,' he told Hugo. 'Be nice to them, eh? Show them your soft side.'

'I don't have one.'

Maurice shook his head. 'Such a petulant child. Tomorrow.' Maurice tipped his hat at him and left him alone to stew over the guests who padded about upstairs, disturbing his solitude.

Frustrated, Hugo took to his room, slamming his bedroom door so that the woman upstairs would hear his annoyance, and flung himself on his bed, wanting to sleep before memories barged their way into his mind.

Whether from the wine or the upheaval, he soon found himself drifting into the murky world of dreams. The last thing he thought of clearly was *the child – a child, a girl...*

SIX

KASIA

Kasia heard the door slam downstairs and felt her jaw tense at the thought of that man – that Hugo! She wished she could contact Marta and ask her why she had chosen this man and his home. He certainly didn't want them here. And besides, she thought, why did she have to stay with any man? Why couldn't she have been billeted to a hotel, or a farmhouse – anything but here, with him.

'Even a barn would have been better,' she muttered under her breath and saw the girl look at her.

'Here, come here now.' Kasia waved the child over. She had managed to move boxes off the small single bed for Elodie, and found a tattered blanket and pillow that smelt damp and dewy.

'It will have to do for now,' she told the girl. 'I'll find you some better bedsheets tomorrow. Here, arms up.'

The girl raised her arms, and Kasia removed the knitted sweater for her. She was sure the girl could dress and undress herself, but she did not ever make an attempt to do anything independently, and instead would look to Kasia with her mismatched eyes, waiting for her to indicate what should be done next.

She removed the girl's skirt and socks and dressed her in one of her own nightgowns. 'It's too big, of course, but we'll get you some of your own clothes soon. This was my mother's, you know? See here, on the lapel there are hand-stitched daisies. She did this. She liked to do things with her hands, sewing, knitting, painting even. She always told me to keep my hands busy as it keeps the mind busy,' Kasia prattled on, feeling the need to constantly have some noise filling the silence that emanated from the girl.

'So, into bed.'

The girl climbed in and Kasia covered her with the blanket. 'You sleep well. I'll be just down the hall so come and get me if you need anything.'

Kasia waited a beat to see if the girl might reply, but she simply turned on her side and closed her eyes.

'Goodnight,' she whispered, then unsure of whether to kiss her on her cheek or not, patted her head in an awkward fashion and left the room.

Kasia's own room was filled with boxes, suitcases, some empty and some full, a desk that was covered with papers, newspaper clippings and childlike drawings. She leafed through them, noting that most of the newspaper clippings came from a Parisian newspaper fifteen years ago. She paused to read one when suddenly a roar of the wind broke loose one of the shutters which smashed against the window, making Kasia yelp with fear. She placed the newspaper clipping back on the pile and checked that the window was closed, feeling the wind seep through the edges onto her fingers. Out in the blackness she could see little, but imagined the sea that was nearby, the waves tossing and foaming against rocks and felt a childish excitement at being near the coast.

She had never seen the sea before; instead, she had spent most of her life in Kraków, first at her parents' home and then with Marta when they went to university together. She remembered begging her father when she was small to take her and her sister to the sea after she had read *Moby Dick* and was desperate to see a whale.

'They live there, I know it.' She had waved the book in her tiny hands and beseeched her father to listen. 'We can find one. We won't kill it. We'll be friends.'

Her younger sister, Maja, had laughed. 'Don't be stupid, Kasia. You won't find a whale and it won't be your friend.'

Kasia had looked at her sister whose dainty features and curly chestnut hair endeared her to everyone she met, yet Kasia knew that her sister had a mean streak, jealous and impulsive. Although Kasia was a year older, Maja would treat her as the little sister, mocking her and taking all of their parents' affections for herself. Yet, when the right mood took her, Maja was one of the best people to be around. She could make Kasia laugh, come up with games that she knew Kasia would like, and could be generous with her love and her toys.

'One day we will go to see the sea.' Kasia's father had raised his head from the students' papers he was reading. 'Not now, though. But soon.'

Kasia had stomped her way to her bedroom to lie back on her bed and imagine what the sea was like, what it smelt like, what all that water felt like when you jumped into it. For months afterwards, Kasia would submerge herself in the bathtub, pretending that the break of the ocean was just above her, the hidden depths of it below.

'I'll see it for myself tomorrow,' Kasia whispered, as she left her daydreaming at Hugo's window and sat on the edge of the mattress that lay flat against the wooden floor: the bedframe was propped up against the wall, still to be properly erected.

The irritation at Hugo flooded over her again. The ham. That bothered her. Why had she eaten it? She had told the truth that her father was not devout, but they had remained kosher, keeping one tradition at least. But Hugo's face, craggy, his hair dishevelled, his small dark eyes almost goading her had made her pop it into her mouth, feeling the flesh on her tongue, making her want to gag. She had stared at him after, hoping he saw a flash of triumph in her eyes that she had bested him. He had simply looked away as if she were an annoying fly, one that had held his attention for a while whilst it buzzed and bashed about at a windowpane, and then it had become nothing to him.

She had lied too about her background. They hadn't been poor – not rich either, but certainly not poor. They had lived on a quiet street not far from the university where her father worked as an academic and lecturer in mathematics. Their house had four bedrooms, an indoor bathroom, parlour, sitting room and office, each cluttered with her mother's family's furniture that had been left to her when both Kasia's grandparents had died suddenly when her mother was in her early twenties. It was then that her mother, a student, had met her father, the new lecturer. Despite his family's protestations at her lack of Jewishness, and the fact she was unwilling to convert, they married and moved to a street that held a mismatch of families from every background and religion.

'We are the new Poland,' Kasia's father would regularly tell them at dinner, her mother bobbing her head with approval. 'Education is what is important – education, not religion, not colour, not our backgrounds. Our education defines us. Science and mathematics give us proof, facts of who we are and how to make sense of the world around us. You must always remember this,' he had warned them.

Education had so far served Kasia well. She had gone to university, following in her father's footsteps and studying mathematics, yet also embracing her mother's love of languages, learning them one at a time, the new words and sounds filling her mind and making her dream in French, German, Polish, English and Italian. But Maja was far superior. Her mind absorbed everything, mathematics came more easily to her, as did physics. Her accents in French and Italian were nearly perfect, and it always seemed to Kasia that whilst she spent hours poring over textbooks, her sister simply glanced at them, laughed as though mocking the information they provided as if she had always known it, and walked away to fix her hair, her face and to find a dance to attend.

'Listen to how Maja pronounces it,' her mother would say. 'Hear how her accent is perfect?'

'Look at how quickly Maja has solved the equation,' her father would add. 'Genius!'

Kasia looked down at her hands. They ached. She realised that her thoughts had made her bunch her hands into fists so that her fingernails bit painfully into her palms. Releasing her grip, she flexed her long fingers. *Would Maja have handled Hugo the same way?* She wondered. Then, another thought, *does it matter?*

Tired and with a stomach that rumbled with both excitement about the sea, about her new job and anxiety about the small girl that she had foolishly agreed to look after, she lay down on the thin mattress, not caring to undress, and fell asleep to the sound of the wind moaning against the house.

SEVEN

HUGO

He woke in silence. The mistral had eased, allowing the house to cease its creaking and settle once more. Every time the winds came, he wondered if the house would survive, noting each time roof tiles smashed on the ground, another shutter come loose, another brick or piece of wood wobbly and ready to fall.

This had been his parents' home, and before them, his grandparents', and in his youth, he had promised them that he would always maintain both the house and the grounds. Yet, here he was, with the house crumbling around him, the gardens wild. *At least I've managed to care for the vineyards*, Hugo mused. The vineyards had been his only family since he had arrived back here from Paris fifteen years ago. He had cared for them and employed others to help him, making sure his cellar was always stocked and his pockets filled with enough money to keep him alive.

The thick darkness of night had left the room, and a deep blue light alerted Hugo to the fact that it was some time before dawn. Irritated, he rolled onto his side. Dawn. He had seen dawn before when he stayed awake all night, but to be awake before the rising of the sun? That, Hugo did not care for at all.

Suddenly, his ears pricked at a creak from above. He held his breath. Was it the woman or the child moving about? The house fell silent once more, and Hugo lifted himself from his bed, reluctantly acknowledging that sleep was forever lost – for today at least.

He decided that he would meet the dawn, sip coffee and smoke cigarettes and try to quieten his mind before that woman, Kasia, appeared to shatter his protected solitude with her demands. Linens he already knew he had to find for her, and he supposed he would have to get them food too.

Again, a creak, then a light thud from above. He waited to hear footsteps, and hearing none, he felt a knot of worry in his stomach. Was it the girl, had she fallen out of bed? He shook his head at the irrational thought – she was old enough to cry out, to put herself back in. Yet, the worry squirmed in his mind like a worm, and he knew it would not settle until he went to check.

He took the stairs carefully, realising that he had not been upstairs for some time. He knew that each room contained his past life, and even some remnants of his parents and he rarely wanted to access them, or to remember them. Now, he would have to move them somewhere away from Kasia's eyes and the small girl's hands. Who knew what they would find?

He stopped outside the door to the bedroom that held the silent girl and he listened for a moment before slowly turning the doorknob.

In he crept, seeing the girl on her side, her hair splayed out behind her. He looked on the floor for what could have fallen and, seeing nothing, he turned to leave. Yet, suddenly, apprehension twisted and turned in his belly. *Was she breathing? Was she alive?*

He knew he should leave the girl, but his body did not obey his mind and led him to the side of the bed where he saw his arm stretch out, his hand resting on top of the girl's head for a brief moment whilst his eyes took in the gentle rise and fall of her chest. Relief flooded through him, and he left the girl as quietly as he had arrived.

Downstairs, he rattled about in the kitchen to make coffee, feeling foolish and uneasy about what he had done. He shouldn't have gone into her room. He shouldn't care. 'They shouldn't be here!' he exclaimed aloud, staring at the coffee cup in his hand as if it would answer him back.

'Do you always talk to yourself?'

Hugo turned to see Kasia in the doorway, her face already neatly made up, a slick of red over her pouty lips.

'I see you slept well,' Hugo replied. He poured coffee into his cup, then stalked out onto the veranda, noting that the sun was already up and that he had missed it.

He heard Kasia behind him, finding her own coffee cup. She was already acting as though she lived here, he thought, so comfortable that she would go about his kitchen. He wanted to turn and glare at her to show her his irritation, but he knew if he did, she would suggest that he act like a host and get her a cup himself, so he said nothing.

'It's beautiful here.' She sat down on a white wicker chair across from him.

He looked at her as she scanned the ramble of gardens, then she turned her head further to see the neat rows of vineyards stretching out towards the town.

'Are they all yours?' she asked.

'*Oui*,' he said.

'And this house, there is just you here?'

'*Oui*,' he said once more, then tucked a cigarette between his lips and lit it.

'Am I annoying you?' she asked, a twinkle of laughter in her voice.

'*Oui*,' he said gruffly, and pulled hard on the cigarette so that the tobacco crackled at the quick burn.

'We won't be here long. Just as your friend Maurice said. It will be a month or so at the very most.'

Hugo shrugged.

'Look at you! Up already,' Maurice's voice sang out from the driveway as he walked his bicycle along the rutted ground.

He wheeled it up to the house, then took the steps to join them.

'Madame Delphine, good morning.' Maurice kissed Kasia on each cheek.

'I thought your name was Kasia,' Hugo said.

'It is. Do you not remember last night when I said that I have to be called Delphine?'

'Ah yes, your alias,' Hugo said. 'How silly of me to forget. But a lot happened last night. My mind has not quite grasped everything yet.'

He saw how his clipped words made her narrow her eyes a little, and he felt a swell of pride at this minor victory.

'Now, now, Hugo,' Maurice said. 'Be nice.'

'Why are you here so early?' Hugo asked his friend. 'As far as I am aware, I am not unwell.'

'So moody in the mornings, Hugo,' the doctor quipped. 'Always were, even as a child.'

'I need my sleep.'

'You have known each other a long time?' Kasia asked.

'Indeed. Since he was a boy. I was friends with his father.'

'Where are your parents now?' Kasia looked to him.

'On Rue Jean Jaurès,' Hugo said. 'You can visit them if you like and ask them questions, but I doubt they will answer you.'

For a moment, Kasia's brow furrowed.

'They're dead, my dear,' Maurice said quietly. 'He's given their address as the cemetery. I'm afraid you will have to get used to Hugo's *esprit*; it can be tiresome at times, so I suggest you ignore him when you need to.'

Kasia laughed and Hugo saw that her eyes lit up as she did so.

'Well, we will have to leave you now.' Maurice stood and held his hand out to Kasia.

'What do you mean, *we*?' Hugo sat up straight.

'Delphine and I, we have work to do.'

'And the child?' Hugo asked. 'She's still sleeping.'

Neither Maurice nor Kasia looked at him, and neither answered.

'No,' Hugo said.

'Just for today,' Maurice said hurriedly. 'After today, we will get something sorted.'

'And what exactly am I meant to do with her?'

'Take her to town, let people see you with her, tell people about your cousin and her child. Buy her some clothes. Clean the house. Buy some food.'

'All of that?' Hugo stood up. 'My God, how long will you be gone for?'

Maurice shrugged. 'It is hard to say. We have much to do.'

'No,' Hugo said bluntly, then slumped back down into his chair and looked out to the sea. 'No. And that's final.'

He felt a hand on his shoulder, then the warm coffee-scented breath of Maurice close to his ear. 'You owe me,' Maurice whispered.

Suddenly, a chill swept over him. Those words. He had waited to hear Maurice say those words for years and thought that he never would. And yet, he had said them.

You owe me.

Maurice moved away from him, and he heard the pair go back into the house. He could not make out what they were saying, a whooshing sound seemed to have taken over and his eyes could not focus properly.

You owe me.

The words tumbled over and over in his mind, and the guilt he had thought he had successfully buried reached out from somewhere deep in his stomach and began to spread like the cancer that it was.

EIGHT

THE POLISH GIRL

She woke to loud voices in a language she did not know, yet although they were raised in argument, she enjoyed the way it sounded. Like a song. The words going up and down, up and down, then round and around.

She lay in the tiny bed that smelt of mould and dirt and remembered that the woman called Kasia said she would make sure they got fresh sheets today. She liked Kasia. She liked how her hair was always so neat and pinned in chignons at the nape of her neck. She liked how she rouged her lips and wore a citrus scent that was exotic and comforting all at once.

The man, who Kasia called Hugo, she was not sure of. His hair was messy and long, his clothes dirty and his feet bare. But she liked his voice and she liked how he had placed his hand on her head, perhaps by accident, perhaps not, as she had tried to get back to sleep a while earlier. She had wanted to open her eyes and look at him, but he had crept so slowly, so quietly, that she oddly did not want to disturb him.

Hugo. Kasia.

She mouthed the words, but no sound came out. She

wondered why the sound had disappeared. She remembered it was fine one day, and then the next day she was with the woman called Sarah and all those people, and her voice had been left behind somewhere. Perhaps it was still in her home in Poland. Perhaps it had been packed away in a suitcase – so many cases, clothes thrown in, shouting, fear. She placed her hands over her ears and scrunched her eyes and willed those images out her mind. Her voice was with those images, with those memories. She opened her eyes. Well, if that was where her voice was, it could stay there – she was never going to think about that day again, she would never remember.

She swung her legs off the bed and plopped onto the bare floorboards, noticing that her warm feet left footprints in the dust. She gathered up the long nightdress that Kasia had given her so she would not trip and made her way out of the room and padded down the rickety staircase holding the rail in one hand, and the tails of her nightdress in the other.

Kasia and the man with the moustache stood in the kitchen to the left, both talking in that singsong language. She walked slowly towards them and stood, waiting for them to notice her.

The moustache man noticed her first and said something, then twisted and turned his moustache and smiled at her. He patted her on the head, then looked to Kasia.

'He says good morning,' Kasia told her.

She was happy to hear a language she knew and nodded slightly.

'Elodie,' the moustache man said. Then again.

'That's your name now, do you remember on the train when I told you that would be your name for a while?' Kasia asked.

She did remember. It was a hazy, misshapen memory of the train, of leaning on Kasia's shoulder and feeling so tired she struggled to keep her eyes open. But yes, she remembered her new name.

'Maurice says if you speak, you can tell us your real name,' Kasia said to her and then looked to the moustache man.

Her real name. She knew it, of course she did, and she let it ring around in her mind for a moment, but only a moment, because the voice that said her name was her mother's voice and she felt a stabbing in her stomach when she thought about it.

'This is Maurice,' Kasia was talking again. 'And you remember Hugo?'

She looked to the open doorway that led outside where Hugo sat and looked out at the garden.

'He will take care of you today. You will need to dress yourself, and he will take you to buy some clothes,' Kasia said.

She chewed on her bottom lip. She wasn't sure about this at all. She couldn't understand him, what if he left her somewhere? What if he wasn't that nice? What if...?

'It's all right.' Kasia had moved to embrace her. 'You will be fine, I promise you. And I won't be gone for long.'

Breaking the embrace, Kasia spoke to Maurice, then looked back at her. She could see how Kasia's face had changed, wrinkles in her brow in the same way as her mother when her father had told them about a man called Hitler, about a star that they must wear. Kasia was worried. She knew that.

She reached out and touched Kasia's arm and forced herself to smile. The smile worked, just as it always had done for her mother, and Kasia's face relaxed.

'I promise you I'll come back, and I won't be long,' Kasia told her again, then took her hand and led her outside to Hugo.

'Hugo will give you some breakfast, then you can dress yourself and he will take you to get some new clothes, all right?'

She watched as Kasia spoke to Hugo, her face animated, her hands moving as if she were creating the words out of thin air. Soon, Hugo looked at her, and she noticed a small smile that quickly disappeared. He nodded at Kasia and said something else she did not understand, then Kasia bent down, kissed her

briefly on the cheek and left with Maurice and a bicycle that
squeaked as he wheeled it away.

'*Merde*,' Hugo said. '*Merde*.'

She silently mouthed the word, *merde*. And she found that
she liked it.

NINE

KASIA

The air was thick with salt as a tail wind whipped up a sea breeze into Kasia's face as she walked, stinging her cheeks pink, and leaving its briny residue on her lips. She didn't care that the sea assaulted her in such a way, even though it was the first time that they had met. She was glad of its freshness, its belligerent nature, and faced it full on so that she had to close her eyes against the fierceness of it.

'Do you think they will be all right?' Maurice's words swirled through the wind and broke her reverie as they walked along the coastal path through naked trees that would be full come summer.

She realised that she should have been the one to ask the question and felt a bubble of guilt at not worrying about the child more. It was the sea that had taken her thoughts and now she was anchored back to the solid ground.

'I hope so,' she said.

'Hugo, he's a difficult man, but he's a good man too, if that makes sense? Deep down he is very kind and caring,' Maurice said, leading them to a rundown house that faced the sea.

Kasia could see the walled town swelling up behind the

house, its ramparts and church spires and felt a desperation to see what was held within.

'I thought you said we had to meet someone,' she said. 'The town is still miles away.'

'We are here.' Maurice stopped and propped his bicycle against a crumbling wall. 'In here.'

Kasia looked at the house, dimpled windows stuck into the brick whilst long-forgotten ivy wrapped and weaved its way in between the wrought-iron gates and the cracks of the mortar.

The pathway was bordered on either side with overgrown grass, dandelions and stinging nettles that pricked at Kasia's legs as she walked. She stopped to rub at her calf, noticing how someone, long ago, had edged the path with coloured broken glass. She ran her finger over a piece of cornflower blue, wiping it clean from soil and dust, delighting when the sun caught it and made it shine. Beach sand had blown over the garden for so long that small mounds of it rested against the house, and Kasia wondered if soon the sea would be here as well.

She looked up to ask Maurice who had thought of doing such a thing, but he was already at the door, pulling it open with such force that she was sure it would be wrenched from its hinges.

She followed Maurice to the front door and went inside, where the smell of damp and the salty air from outside mixed in Kasia's nostrils. Sand had found a way inside too, and covered the hardwood floor in a thin layer, scattering now and again as soon as a light breeze blew through. Oil paintings of the countryside and the sea clung to the walls, their colours muted and sad and, to the left, a sitting room still held furniture that seemed to Kasia to be all the shades of grey, the tables and mantlepiece covered in thick layers of dust. Although abandoned, unloved and with a slight air of eeriness, Kasia liked the house. There was something about it that called to her to make it a home once more.

Maurice disappeared into a back room, and Kasia could hear him talking low and quick.

'Come.' Maurice popped his head around the door, and Kasia quickened her step.

The room in which she found herself in had once been a grand dining room, the chestnut table still standing proud with a clutter of velvet-clad chairs around it. A chandelier hung from the ceiling, ornaments and gilded paintings giving the room some opulence. It was too much for a small beach house and seemed to Kasia to have been brought from a grander home.

'It's a strange room, isn't it?' Maurice broke into her thoughts. 'Not a usual home – each room is so different – luxury here, a study painted pink! It has a history, this house. Remind me one day to tell you about it.'

It was then that Kasia noticed the other occupant of the room, a thin man with sandy blonde hair, and for a moment her heart jumped. But when he raised his head, she could see she had been wrong to feel fear. His face was angular, as if someone had chipped away at a block of marble to get the features with harsh edges. His eyes seemed too large for his face, big, wide and restless.

'Delphine?' he said.

She nodded.

'Maurice has done well,' he said.

'And you are?' She held out her hand to the man with a face like a stoat.

He shook his head. 'My name is irrelevant. You won't see me again.'

Kasia was already glad to hear this as there was something about him that she disliked immediately.

'Your position here is highly unusual,' the stoat continued. 'I hope I don't have to remind you of how generous we are being.'

'And who is we?' Kasia asked.

'We are the British Government,' he said, his chest almost

puffing out with importance. 'Not that you work for us, at least you don't officially.'

'Then who do I work for?'

'*La Resistance!*' the stoat said in a comically thick French accent. 'At least on paper you do. You see, to work for us officially, you would have to come to England and go through extraordinary training, but your reputation precedes you and we are willing to take a risk. Your role is simple: relay messages from the resistance, and sometimes from our agents to both the home base in England, and to a French network. Maurice will tell you which message is for whom.'

The man bent down and picked up a small suitcase, then laying it on the table, opened it to reveal a radio transmitter. 'This is yours now,' he said. 'You know how to work it, I assume?'

Kasia looked at the equipment. It was smaller than the one she had used in Poland, but it seemed to be similar. The coils and wires were all in place and she reached out to touch the dials.

'Wait,' the stoat said. 'Let me explain. It has a range of over five hundred miles. We suggest local transmissions. You have twenty minutes for each transmission, and Maurice here will keep you moving about to relay any messages that come in from the field agents and ask for supplies. Oh, and there is this – memorise it.' The stoat handed Kasia a piece of paper upon which a poem was written. Kasia read the first stanza:

> *Is de Gaulle's prick*
> *Twelve inches thick*
> *Can it rise*
> *To the size*
> *Of a proud flagpole*
> *And does the sun shine*
> *From his arsehole?*

Kasia laughed.

'It is funny, I know. But more than that, it should be easy to remember. We tried other poems – Shakespeare, Keats – but our German counterparts cracked that pretty quickly. Thus, this has been made up, and hopefully will be harder to crack.'

'I'll remember it,' she said.

'You must. Word for word, letter for letter. This is where we are having problems. A lot of our agents have misremembered the words or forgotten how certain words are spelled. Once you've encoded it, and we try to decode it, if there is a mistake, we have no idea what it means.'

The stoat then went on to explain to her how to encode the poems by choosing five words at random and giving each letter a number corresponding to the alphabet. She was to insert an indicator group at the beginning of her transmission so that it could be decoded quickly.

'I don't have to tell you the difficulty of this way of transmission, do I?' the stoat asked.

'It seems straightforward to me. We used something very similar in Poland. I'm sure I will be fine,' Kasia said. Indeed, to her the coding was too simple – it was a game she and others had played at university, and oddly she felt a little disappointed at the lack of challenge.

'No. What I mean is, if you're captured, the poem can be tortured out of you and our German friends will then be able to transmit as you, or intercept messages going forward.'

'I don't expect to be captured,' Kasia said.

The stoat laughed at this, and lit a cigarette. 'So naive, my dear. You know the average life span of a radio operator is just six weeks?'

The stoat then looked to Maurice. 'Are you sure about her?' he asked.

Kasia felt her face flame and was ready to say something to the angular man when she felt Maurice's hand on her arm.

'She is the best. If you don't remember, she was requested especially due to her work on earlier ciphers and codes that aided the British and their machine.'

The stoat nodded. 'Yes, yes, I know all this. But this is different, Maurice. To be a pianist...' he tailed off and raised his hands in question.

'A pianist?' she asked.

'That's what you are – a pianist. A radio operator. That's what you are called.'

'And what are *you* called?' she repeated her earlier question, happy to see that he narrowed his eyes at her – he was annoyed.

'Maurice is your handler, as you know.' He slammed the case shut. 'You, to all intents and purposes, are a nurse. He will get you around the towns and ensure you keep moving.'

She felt a flutter of excitement and wanted the man to leave so that she could have time with the radio alone.

'It isn't ideal, this setup. It is against protocol. But as you're not officially with the home office, I suppose it can be overlooked. You should be living alone, moving about regularly. Six weeks, remember?'

Kasia set her jaw. 'Monsieur, it cannot be any more dangerous than bribing Nazi guards, sneaking in and out of ghettos and helping people escape. I have had my fair share of danger and fear. This will not faze me.'

Maurice laughed. 'You see? She's perfect for this role. And whilst you may think she should be alone, how much better is it if she is seen with a child, staying with family? A woman alone is surely more of a target, no?'

The stoat shrugged, 'Let's just hope that the child and that man don't slow you down. If you need to leave, you run, you understand? You run, disappear, then get a quick message either to Maurice or use the radio for a brief transmission to let us know where you are.'

Kasia simply nodded.

'Your home office times are Wednesday for England and Friday for the French network – afternoons at three p.m. on the dot. Do not miss this time. Again, it is out of the ordinary to allow you to transmit during daylight hours, but as you will be travelling at those times as a nurse, we have decided it could be safer for you.'

Maurice shook hands with the thin man, who now gathered his coat and slim briefcase, nodded his goodbye at them and left.

'Who was that man?' Kasia breathed a sigh of relief and sat down at the dining table.

Maurice ignored her. 'He forgot to give you this.'

Kasia watched as he delved into his pocket, then sat next to her. He uncurled his closed hand and within it lay a small silver pill box.

'It's—' Maurice started.

'I already have one,' she said, not willing to have the conversation about what pill lay inside, what it did, and the reality that, odds were, she'd have to take it. 'Sewn into my underwear,' she added, and saw Maurice stifle a laugh.

'You may think it funny, but it's the best way. All my underwear has a small pocket and each day I place it inside.'

'No, no, I agree! It is the best place, but just the thought, you know...' He gestured at his crotch. 'Cyanide in underwear! Whatever next?'

Despite the fact that Kasia found the topic unpleasant, she couldn't help but laugh. Maurice's moustache twitched and bobbed as he too gave into the absurdity of their lives now.

Once they had gathered themselves, Maurice set up the radio and together they ran through the poem, making pretend messages and playing with the radio to understand the quickest way to get it up and running. Kasia's hand hovered over the power switch.

'Don't!' Maurice warned.

'I wasn't going to,' Kasia replied, and wanted to tell him

about the barbed wire in Warsaw and how she experienced a pull to touch it. The switch was the same.

'Now,' Maurice said, giving her no chance to explain her strange train of thought. 'I have to go and get your bicycle. It's a mile or so away.'

'I'll come with you,' Kasia said.

Maurice shook his head. 'The house is close to a checkpoint leading into the town. We will have to go that way one day, and you will be questioned. But not today. Stay here, memorise the poem, then I will be back.'

The doctor left and Kasia was happy to be alone. She didn't look at the poem; instead, she wanted to investigate this strange house and see the pink room.

She started in the dusty sitting room, the walls painted white, contrasting with the thick red rugs on the floor, which she assumed had once been vibrant but now lay dull and uncared for. All of the furniture in the room was of a dark, heavy wood, and there on the wall opposite the window, she saw a mural, painted by hand, of cherubs flitting through clouds, tall trees trying to reach them in the heavens. She stood back and looked at it for a moment, then placed her fingertips on the leaves, then the clouds, tracing the beauty of the image. She had seen similar paintings on the ceilings of churches, but never in a home, and she wished that she could draw and paint to create something so divine.

The room off the sitting room was the pink room – a study of sorts with shelves full of books, a small desk and a chaise longue covered in the lightest of pinks. Again, the painter had found themselves in this room, decorating the paler pink walls with deep rouge roses that spiralled up from the very base of the wall, curling and trailing as if they were truly alive and growing in front of her eyes.

She felt a sense of peace in the room, and could imagine sitting on the chaise longue, reading a book, whilst all around her the outside world had been brought in – her own private garden.

Kasia eased a book from the shelf, one bound in green leather with the title stamped in neat gold lettering on the cover – Charles Dickens, *Great Expectations*. She felt a shiver of excitement at the find, reliving the characters and stories that she had so treasured as a child. She sat on the chaise and began to read, the high-pitched chatter of seagulls outside as they fished and swooped at the sea setting a relaxing tone as she read.

'The ones upstairs are far more interesting,' a voice behind her said.

She jumped at the interruption and looked up to see Maurice, a strange look on his face that she could not place.

'Emerald-green in the master bedroom, full of hand-painted birds. Blue for another room where the sea roams on every wall and clouds line the ceiling.'

'I'm sorry I got curious,' she said.

He smiled sadly. 'It is a curious house. Full of surprises. You know, in the dining room there is a hidden door, behind which is a corridor that leads to all the rooms in the house. The dining room has yet to be completed. I believe there was a plan to paint it with Greek gods and mythical beasts.'

'When will the artist finish?' she asked.

He shrugged. 'Not for a while yet.'

'I'd like to meet them. They make it feel so real – so alive.'

Maurice opened his mouth to speak, but no words came forth. He shook his head. 'Come. We have some work to do.'

TEN

HUGO

Hugo stared at the child, who stared back. He wanted to look more closely at her eyes – one brown and one green, yet he could swear that there were flecks of gold in them too. As if sensing what he was thinking, the girl rubbed at her eyes, then turned away from him and walked into the house, her night-dress dragging behind her.

What had Kasia said her name was again? Esme? No, Elodie. He snapped his fingers. *Elodie.* And Elodie was his charge.

He felt sweat collect on the back of his neck. What was he meant to do with her? With a girl that didn't speak and even if she did, he would not understand her anyway. Hugo followed her inside and saw she had climbed the stairs. Perhaps she would go back to sleep, he thought. Perhaps he wouldn't have to take care of her at all.

With this soothing thought, he made himself more coffee and began to whistle quietly. Then he turned and saw a shadow in the doorway. Suddenly scared, he spilled the coffee on his hand and yelped.

It was the girl.

'Don't do that!' he yelled at her. 'I've burned my hand. Didn't your parents ever tell you not to sneak up on people?'

He blew on the scaled skin and saw she had dressed herself. She walked up to him and gestured for his burned hand.

'It's fine, it will be fine,' he said.

She looked intently at the skin, then pulled him to the tap where she ran cold water over it. Each time he tried to pull his hand away and told her it was fine, she tightened her grip and kept it under the running water.

He wondered how long she was going to make him stand there with his hand under the water. Did she think it was a game? Then, just as the thought entered his mind, she let go of his hand and turned off the rusting tap that squealed in protest. She narrowed her eyes at the noise, then looked to Hugo.

'Yes, I know, it is something else I need to fix,' he said.

She tilted her head to the side, then went to the cupboard, opened it and began to rummage around.

'Ah, food!' he shouted, startling her.

'No, no.' He waved his hands. 'Don't be scared. You want food, yes?' He mimed moving imaginary bread up to his mouth, then chewed.

The girl nodded, then held out her hand for him to take and began walking to the front door. Shopping, yes. She was right, he needed to get food for her. And clothes.

He went to open the door and saw that she was looking at his bare feet.

'It's fine, I don't wear shoes. I'll be fine.'

Her eyes wandered up from his feet to his still-dirty trousers and creased shirt.

'I look like this all the time. Honestly, it is normal for me.'

Elodie folded her arms and narrowed her eyes at him, and she reminded him suddenly of his mother. A tiny version of the woman who with one look could make Hugo do anything she wanted. And the girl had it perfected at her young age! He laughed.

'All right, you win! I will change and find shoes, are you happy now?'

He turned from her and made for his bedroom, looking over his shoulder just the once to see Elodie, her arms still crossed, watching and waiting.

Hugo looked around his bedroom, at the clothes dumped on the floor, thrown over the backs of chairs and even a shirt that in a moment of passion with Cécile had been flung high enough to catch itself on the light fitting. Normally, he would smile at the memory and ignore the chaos. But now it annoyed him. He dug around trying to find clean clothes and sniffed at them much like Monsieur LeBlanc's pig that snuffled for truffles.

I'm a pig now, he thought as he searched and sniffed.

Finally, he found a creased pair of brown trousers and a light blue shirt that he had forgotten he owned. It had no dirt, no ink or wine spilt on it, and he wondered why this one shirt had avoided his daily life.

He washed his face in his small bathroom off his bedroom and decided it might be time to shave. Dragging the razor over his days-old stubble, he looked in the mirror and noticed how red the whites of his eyes were, and how some new lines and creases had appeared on his forehead. And look there! Another grey hair in his black mane! He stopped shaving and plucked out the offending hair, before noticing that not just one, but a hundred, had taken residence.

'*Merde!*' he yelled.

Hugo finished shaving, cutting himself twice with tiny nicks on his chin. He wiped the blood with the back of his hand, then looked at it. The hand that had been burned. He had expected it still to be painful, to be blistered, but Elodie and her prolonged water stream had cured it.

Dressing quickly, he searched for shoes, finding only a pair of soft leather sandals with the heel flap folded down from where he had worn them as slippers. He shoved his feet into them and immediately felt claustrophobic. He wanted to flick them off and once more feel the ground beneath his soles, yet he knew the girl would eye him with distaste.

Why do I care? he wondered. She could think what she liked of him.

The door creaked and she appeared.

'*Et voilà!* What do you think?' he asked her.

She cocked her head to the side, then straightened it and gave him a small nod.

The shoes would stay.

At the front door stood an armoire with tiny drawers. Hugo stopped at it and found his ration tokens along with some money. He could feel the girl watching him and for some reason handed her a franc so that she did not feel left out.

It took them almost an hour to walk into the town, with Elodie struggling to keep pace with Hugo's long strides. He tried to slow at times and pointed at the sea, '*la mer*' he told her, once, twice, three times, hoping she would repeat it or at least understand, but she seemed uninterested in the crashing waves and tiny beaches. It wasn't until they reached the town, entering through one of the medieval gates that she became animated.

He took her into the Ramparts Gardens where the river Marle flowed steadily through. He watched as she reacted. First, she stood, her hands by her side, and turned in small circles as she looked at the fortified walls, the town peaking behind them, the manicured lawns, the few flowers that still remained until next spring when the gardens would truly come alive.

Then, her eyes locked upon the river and as if she was in a trance, she approached it, then picked up her pace and ran.

For a moment, Hugo did nothing. Then, as she got further

and further away, his heart quickened and he followed suit, shouting her name that she had been given just a day before. He reached her just as she reached the bank, and she looked up at him with surprise in her eyes.

'It's not safe to run like that. What if you fell in?'

As if she understood him, she shrugged, then knelt down and put her hand in the river, making small waves.

He pulled her up and took her wet hand in his and began to walk, feeling her slow reluctance just a few steps behind him.

'One day I will take you to the river. To the river proper, where you can fish and swim and play. But you cannot go there alone, do you understand?' He stopped and bent down to her height, holding her shoulders in his hands. 'Do you understand? The river—' He pointed at it. 'No, never,' he waggled his finger in her face. 'Not alone.'

The girl blinked a few times, then, again, gave a nonchalant shrug. Exasperated with the exchange, or lack thereof, Hugo stood, took her hand in his and made his way away from the gardens, along the river and past the manicured lawns, advancing on the cobbled streets of the town. Just as they reached the high domes of the Cathedral Saint Pierre, Hugo saw two soldiers checking papers.

He let go of her hand and rummaged in his pockets. '*Merde*,' he mumbled. He looked behind him – they could simply walk home, but they had come to an almost stop and it would look suspicious if they simply turned and walked away. Had Kasia even given him the girl's papers? He couldn't remember. The bakery was a few yards after the checkpoint, just one turn to the left. Making up his mind, he took her hand once more and moved forward in the small queue.

'*Papiers*,' the German guard asked as Hugo moved forward.

Hugo let out a sigh of relief. He knew the guard. He liked merlot. What was his name?

'You still liking the merlot?' Hugo asked in German.

The guard took notice now and looked at Hugo with recognition in his eyes. 'Ah! The winemaker!' The guard slapped him on the arm. 'We are getting a bit low.'

'Well then, let me see what I can do,' Hugo said.

The guard took a cigarette from his breast pocket, and Hugo quickly removed his lighter and lit it for him, then stepped forward thinking that their business was concluded.

'You know,' the guard relaxed now, ready for a conversation, 'I had always preferred beer before. My whole life – beer. And then, I tried your wine and that was it! Extraordinary, don't you think? I even wrote to my mother and told her, and she wrote back and said she did not believe me! I've asked one of my friends to take some photographs of me with your wine so I can send her the proof.'

Hugo could feel Elodie's hand squeeze his and then clamp on like a vice.

'I'm more than happy to oblige,' Hugo said, and made to step forward once more.

'Very good! Bring some by the end of the week if you can.' The guard stepped to the side to let him through, and it was then he noticed the child and blocked their path once more.

'Who is that?' he asked.

The girl was squeezing and clenching at his hand now, and Hugo had a moment when he couldn't remember her name, what he was supposed to say.

Then, it came to him. 'Elodie. She is my cousin's daughter,' he said, his mouth dry and the words slapping against the parched roof of his mouth.

'Cousin? I didn't know you had one.'

'They only just arrived. Her husband died, and I said they could stay.'

'Her papers?'

'I forgot them.' Hugo forced out a laugh. 'Too much wine

last night and *poof*! My memory disappears. You know what it is like? Can't remember which way is up the next day!'

The guard narrowed his eyes, looked at the girl, then grinned. 'I know! My head two days ago was terrible. I had to lie down in a dark room for hours.'

'Next time, I promise, I will remember,' Hugo said.

The guard laughed once more, stepped aside and let Hugo and Elodie go on their way. As soon as they rounded the corner, the girl loosened her grasp. He pulled her under the awning of the patisserie, and bent down to look at her. She was not crying, her face was blank, but her skin was pale, her eyes wider than usual.

He stroked her cheek. 'The guard, he scared you? I know, I know. It's not good. The Boche are everywhere. We will go to the river again. It will make you happy. You want to go to the river?'

The girl leaned into him and put her head on his shoulder. For a moment, he felt a surge of warmth run through him, then she pulled away.

'Here, come,' he stood and held out his hand. 'We will get you anything you want.'

What had she seen in Poland? he wondered. He had not even asked Kasia where she had found the child and indeed what she was really doing here. Had she never talked? Or had what she'd seen made her dumb? With his free hand, he rubbed his palm across his face.

'Ah, Hugo!' Henri waved at him from the doorway of the bakery. 'You are late again. Nothing left for customers – only a few bits for Cécile and myself.'

Hugo saw Henri's eyes dart to the child, then back to Hugo. He raised his eyebrows in question.

'My cousin,' he replied. 'I mean my cousin's child. They are visiting.'

'Your aunt Brigitte?' Henri asked. 'I didn't know she had a daughter?'

Hugo felt cold all over. Of course, Henri knew his mother, his mother's sister. He knew his father's side of the family too. What should he say?

Before he could think to answer, a squeal came from behind Henri, and Cécile appeared, pushing her father out of the way.

'Look at her eyes!' Cécile bent down and took the girl in an embrace, then held her face between her hands. 'Look, Papa. One green, one brown! Have you ever seen anything like it? What is your name beautiful girl?'

Elodie shifted her eyes to focus on Hugo.

'Ah, she does not speak,' Hugo said. 'Her name is Elodie.'

'She does not speak?' Cécile stood and dusted down her skirts. 'Why?'

Hugo shrugged. 'Born that way.'

'But she can hear, yes?'

'She can,' Hugo said. 'But sometimes she does not understand much.'

'Oh, you poor girl.' Cécile swept down once more and pulled the girl to her again. 'Come with me, you poor thing. Let me find you something.'

Cécile took Elodie's hand and walked into the bakery, Hugo following behind.

'But Cécile, we have nothing left!' Henri shouted at her.

With a quick look over her shoulder, she silenced her father and disappeared into the kitchen with the girl.

'Bloody women,' Henri mumbled, following Hugo. 'She thinks she is the boss of me, you know.'

'It's because she is,' Hugo answered.

'You may be right.'

In the kitchen, between the large ovens, Elodie sat at a small table and Cécile plated up pastries and bread for her.

Hugo sat beside her and tore into a fresh croissant and motioned for her to do the same.

'I will put some of these in a bag for you,' Cécile said. 'You must come earlier. The queues grow larger each day and the ration cards smaller.'

Henri placed his meaty hand on Hugo's shoulder. 'Do you think you can help?'

Hugo turned. 'I'm not sure what you mean.'

Henri manoeuvred himself and his large stomach through the narrow kitchen and plopped himself on a wooden chair that Hugo was sure one day would give way under his great girth.

'I've heard that you have helped Maurice with a few items.'

'Says who?' Hugo asked, feeling a creeping nausea rise. It was meant to be between him and Maurice. Who else knew?

Henri shook his head, but he gave himself away with a quick glance in Cécile's direction. *Merde.* He remembered now that he had told Cécile. Promised her perfume and stockings after drinking a copious amount of wine. Cécile refused to look at him and instead trained her attention on Elodie, whom she fussed with and cooed over as if she were a tiny baby.

'What do you need?' Hugo asked quietly.

'Flour. Butter. We are fine for eggs – in fact, now you have guests go and see LeBlanc. His hens are laying like crazy. Get them whilst they are there. He also has a few chickens and rabbits.'

'I will see what I can do,' Hugo said. 'But this can go no further, you understand?'

Henri grinned. 'I'm nothing if not trustworthy.'

'Does she have anything prettier to wear?' Cécile was plucking at the girl's cardigan that had a hole in the elbow.

'We need to get her some new clothes.'

'They did not bring luggage?' Henri asked. 'Why not?'

'There was a fire,' Hugo said quickly. 'Everything was gone.'

'Oh, you poor, poor thing. Come with me.' Cécile held out

her hand and Elodie, her face now flushed from eating so quickly, took her hand without hesitation. 'And you,' Cécile extended her palm to Hugo, 'Give me whatever money you have, and I will go and get this little mite some pretty girl clothes.'

Hugo knew he was beaten and handed over a scrunched-up ball of money and ration tickets.

'Whilst we are gone, go and get some food. Proper food. See LeBlanc, then go and see Armand. He has vegetables still, even though he will say he has none. Tell him Cécile sent you.'

As she said Armand's name, Hugo noticed Cécile blush. 'Ah, our young Armand. How is he?' Hugo asked.

'He is well,' Cécile said.

'And you two are—'

'We are,' Cécile answered, then led Elodie out of the kitchen.

Hugo had known deep down that Cécile had used him, just as he her. She had wanted Armand back for months, and Hugo knew that jealousy was a way to get to a man's heart. If he thought his prize were being taken, then he would act. And Armand had done so – and quickly too.

He searched his own feelings for jealousy. Was he upset that Cécile had moved on so quickly? No. It had been fun. They were friends before, and still friends now, and each had got what they wanted – him some companionship, however brief, and she, the man she truly loved.

'I cannot keep up with her.' Henri leaned back in his chair and wrapped his arms around his belly, clasping his hands in front.

He could see the man's eyes closing. 'You need a sleep.' Hugo stood.

'Up at dawn. As usual. The cockerel is always annoyed at me for being awake before him. I've taken his job...' Henri mumbled as his face got slacker, his breathing heavier. 'Cockerels, bread, women who shout at me...'

Hugo smiled, wanting to laugh at the way Henri spoke as he fell through the membrane from this world into that of dreams.

'Women – bloody women,' Henri said, his head dropping onto his shoulder.

Hugo left his friend to sleep and sought out provisions. Armand indeed told him he had nothing left, yet as soon as Hugo mentioned Cécile, he somehow managed to find potatoes, carrots, onions and a cabbage.

'Thank you,' Hugo said, and held out his hand to shake Armand's.

Armand did not reciprocate, and Hugo smiled at him. 'The better man won,' he said. 'No hard feelings.'

Armand nodded. 'You are right. The better man won.'

Laden with a basket full of eggs, a chicken and a freshly shot rabbit, and a bag full of vegetables, pastries and bread from Cécile, Hugo sat at *la café* Mirabelle and added a thick black coffee to his tab, which he assured Madame Dupont would be settled soon. The town streets were still too quiet. Businesses were open, and yet customers came early, then returned home, even though there had been no rule forbidding them to be about during daylight hours. He knew of the other rules – not to lock your door, not to hoard food, shutters closed, curfew from 8 p.m. until dawn. He had listened to the new rules as soon as they had been announced, but, as yet, he hadn't taken them seriously – his wine kept him friendly with his occupiers and he had stupidly thought he was invincible.

Yet today, with the young guard who liked the merlot, he had felt a thread of fear. They could turn on him, wine or no wine. And now, he had the child and Kasia too. He picked at his fingernails, pulling away the skin and making them bleed.

Over an hour later, Cécile appeared with Elodie who was now dressed in a light blue skirt and matching cardigan, a primrose yellow shirt underneath. He smiled at the sight of her as her eyes darted about the town, her cheeks flushed pink, her skipping step signalling that she had found a little happiness with Cécile.

'What do you think?' Cécile asked.

'I think I've been waiting for a long time,' Hugo answered.

'Always so grumpy.' Cécile sighed and handed him yet another bag. 'Nightgown, underwear, some shorts, sandals, and a few dresses.'

Hugo held out his hand. 'Where is the change?'

Cécile laughed. 'You're lucky it didn't cost more. I've asked Madame Laurent for any clothes she may have too.'

'Madame Laurent?'

'Yes, you know she runs the school? She always has things. She says she will knit the girl some winter clothing, find her some winter boots too. She said to bring her mother next time as she may have some clothes of her own to give her.'

'I will.' Hugo stood and balanced the bags in such a way that Elodie could hold on to his little finger as they walked.

ELEVEN

KASIA

Clouds heaved across the sky, sucking out the afternoon light as Kasia and Maurice cycled down a rutted track nearing a farmhouse in the distance. They had cycled for miles, down lanes, around abandoned shepherd's huts, near the coast, away from the coast, down narrow roads with houses on either side where cars would be scraped by the bricks. Each place was good for her to transmit, Maurice had explained. The more rural, the better. He would take her to some nearby towns over the coming days, ostensibly as his nurse.

'The Boche have to see you with me, they have to get used to you. The more we travel, the more you will see and the more options you will have.'

'And the "patients" you see?' she had asked.

'Most of them are patients. Some perhaps you can help with, but some you cannot come in. These will be the ones that are going to give us messages to take.'

Maurice stopped in front of the farmhouse and led her to the rear. From his panniers he produced a blanket and some bread, cheese, water and chicken.

'We must eat,' he said.

'Can't we go inside?' she asked.

Maurice shook his head. 'I can, but you must stay here and wait.'

He left her picnicking on the craggy field, lumps of rocks underneath her buttocks so that she couldn't get comfortable on the blanket. She ate quickly, barely tasting the food, realising she hadn't eaten much since leaving Warsaw. It was then that she wished for her mother's cooking – *rosol*, the chicken soup she added strings of noodles to, and the *pierogi* dumplings filled with cheese and fresh mushrooms.

Suddenly, her mind took her back there, to the kitchen where she had sat with her sister crimping closed the dumplings with her stubby child's fingers, the air gooey with the scent of honey for the sweet pierogi, frying mushrooms with pickled cabbage sizzling on the stove, her mother wiping her hands on a red apron, her hair wild from the steam and heat.

Her father entered the memory, an unlit pipe clenched between his teeth. He grinned, removed the pipe and kissed the top of his younger daughter's head.

'Well, look at what Maja has done! Aren't they perfect, *kochanie?*' he asked her mother.

He held up the crimped dumpling and her mother clapped her hands, then kissed Maja on both cheeks. Kasia had held up her own dumpling, bent and sagging, the edges not closed and thin strands of sauerkraut sticking out.

'Keep trying, *misio,*' her father had said.

Misio – teddy bear, a name given to her for her squishy stomach, or so her sister had said.

Now she shook the memory away and bit into a cold chicken leg, tearing the flesh with her teeth.

'You were hungry.' Maurice was back.

She nodded, her mouth full of the chicken, her cheeks bloated. Perhaps she was a *misio,* after all.

'Nothing for today,' Maurice said. 'Tomorrow, though, we

will be busy; it's Friday, after all. I will take you home soon and then I will fetch you early, perhaps at six. Is that all right?'

She swallowed. 'I barely sleep. Anytime is fine.'

'Remember to store the radio somewhere safe – a hiding place in the house or in the outhouses. Look at it if you must, but don't transmit from Hugo's, it is too obvious and will be found quickly.'

A plane hummed overhead and Kasia followed its trail, the sound of its engines lingering long after the sight of the metal bird had disappeared into a thick cloud.

'It feels so quiet here,' Kasia said. 'Granted, I've only been here a day, but it is so different to Poland.'

'We have air raids, of course. Bombs have been dropped nearby, but yes, I'm sure that compared to what you have lived through, it is relatively quiet.'

'There were times when we were trapped in a cellar because of the bombings,' Kasia said. 'Sometimes several days. When we could finally leave, I almost didn't want to – I didn't want to see what had become of the city.'

'Warsaw?'

She nodded. 'Rubble everywhere. Homes gone. Things, places, just seemed to disappear. Kraków was different – my home. Less bombs but still the fear – the constant fear.'

'But you survived,' Maurice said.

'I had to. I had no choice. My mother died, my father left to live with his brother in America; I was alone.'

'You had no one else?'

Kasia shrugged. 'No one that mattered.'

'So you gave yourself to the cause. It became your life.'

Again, she shrugged. 'I gave myself to codes, to ciphers, to mathematics at university and it consumed me. Then, before the war, I was recruited to join the cipher bureau in Warsaw.'

'What was that like?' Maurice asked. 'Exciting? I imagine that it would have been.'

Kasia laughed. 'Not as exciting as you might think. A lot of it was desk-based. There were three men, all mathematicians who headed up the research into cracking German codes, Enigma it was called. A machine that Rejewski originally deciphered as early as 1932. Then, as the keys changed, they had to change the way they cracked the codes. Myself and others were brought in to help decipher, help with equations. If you like that sort of thing, then yes, it was exciting, but I imagine that for most it would seem boring.'

'But you joined the resistance?'

Kasia nodded and chewed thoughtfully on a piece of bread. 'When war broke out, the bureau headed for France. I was going to go with them, but my best friend Marta had set up a local resistance group – all Jewish and Polish women, some with special skill sets, others just women who wanted to fight but could not do so with the army. She begged me to stay with her to be the one who was able to transmit and relay messages through the radio and to train others. I couldn't deny her, nor those other women who needed me.'

'How is it that you were never caught? You are Jewish, and you said the others were too,' Maurice asked.

'What choice did some of us have? As the war progressed, women from all over began to join local resistance groups; groups which have been established before the Germans arrived as we knew what was going to happen. I was chosen, as were others, because when we dyed our hair, we did not look Jewish any more. I was already fair enough, and my languages meant that I could move about pretty much undetected. I had taken my mother's maiden name very early on in 1935 and fake documents meant that I was able to go somewhat undetected. Others were not as lucky as me – many were found, sent to prison, work camps, the ghetto. And the more women that were arrested meant that I could no longer simply help with the radio and messages, I had to fill in the gaps that were left and go into the field – namely going in and out of the ghetto.'

'You make it sound so easy – so simple...' Maurice raised his hands.

'It wasn't, it isn't. Even with new papers, with dyed hair, there is always the constant fear that it won't work, that they will find out who you truly are.'

She saw Maurice shake his head. 'I am amazed by you – truly I am. You are the bravest person I think I have ever met!'

Kasia laughed once more. 'I will let you into a little secret of mine, Maurice. I am not brave, not really. Inside I am scared and that is why I do what I am doing. It is the fear that drives me. I can't imagine sitting and doing nothing – just feeling the fear consume me day in and day out. At least this way I am doing something with the fear – fighting against it. Does that make sense?'

Maurice nodded. 'I think I am the same way. Can I ask, though, why did you want to come to France? Your handler in Poland was insistent that you come here.'

'I knew I could help,' Kasia said simply. 'Look, it's going to rain.' She pointed at the sky where a full grey cloud hung low overhead.

Within seconds, fat raindrops fell, then quickly gathered speed to become icy sheets of rain that obscured the view in front of them.

Gathering the picnic up, they cycled away from the farmhouse, Kasia's bicycle hitting potholes, splashing muddy water onto her stockings.

No one left that mattered, she had told Maurice. *No*, she thought, *that wasn't entirely true...*

TWELVE

THE POLISH GIRL

She sat on her bed, her feet swinging back and forth in the new shoes that the lady with the flowing skirts had bought her. These shoes were shiny and yellow, and she loved them and had refused to remove them when she and Hugo had returned home.

She watched as Hugo moved boxes from her room and traipsed down the stairs to his bedroom. She was a little sad to see the boxes go as she had thought that she could have time to look inside and see what was in them.

There was one box left. It was small and made of wood with little golden clasps that reminded her of a pirate's treasure chest. She could still hear Hugo stomping about downstairs, now and again saying that word, '*merde*'. He said it a lot and she still liked it and found herself mouthing it when he wasn't looking.

The new words she had learned almost had flavour to them – *merde* – that was a spicy. *Bonjour* – this was like butter in her mouth, it covered and swelled the top and bottom of her gums, coating them in warmth. *Vous,* and *tu,* were singsong-like, lemony in their taste.

Whilst Hugo was downstairs, she quickly clambered off the

bed and made her way to the box. With deft fingers, she opened it, and inside held a teddy bear, an eye missing, a red bow tied around its neck. She carefully removed it and held it to her. It had the odour of the cellar at home and, whilst she had always hated that smell, in this moment, she felt safe, calm.

She did not hear Hugo approach her, but there he was, his long legs and now bare feet in front of her and she suddenly felt fear. She handed the bear to him and made her way back to the bed. Hugo held the bear away from him and stared at it for some time. Then, with watery eyes, he smiled.

'*C'est à moi*,' he said, and pointed to his chest.

She nodded. It was his bear. Not hers. He knelt in front of her and spoke quietly. She tried to make out some of the words, but it all sounded like a song to her.

'*Il s'appelle* Georges,' he said. He repeated it to her. Then, he pointed at himself and said 'Hugo', then to her, 'Elodie', then to the bear, 'Georges'.

She understood. The bear had a name. He was called Georges.

He held the bear out to her. '*Il est pour toi.*'

She took the bear and held it close. Then, she smiled at Hugo and kissed the top of the bear's head. She had a bear. And his name was Georges.

The rest of the day was spent in a flurry of activity. Hugo went from room to room, finding bedding, moving boxes, setting up the bedframe. All the while he spoke and pointed at things. *Un lit*, she found was a bed – a flat word that tasted of bread. *Une armoire* – a cupboard. Bread was *le pain*, a book, *un livre*. So many words with a mixture of tastes that she could not place them all.

She learned quickly and mouthed each word silently – *un lit, une armoire, un livre, Georges, la mer*. And, of course, Hugo's favourite word, *merde*, which she did not know the meaning of, yet she realised he said it when he dropped something, or when his brow creased when he thought of something. It was a bad word, she was sure. It made her think of Papa, when he would stub his toe on the coffee table, then yell out 'damn it to hell!' and her mother would shout at him and then tell her she was not allowed to repeat what he had said.

Snippets of memories kept breaking through all day. The scent of her mother when she hugged her, like fresh flowers; her father laughing at something he had heard at work, her sister and brother fighting over who had won at cards. Each time a memory came, she squeezed her eyes tight and willed them away. She thought instead of the words she was learning, of the nice lady in the town, of her bear Georges.

One thought that she could not get rid of was that of the German guard she had seen earlier that day. As soon as she had heard him speak, her hands had felt clammy, a shiver of cold had run down her spine and her mouth went very dry. Hugo had not let go of her hand. He had kept her with him. He had smiled and laughed with the man, even spoke in German to him too.

Hugo had understood the fear that she had felt, as he had stroked her cheek and let her rest on him a moment. He would keep her safe, she thought. But then another thought came – *but why couldn't Mama and Papa keep me safe?*

She knew the answer to the question and did not allow herself to answer it. Instead, she kept Georges close to her and listened to Hugo as he pointed at things and taught her words. *La mer, une armoire, merde.*

THIRTEEN

HUGO

As the rain intensified, a rumble of thunder rolled across the sky, out towards the sea. Hugo stood on the veranda and watched the water fall in sheets, the gush of it flowing through the gutters, and the sound of it hitting the roof like pebbles soothed him. Elodie joined him and sat on a tiny stool that he usually stood on to retrieve the spiders that loved to make their home in the eaves of the veranda roof. He watched her out the corner of his eye and caught her mouthing words to the bear, then he saw her smile and kiss the bear's furry head.

Georges. His bear from childhood. He could not remember when Georges came into his life, but the stuffed toy seemed to be always with him. He remembered how he would follow his father into the vineyards, pulling a little red wooden cart behind him, and inside Georges would sit along with a few other toys he would bring to entertain himself whilst his father worked.

His arm fell off once and his mother wiped away his tears and performed surgery on him on the kitchen table. Her quick hands sewed almost invisible stitches so that he could barely tell that Georges had had an accident. She even wrapped his arm with a scrap of an old sheet and made a sling.

The last city that Georges had seen was Paris, where he had belonged to someone else for a time, and since then he had been hidden in the chest in the spare bedroom, and Hugo felt a pang of childish guilt at forgetting about his once best friend.

Now, though, he had a new owner. When he first saw Elodie with the bear, the years came rushing back to him – memories of his past life – and he wanted to snatch Georges away and put him back into the box and lock it forever. But then he had seen her face. She was smiling, and despite the memories Georges would make him face, he could not take that away from her.

A clap of thunder directly overhead made him jump, and he looked to Elodie to see if she was scared by the noise. But she was not shaken; she was still mouthing words to the bear. He was sure he saw her mouth the word '*merde*' but could not be sure. Perhaps she would talk soon, he thought. Perhaps Georges had made her feel safe enough to talk.

He turned to her. 'Are you hungry?' Then, he mimed eating. She nodded and held out her hand for him to take and together they went into the kitchen.

Feeling lighter than he had done in years, and with a bubble of excitement that he could not place, he put a record on the gramophone, poured himself a glass of wine and set about making a meal.

He did not hear the door open and close; instead, he sang as he chopped the vegetables, now and again singing loudly in Elodie's direction, and sometimes getting a smile back in return.

'You have been busy.'

He turned to see a drenched Kasia in the kitchen doorway, a small pool of water at her feet.

'I see the storm found you,' he replied.

She laughed and placed a small suitcase on the floor, then went to Elodie, talking to her in rapid Polish and admiring her new yellow shoes and her bear.

'You've taken good care of her.' She turned to him, surprise on her face.

He shrugged and continued stirring the thickening stock, adding carrots and onions, watching the steam circle out of the pan, bringing a comforting herby aroma. When was the last time he had cooked? A year? Maybe more.

He had been enjoying the process, and, if he admitted it to himself, he had even enjoyed cleaning and shopping too. But now Kasia was here, he felt a bristle of annoyance. Why should she be surprised that he could take care of the child? Did she really think he was so pathetic, so untrustworthy?

He drank the rest of the wine and slopped more into the glass.

'I'm just going to change.' He heard Kasia clop her way to the stairs, then the pitter patter of Elodie's feet as she followed her like a duckling.

Alone in the kitchen, Hugo tried to sing along once more to the record, yet his voice had lost enthusiasm, and soon he found himself bashing pan lids, swearing when he could not find a ladle, which finally culminated in him burning himself on the stove top.

Running his wrist under the tap, he tried to figure out when his mood had changed. He was sure it was when Kasia had arrived, but why? He did not know her so couldn't say he disliked her. But there was something about her, the confidence perhaps, that got under his skin and turned his mood black.

They ate in near silence. Kasia spoke to the girl who barely looked up from her plate, shovelling in the chicken and vegetables, then mopping up the juices with bread.

'She has found her appetite, if not her voice,' Kasia said. 'It was very good, thank you.'

Hugo nodded, then pushed back his chair to stand just as a quick rap at the front door alerted him to a visitor.

Kasia looked to him. 'Maurice?' she asked.

He didn't answer, knowing that Maurice would simply barge his way in unannounced if he wanted to. On the front porch, with shiny slicks of rain on his dark mac, was the gendarme, Pierre.

'Evening,' he started, tipping the brim of his hat. 'I hope I'm not disturbing you?'

Hugo glanced over his shoulder.

'You have visitors, I hear?' Pierre said, then stepped inside, pushing his way past Hugo.

'And here I was thinking you came for the wine,' Hugo responded. 'I have it ready for you.'

Pierre ignored him, removed his hat that trailed droplets of water onto the floor and walked into the kitchen.

'Madame,' Pierre began. 'You are Hugo's cousin, I believe?'

Hugo saw a flash of fear in Kasia's eyes, and he too felt an uncomfortable knot in his stomach.

'I'm sorry, but I did not know your mother,' Pierre said. 'So you are?'

'Please forgive me,' Kasia stood, a welcoming smile appearing on her face and held out her hand by way of introduction. 'Delphine.'

'Very pleased to meet you, I'm sure,' Pierre said.

'Please, sit, dry yourself, can we offer you some food, a drink perhaps?' Kasia guided him to the table, and Hugo, as if in a dream, followed and sat back in his place.

Pierre waved away the invitation, then his small moustache twitched. 'Perhaps one glass would be suitable.'

Kasia nodded and retrieved a fresh glass, pouring in a hefty measure of the merlot that Hugo had recently opened.

The gendarme drank it back, then smacked his lips in appreciation. 'And who is this?' He gestured to the girl.

'This is Elodie, my daughter.' Kasia placed a hand on the girl's shoulder. 'She doesn't speak, I'm afraid.'

'An illness,' Hugo barked out before Kasia could say more. 'A childhood illness. She barely understands anything either.'

Kasia narrowed her eyes at Hugo, then looked to Pierre and nodded.

'Such a shame,' he replied. 'For such a pretty girl, such a shame.'

Hugo wanted to ask him if it would be agreeable for her not to speak nor understand if she were perhaps ugly instead, but he said nothing.

'I only came this evening, in such a weather, as I wasn't sure whether Hugo had heard that from now on a list of occupants must be posted on the door at all times. It was a decree that came about last week, but as Hugo was alone, I thought it unnecessary to ensure his compliance. But now,' Pierre gestured to Kasia and Elodie, 'It's for the best I'm sure. You are not expecting anyone else, Hugo?'

'I highly doubt it,' he said.

'Forgive me for asking, but your accent, have you lived abroad recently?' Pierre asked.

Kasia opened her mouth to answer when suddenly Elodie scraped back her chair, causing a cry from the wood of the chair and floor as they met.

'You should lift it!' Pierre said, scrunching up his face with distaste from the high-pitched noise.

'You must forgive her.' Kasia stood too. 'She is tired, ready for bed. I must attend to her.'

'Of course, of course.' Pierre stood.

'It was so lovely to meet you,' Kasia said, and Hugo noticed that the way she had leaned into Pierre, the way she had smiled at him had made the gendarme's cheeks flush.

'Yes, yes,' Pierre blustered. 'We shall meet again, I'm sure.'

Hugo saw that Pierre did not take his eyes off Kasia until

she was completely out of sight, then he sat back down in his chair with a sigh.

'Beautiful cousin you have there, Hugo, absolutely. Her husband is dead, yes?'

'He is, but she is still in mourning,' he said.

'Yes, of course, of course. Not that I meant anything by it.'

'The wine? Are you still in need?' Hugo stood and walked to a low cupboard at the rear of the kitchen.

'Not in the cellar then?' Pierre asked.

'Not these. I told you, I had them ready for you.'

Hugo handed over four bottles, and knew that Pierre would most likely drink one and sell the others for an extortionate rate.

Pierre carried the bottles in his arms to the front door. 'Remember now, eh? Names on the door by tomorrow. And keep your shutters closed. I don't want to have to remind you again.'

Hugo watched as Pierre tucked the bottles into his panniers and cycled out into the night.

'He's gone?'

Hugo turned to see Kasia paused on the stairs, her eyes darting about the hallway.

'He has.'

'I'm so sorry. We should have discussed exactly who I am, your family, everything.'

'It's fine. He's only been here a few years and never knew my family, you're fine.'

'What if he checks?' she asked.

'He won't. As long as he has wine, he won't do a thing. Besides, I think he's rather taken with you.' Hugo closed the front door and locked it, despite knowing it was now against the rules, and headed for the sitting room.

'Still, I think you should tell me about your family so that if there are any questions—'

Hugo held up his hand to stop her. 'You will be with

Maurice, yes? He will speak for you. Let's not go into things now, I'm tired. I've had a busy day, or hadn't you noticed?'

Kasia had her hands on her hips, and he was sure that she was going to press him to talk more. Instead, perhaps feeling the day's events herself, she let her arms fall to her sides, then flopped onto the chaise longue.

She took a silver cigarette case from her pocket, removed one and offered one to Hugo. He accepted and lit hers first, noticing how her eyes did not leave his as he did so.

'It's unlucky,' she said, blowing out the first plume of smoke, 'not to make eye contact with the person who lights a cigarette for you.'

'Says who?'

She shrugged. 'I've heard it before. Someone said it. By the way, I need you to do something for me.'

Hugo rolled his eyes. 'No, wait, don't tell me, you'd like me to wash your clothes? Or perhaps bring you breakfast in bed?'

'Here.' She flung a piece of paper at him, a scribbled address.

He read the address. 'America. You want me to go there, perhaps?' He smirked. 'You'd like my home for yourself?'

'Are you always this disagreeable or do I bring this out in you?' she asked.

'Who's to say?'

'Look.' She ignored him. 'That's an address that Elodie had in her pocket when she was found. You are to write to them – Maurice says you know English, correct?'

Hugo nodded.

'Well then. Write to them. Explain that a child was found with this address with her, in Warsaw. Explain that her parents are dead. I would do it myself, but there's the possibility that it would be opened as the postmaster does not know me. But Maurice said you are friends with everyone, so you sending a letter to America would not be found strange.'

'Dead?' he asked.

'Didn't I tell you that?'

'No.'

'Well now you know.'

Hugo looked to the chair by the living room door, a chair that usually held books, papers, letters, but now had blanketed upon it Elodie's small coat. He stared at the coat and thought of her parents – what she had perhaps been through. No wonder she didn't speak.

'Are you all right?' Kasia asked.

'How can you be so nonchalant about it? Her parents are dead and you just say it, just like that.' He snapped his fingers.

'How else would you like me to say it? With tears running down my face? Tearing at my clothing?' She suddenly laughed. 'You have no idea how much death I've seen, how many people I've seen suffering. If I were to feel it all, to allow myself the luxury of being emotional, then I dare say I would never stop crying.'

Hugo was unsure of what to say. He wanted to ask what she had seen, but he was afraid to hear it at the same time.

'You are fearless,' he said almost to himself, his voice dipping as he said the final word.

'Is that a compliment?' she asked.

He shrugged. 'Yes and no.'

'And what's wrong with being fearless?' Kasia said, leaning back into the chaise and blowing smoke rings above her head.

'You're a woman – have you no sense, no compassion?'

'So you think being fearless is for men alone? Bravery is for just those with something dangling between their legs?' She laughed.

'I think you should be more careful,' Hugo said. 'In just a day you have had me questioned by a guard, I had to lie to a gendarme, and he is now sniffing about the house. It's as though you don't see the danger that you're putting yourself in.'

'You're a typical man, you know that? A man who thinks he must take care of a woman and then when things get difficult, he simply disappears!'

'You have no idea who I am,' he said.

'I know exactly who you are.' She sat forward now and stubbed her cigarette out into the ashtray. 'You are like every man. You say you want a woman who will conform, who will obey and offer you some excitement in life. Yet, when the excitement is too much for you, when it threatens you, the woman is no longer exciting but an annoyance – a thorn in your side, eh?'

'I'm not that man.' Hugo stood at the same time as she did, the pair of them eyeing each other over the coffee table. He pointed his finger at her, ready to give his final say on the matter when there was a small yelp from the doorway.

Hugo saw Elodie, her mouth open, the bear Georges in her hand, her eyes wide with fright. Kasia rushed to her and stroked her hair, whispering words in Polish to her, whilst Elodie stared at Hugo, a single tear escaping her eye.

FOURTEEN

THE POLISH GIRL

She slept badly. Dreams merged with memories, changing her childhood home from the three-storey townhouse to one where the stairs never ended and no matter how fast she ran up them, she never could reach the top. Behind her, Papa shouted for her to hurry, to pack and find her coat. She tried to get off the stairs onto the landing that would lead to her bedroom, but as she did, she fell into nothingness.

Expecting a thud as her body hit the ground, she awoke into another dream. A man in a uniform was shouting words at her – no, not her, at Anna, her aunt. Anna was crying and the man was pointing at her, yelling, then in his hand was a gun. She tried to open her eyes, tried to break the barrier between sleep and wakefulness, but she couldn't – the dream pulled at her so that she kicked her legs in the bed hoping that, eventually, it would let her go.

Suddenly, the man disappeared, and she was in the dark. She knew this darkness, and felt along the damp brick walls, trying to find her way to Papa, to tell him to find the matches and light the candle. Underneath, she stepped on something soft and knew it to be her brother. She tried to reach down into the darkness to pull him up, to wake him, but her hands could not grasp him. She knew what would happen next. She knew she would open her mouth and scream and say his name. Both in her dream and on her bed as she slept, she began to cry; no matter what she tried now, it was too late, she would speak.

Then, she was awake. She was fully aware of the blanket that had twisted itself around her legs and the sweat that had made her armpits and back damp. She sat up and looked around her. It was still dark, but the sky was lightening, slivers of light creeping through the shutters. She did not want to be in the dark and got out of bed, opened the window, then pushed the shutters open.

Outside, she could hear the sea as it crashed against the shore, then quietened as it pulled back. She concentrated on the sound, letting herself breathe along with the rhythm of the waves. She was not in the dark any more, she had not spoken.

Out in the distance, she could see a light that was quickly extinguished, then it came back, once, twice, three times. Who was out there, on the waves? Who was flashing a light towards the shore? She heard the door click shut, then below her she saw the shadow of Kasia running down the drive, following the light.

She wanted to cry out – to stop her. She was leaving, she knew it would happen. After last night when she had cried because of their raised voices, she knew that they would think her too much trouble, but she hadn't been able to help it. And now, Kasia was running out to the sea, and she would never see her again.

The girl waited at the window until she heard the first bird sing, announcing that the night had finally ended, then she got back into bed, leaving the window open, breathing once more with the ebb and flow of the sea, trying to calm herself, trying not to cry. Just as her eyes began to close, she heard quick footsteps on the stairs. Jumping out of bed, she went to her door and opened it just as Kasia reached the landing.

'What are you doing awake so early?' Kasia asked her.

She felt foolish. Of course Kasia would not leave her, she had promised to keep her safe. *Just like Mama and Papa did?* A voice asked in her head.

'Do you want some breakfast?' Kasia asked.

It was then that she noticed Kasia holding a suitcase. She looked to it, and then to Kasia, and could feel her eyes beginning to well up.

'No, no.' Kasia placed the suitcase down. 'I'm not leaving. Hush, hush.' She embraced her and patted her back.

'This is no ordinary suitcase.' Kasia pulled away and wiped her tears with the back of her hand. 'Come, come with me and see.'

She padded after her, into Kasia's bedroom and sat on the bed next to the suitcase that Kasia had placed there. Kasia opened the case, revealing coils, switches and buttons. She reached out to touch it when Kasia told her not to.

'It's a radio,' she said. 'It's so I can talk to people and help them.'

Elodie did not understand. She remembered the radio that Papa had, which sat in his study and voices and music came from it, but she had never heard him talk back to anyone before.

'It's a different kind of radio,' Kasia explained. 'You take this wire here, and it sets up an antenna, then I flick this switch and turn this dial and then I can either speak or I can send a message by tapping this.' She pointed at a small lever attached to a black box.

She stared at the radio for some time, until Kasia told her it was time to go back to bed, wondering how far you could send your voice or your message and wondering why Kasia didn't simply use the telephone.

· · ·

That morning, she woke from a fitful few hours' sleep to a quiet house. She dressed quickly in a red dress that was too big for her frame, but the pretty woman called Cécile who had bought it for her had told her she would grow into it. She paired it with the yellow shoes and was sure that if her sister Zara had been there, she would have told her that she looked like a little girl and that she was growing up – she should wear something different. She didn't care, though. She liked dresses and colourful clothes, whereas Zara had always wanted to dress like a boy, insisting that trousers were more comfortable and if Benjamin got to wear them, then why couldn't she?

She opened her mouth ready to tell the memory of Zara that she could wear what she liked when she promptly stopped herself. She was thinking of them again and it had taken her by surprise. Leaving her bedroom, she resolved she must be more careful with her thoughts, she must not think of them – of any of them.

Downstairs the rooms were empty, and she felt a moment of panic that she had been left alone when she heard heavy foot-steps seemingly coming from underneath the house. Suddenly, she saw Hugo appear from a door at the rear of the kitchen, his hair mussed, an unlit cigarette dangling at his lips, his arms carrying three dusty bottles. He did not seem to notice her and banged the bottles on the table, scratching at the back of his neck and muttering to himself.

She walked heavily towards him so that he would look up, and when he did, he smiled.

'*Bonjour,*' he said to her. Then, he nodded at her.

He handed her a piece of paper and upon it was written a note in Kasia's messy handwriting, explaining that she had to go to work and that she should do as Hugo says. She went to place the note in her pocket, but Hugo took it from her and scrunched it up into a ball.

·   ·   ·

After breakfast, Hugo took her hand, and together they walked away from the house, down dusty rutted tracks to a large shed. On either side of the shed, she could see rows and rows of small trees, all neatly planted.

'*Mon travail*,' Hugo said, pointing at himself and then at the trees.

Then, he waved at a large man who was approaching them, dirt smattered on his trousers and shirt. Hugo let go of her hand and became busy talking to the man, who now and again looked at her and scrunched up his brow as Hugo spoke to him.

She saw then that the large man was not alone. Just behind him stood a tall, skinny boy that reminded her of a thin willow branch. She wondered if a strong wind came whether it would blow him over or snap him clean in two.

Hugo walked up to her with the man and the boy in tow and said something she didn't understand. Then, he pointed at her and said, 'Elodie,' then pointed at the boy's chest, 'Antoine.'

She nodded her understanding, then was unsure of what to do. Antoine listened as Hugo spoke, and she saw that he had green eyes, and when he listened, his eyebrows would become heavier so that his eyes narrowed. The boy nodded at Hugo, then held out his hand for her to take. He had big hands just like the man Hugo had spoken to, and she wondered if he was the boy's papa.

She took his hand and looked to Hugo who smiled at her and said '*allez, allez*,' and as much as she was unsure of this boy, she knew she was being told to go and play.

Antoine led her through neat rows of bare stalks, and she stopped to touch one. '*Les raisins*,' he said to her, once, twice, three times, then mimed popping something in his mouth.

Seeing that she did not understand, he beckoned for her to follow and jogged ahead of her, his boots stirring up clouds of dust. *Les raisins. Allez.* Two more words that she rolled about silently on her tongue like the boiled sweets her papa would give her every Saturday from a paper bag that he kept in his pocket, still not quite understanding their meaning. She supposed that it was food that was grown on these stalks, but she didn't know what. Perhaps it meant potatoes? No, Papa had once told her they had grown under the ground. 'They like the dark,' he had said, showing her a grubby potato in the pantry at home. It was a long time ago that that happened. How old had she been? She didn't know, but she remembered that she had worn pink shiny shoes that day. Why had they been in the pantry?

'*Allez!*' Antoine sang out. He was quite a way away now and she ran after him, feeling her feet skip across the soft ground.

They were soon on the other side of the neat rows of trees and in a field with grass that reached her knees and tickled her skin and made her itchy. The boy, Antoine, did not stop to wait for her, and she soon felt tired and hot and wanted to stop. The irritability she felt pulled her back in time to when Benjamin had made her go on a walk to fly his kite from the top of a hill. She had felt exactly the same way – hot, annoyed and thirsty.

'Come, come quickly,' Benjamin had shouted back at her.

She searched the memory – where was Zara? Where was Mama and Papa? She wouldn't have been alone with Benjamin, surely?

'Come, come quickly, see, it's flying!' She saw Benjamin in the distance, the blue and red kite lifting up into the puffed clouds.

'*Allez!*' Antoine's voice broke through the image and Benjamin and the kite disappeared, and she suddenly felt a tug of loss in her stomach.

She must be more careful, she had to remember not to remember them.

Antoine was just a few feet in front of her now and he

pointed at a thicket of trees, where a small, beaten stone hut peeked out. She followed him to the hut, seeing that the roof was missing, a wall half-crumbled.

'*C'est un secret*,' he said, then placed his finger on his lips.

She nodded, she understood, a secret. She was not to tell – well she wouldn't, couldn't. Inside, she felt along the cold stone, seeing tiny drawings of stick men scratched into the walls. Antoine beckoned her over to the corner where he removed a few stones to reveal a small wooden box. He sat, opened it and patted the ground for her to join him.

He delved inside and held his palm out to her to show her a silver bullet. She recoiled from it, and he laughed, then dropped it back into the box and produced a monocle on a gold chain which he balanced on his eye, squinting and screwing up his mouth to keep it balanced.

She had seen a school master wear one once and held out her hand for him to give her a try. The lens was too big for her face and no matter how hard she tried to screw up her face like Antoine, she could not keep the monocle secure. Antoine laughed at her endeavours, and she soon found that she was laughing too, a proper laugh where she could hear her own voice.

It sounded strange to her ears – was this really what she sounded like when she laughed? Antoine didn't seem to care and soon his hand was back inside the box, this time producing a small silver-wrapped rectangle.

He peeled away a piece of the silver foil to reveal the hidden treasure – chocolate.

'*Je suis une pie*,' he told her, breaking off a piece of the chocolate and handing it to her. '*Une pie*,' he said, then flapped his arms and squawked at her. '*Je découvre le trésor*.'

'*Une pie*,' he repeated and raised his eyebrow at her in question.

She nodded, he was being a bird, perhaps a *sroka* – a

magpie – that would steal treasures from people, hiding them away in their nests, and this here was his nest.

Une pie, les raisins, allez, bonjour. New words that she rolled around in her mind as the chocolate melted in her mouth.

FIFTEEN

KASIA

She met Maurice as the sun rose at the strange, almost magical house on the beach. He was waiting for her as she arrived, sat on the steps of the house, his gaze focused on the blue-green sea. She pedalled hard towards him, the panniers full with the heavy radio and a change of clothes, then screeched the brakes with such force that she almost toppled over the handlebars.

'Oil,' he said, as she dismounted.

'I'm sorry?'

'Oil. The brakes. They need some oil. I'll fix them later today. We can't have you screaming about the town with those.'

She made to walk to him, hoping they would be going inside the house so that she could resume her investigation of the strange rooms, but he stood and picked up his own bicycle and met her at the rickety gate.

'How did it go?' he asked.

'It went well, very well,' she said, remembering the exhilaration she felt early that morning when Maurice had quietly entered Hugo's house and woken her with an urgent message.

'The boat will be nearby at four a.m.,' he had told her as she sat in bed, bleary-eyed, wondering whether she was still dreaming.

'It's dangerous – we would not normally do this, so close to the coast and so close to your home, but it must be done.'

'But the man said yesterday to stick to three p.m.,' she said, confused with tiredness.

'We have to make an exception in this case – we really do not have a choice. And do not tell Hugo about it – nothing – don't even mention the radio. He doesn't need to know. The fewer people that know the better, and if he found out you were doing this near his house, he would be furious.'

He had handed her a message, a quick short message that she did not understand – *the fish are out at sea.*

'They can land, at a beach nearby,' Maurice explained. 'They have supplies. They were meant to land further down the coast, but things changed quickly. They will understand what this means. There is an outcrop, not far from here, a few rough steps lead to a nook of rock carved out for this very purpose. You will have a few minutes, no more. They will alert you to their presence with a light. But you must be brief, you understand?'

She nodded and dressed quickly, grabbing the suitcase that she had hidden under a loose floorboard under her bed, and rushing out into the night, making her way to the sound of the waves, following Maurice's shadow that stayed a few feet in front of her. Suddenly, his arm jutted out, pointing at the rocky steps, then he disappeared into the night.

She felt her way down carefully, glad that the dark did not allow her to see how far up she was from the water below. The rock soon smoothed out and she found she was on a ledge, just large enough for her to crouch down and set up the radio. Removing her binoculars, she waited, not noticing the slight chill in the air, instead feeling warm, sweaty almost, with nerves.

There, suddenly, was a quick flash of light. Then another.

With shaking fingers, she lifted the microphone, turning the dial until the radio met with the same frequency as the boat. There was a crackle of static, and she waited for the all-clear. Another flash of light. Quickly, she tapped out the message in morse code, then the radio fell silent. She looked about but could see no flash of light letting her know that the message had been received. She waited a few minutes, then, further out, a small flash. She smiled. They had received the message and were moving towards the destination.

'You enjoyed it, didn't you?' Maurice asked, as they walked side by side, each wheeling their bicycles.

'I did, I can't deny it. The fear, the anxiety, but then that rush when you have done the job and know that all is well.'

'It won't always be like that,' Maurice said. 'Today for example we are to make our way to Theix, a neighbouring town, inland. As it happens, I have a patient or two there that I must check on, so it works well for us.'

'And what is the message I am to relay?' she asked.

'All in good time,' Maurice said.

'Your patients you're seeing today, are they actual patients?' she probed.

'One or two, perhaps.' He turned and winked at her. 'I have these for you.'

He handed her some papers, her alias Delphine Garnier, a widow with one child. A passport.

'I already have documents,' she started.

Maurice shook his head. 'Not good enough. A good enough forgery to get you here, I'm sure, but not good enough that they would hold up under scrutiny. These, my dear, are originals, sent by our British friends. They will keep you and the girl safe.'

The ride to Theix was pleasant, despite the tiredness that Kasia was now feeling. The sun was warm on her back, and the small, nestled villages and church spires kept her eyes entertained as she pedalled.

Maurice was a careful man and took many a detour down rutted pathways and fields so that she was sure if she had to make her own way here again, she would not be able to do it. As they reached a cluster of stone houses that circled their way around a church, cobbled pavements stretching out like spider's legs into hidden streets, Maurice stopped.

'What's wrong?' she asked.

He did not answer and looked about him as if expecting someone to arrive.

'They are not here, which is good,' he said.

'Who?'

'The *Boche*, of course. Two days ago, they had a checkpoint set up here. I was worried that they would make it a permanent fixture, but it seems not.'

'So we are fine?' she asked.

'For now. Who knows when they will decide to do it again? But they are all around us, don't forget that.'

'This is Theix,' she said, looking about her, at the quiet streets.

'A small part of it, yes. A fair few people left when the *Boche* arrived and made their way south. It is sometimes a little livelier than today, but I daresay that checkpoint a few days ago has made people worried about leaving their homes.'

They walked up one of the spidery-legged streets, and Maurice stopped outside a small café, its red awning billowing with a sudden breeze. Outside, an old man sat with a white and brown terrier at his heels, now and again reaching down to give it a titbit of food from his plate.

Maurice propped his bicycle against a wall, and Kasia followed suit.

'You shouldn't feed him that,' Maurice said to the old man, who laughed with a gummy smile.

'And what else will I feed him, eh? You know how hard meat is to come by,' he replied, then tore away a piece of bread that he had on his plate with sliver of butter.

'Claude, this is my nurse, Delphine.' Maurice nodded at her. 'Delphine, this is Claude.'

For a quick second, she wanted to correct Maurice – she was Kasia – and then she realised her stupidity.

'Pleased to meet you, Claude,' she said. 'And who is this?' She bent down to fuss at the dog who welcomed her touch with a moan of pleasure.

'That? That's Remi. He's an old one, likes the ladies, though.' Claude chuckled. 'Arthritis in his joints now so loves a nice stroke from a pretty lady.'

'Come now,' Maurice chided. 'She's too young for you.'

'I know that.' Claude popped a piece of bread in his mouth and chewed on it slowly. 'Can I not recognise a pretty face when I see one? Anyway, what do you want, Maurice? I told you last time I'm fine.'

Kasia watched as Maurice rummaged around in his doctor's bag, bringing out a fresh piece of gauze and a bandage.

'Let me see that foot, please.' Maurice bent down to remove Claude's worn boot.

'I will, but only if you let her do it.' Claude grinned.

'I think it would be better—' Maurice started.

'It's fine,' Kasia said. 'I can do it.'

She slowly removed the old man's boot to reveal a sore the size of a large coin on the sole of his foot.

'Just a sore. I thought it would go away, but this one keeps on coming back,' Claude muttered, as Kasia examined the foot.

'It doesn't look infected,' she said.

Maurice nodded in agreement. 'It won't get infected if he keeps it clean.'

'He who?' Claude asked. 'I'm here, you know; I can hear you.'

Kasia ignored him and cleaned the wound as best she could and wrapped the gauze and bandage around his gnarled foot.

Once finished, Claude inspected her handiwork. 'Not bad, not bad. You can come again, my dear, but tell this meddling doctor to stay behind next time, eh?'

Ignoring him, Maurice began to tell him what he must do whilst Kasia entered the café in search of a basin to wash her hands. Behind the bar an attractive woman sat on a stool, idly flicking through a magazine. As Kasia entered, she looked up in surprise and hopped off her seat.

'What can I get you?' she asked. 'Not that we have much, but there is some bread left and a little cheese?'

Kasia shook her head. 'I'm here with the doctor, tending to Claude,' she said. 'Do you have somewhere I can wash my hands?'

With a look of disappointment, the woman pointed at the toilet and hopped back onto her barstool. When she returned, the woman had resumed flicking through the magazine.

'Thank you,' Kasia said.

'It's old, you know? I've read it a hundred times, but there's not much else to do.'

Confused, Kasia stared at her.

'The magazine!' The woman picked it up and waved it at her. 'Look at this place – a ghost town. Nothing to do, nothing to read.'

'You are lucky it is so quiet,' she said, remembering the bombed-out buildings of Warsaw, the constant rumble of guns, the smell of smoke in the air.

'Perhaps. The *Boche*, you know, they come in and eat – but only the best. They drink only the best and then when I run out, they go somewhere else, leaving me reading this godforsaken magazine and talking to Claude. It's no life, is it?'

Kasia shrugged. 'I still think you're lucky.'

Outside, Maurice had managed to wedge Claude's boot on

once more and was ready waiting with the bicycles. With a quick wave to Claude and Remi, they made their way further up the cobbled street, passing a few women with their shopping baskets half-empty.

'Why do you tend to Claude at the café?' she asked.

'It is where he sits most days. Always has since his wife died. He can't bear to sit in the house alone, so I indulge him and go and find him wherever he might be that particular day.'

As they reached the top of a small incline, Maurice told Kasia to wait and he disappeared around a corner, returning in less than a minute, a white paper parcel tucked under his arm.

'Come, let's go,' he said.

He placed the parcel in his pannier and climbed on his bicycle, pedalling away down the street like a child who was thrilled by speeding down a hill. She followed and noted that he did not slow down, his legs pumping at the pedals as quickly as he could, taking them away from the town, down a main road, then left, heading to a clump of trees in the distance.

Suddenly, out of nowhere it seemed, a jeep barrelled up to them. She slowed her bike, noticing that Maurice had done the same as it passed him. Feeling relief that they were moving on, she had begun to pedal faster when the jeep came to an abrupt halt.

A German soldier stepped out of the vehicle and shouted for Maurice to come to him. As she approached, she could hear the soldier asking where Maurice was going, who he was, where his papers were.

'And this is?' the soldier asked, his French muddled with his mother tongue.

'My nurse,' Maurice said.

The soldier looked to her panniers, then to Maurice's. 'Open, open them.'

Maurice did as he was told, revealing his doctor's bag and the paper-wrapped bundle he had just procured.

'This? What is this?' The soldier held out his hand for Maurice to pass the bundle to him.

He opened it, then recoiled in disgust.

'A fish,' Maurice said, 'for supper.'

'And you?' The soldier almost flung the fish back at Maurice.

Kasia opened the first pannier that held a change of clothes and then the other with the suitcase which she hoped they would not open.

'Where are you going?' he asked.

'She is my nurse. We are going to see a patient; those are simply medicines and clothes for the needy.'

Kasia could feel the thumping of her heart at her breast. Her mouth had gone dry. Then, she heard Marta's voice in her head – 'smile, flirt, do what you must.'

Regaining herself, Kasia stepped forward and said in perfect German, 'They are just supplies, Major, simple nursing supplies.'

'You speak German?'

'Of course I do. Why, shouldn't we all be speaking German now? I mean, it is time, is it not, to speak the language of our Führer?'

The soldier smiled at this. 'I'm not a major,' he said.

'Oh, forgive me.' She placed her hand on his arm for a brief second. 'It was just that you look so important and carry yourself with such a respectful air, I was sure that you must be.'

The soldier grinned at her now and she knew she had won.

'Here.' She delved into the bottom of her pannier and brought out an apple she had taken that morning, supposedly for her lunch. 'Please, forgive my mistake.'

He took it from her and bit into the apple showing a flash of his white teeth, the juice dripping onto his bottom lip.

'No apology necessary,' he said. 'I hope we meet again?'

'Of course.' Kasia nodded and climbed onto her bicycle,

telling her legs that felt shaky underneath her not to betray her real feelings.

The soldier, satisfied that nothing was untoward, climbed back into the jeep that sped away from them, leaving a trail of dust in its wake.

'Amazing!' Maurice exclaimed. 'Absolutely amazing! Look how you charmed him. He was smitten with you; I could see it.'

'The fish.' She pointed to the parcel. 'That is what you scurried away to get?'

'It is not just any fish,' Maurice said, his moustache twitching with a smile. 'Come, we haven't much time.'

They reached the thicket of trees within a few minutes, and Maurice skirted around them, bringing them to rest in a field that sloped down towards the coast.

'Sit, sit.' Maurice patted the grass next to him. 'Take a moment.'

'Are you sure we are safe here?' Kasia asked, thinking that more Germans could appear.

'As safe as anywhere,' he said. 'The track they came crashing down in that jeep of theirs leads to a farm. They were most likely getting what supplies they could. I highly doubt that they would come off road to come here.'

Kasia was not so sure and looked about her to see if she could spot any oncoming traffic.

'It is a good spot. I can see for miles around us. It will give you time to do what you must.'

'But we haven't received any messages.'

'Oh, haven't we?' Maurice reached into his pannier and brought out the fish.

As soon as he opened the paper, the scent assaulted her nose.

'It isn't fresh, but then I didn't need it to be,' he said, then she watched as he stuck his hand in the gaping hole of the fish's mouth and drew out a scrap of wax paper.

'Here.' He handed it to her. 'Inside.'

She unrolled the paper to reveal a short message:

Gabriel to go south in one week. Supplies in demand prior to leaving. Café Roubel still safe. Alexander and Carol arrived safely and have already moved to destination.

She took the message and the code along with the radio towards the trees.

'Not too close,' Maurice called after her. 'The trees will block the signal.'

She unpacked the radio as quickly as possible, setting up the antenna and finding the correct channel that Maurice had told her to use. Before she began, she quietly recited the poem, certain that her memory could be relied upon, then on a small pad, scratched out the five chosen words, assigning the numbers to the first word, filling in the blanks with x's. Then she did it again for the second chosen word, and the third, fourth and fifth until the message was deeply encoded with multiple numbers.

She checked her watch – she had just three minutes. At 3 p.m. exactly, she tapped out her message, beginning with Delphine, and the indicator codes.

Receiving, came the *beep, beep* of morse code in her headset. With quick fingers, she tapped the message, her heart beating fast in her chest, sweat collecting at the nape of her neck. When she had finished, she saw that her fingers were shaking – had she encoded it correctly – had she remembered the poem?

Message received, came the reply, then static.

She packed the radio away quickly and scrunched up the coded message she had written down, ready to burn it as soon as she reached home.

Maurice already had the bicycles waiting when she emerged. 'It went well?' he asked.

'It did. I was more nervous than I thought I would be.'

'Come now, I'm sure your work in Poland was more nerve-wracking?'

Kasia climbed onto her bicycle. 'Not really. There I had more time. At first, I thought the transmission with the poem was too easy, almost a game, but then I see now with the time constraints, and relying on memory and knowing that danger is literally around the corner, it is not as easy as I thought.'

'You will be fine,' Maurice said, pedalling away from her. 'Have faith in yourself.'

Kasia waited a beat before following. *Have faith in yourself* – where had she heard that before?

SIXTEEN

HUGO

'Your cousin?' Etienne asked as Elodie and Antoine ran amongst the rows of vines. 'I did not know you had a cousin.'

Hugo shrugged. 'Has it arrived?' He started to walk towards the barn.

'It has. I was sure your mother's sister did not have a child and your father, I know, was an only child.'

'Distant cousins,' Hugo said, not turning to look at Etienne as he spoke.

Inside the barn, a large crate was already open. Hugo looked inside to see empty green bottles. 'This is all of them?'

'As many as I could get,' Etienne said, removing his cap and smoothing down the few strands of hair that were already stuck to his balding head. 'It's getting harder to find what we need.'

'We need to bottle in the next week,' Hugo said as he reached down deep to the bottom of the crate, feeling a padded parcel.

'It's too soon!' Etienne said. 'The wine will taste like piss. It needs a month or two at least.'

'We haven't the time. Our German friends are drinking us dry, and I have only a few left in the cellar.'

'*Bâtards!*' Etienne spat. 'Who cares what they want?'

Hugo stood. 'You can say that and I agree, but we don't have the luxury of annoying them right now. They want the wine, we give them the wine and we will be left alone.'

Etienne leaned against the barn door. 'You're dreaming, you know that? They won't leave us alone. Not ever. Two people from Nantes got two years in prison for breaking curfew, did you know that? And my wife's brother was beaten for hoarding flour. And you think that a few bottles of cheap wine will placate them? You're dreaming.'

Hugo ignored him and went to the fermenting barrels to check on the wine. He tasted it and wanted to grimace at the sourness, but did not want to give Etienne the satisfaction.

'Two more weeks, that's all we can afford,' Hugo said.

Etienne spat on the ground. 'You're the boss.'

'Don't be like that, Etienne. We have few options. Two weeks, yes?'

Etienne replied with a grunt, then said, 'You'd want to check at the bottom of the crate. I think your supplies came in.'

Hugo tried to think of something to say – a reason why medical supplies would be stashed in the bottom of the crate.

Etienne held up his hand. 'I won't tell. Don't worry. I knew you'd be up to something. You could have told me, you know.'

'Only Maurice knows,' he said, 'and Henri. Not that I told him.'

'You shouldn't tell anyone else,' Etienne said.

'I won't be.' Hugo grinned, closing the barn doors behind him.

'So. A cousin, eh?' Etienne said. 'Strange that you've never mentioned a cousin and her child.'

'What do you want, Etienne?'

'Cigarettes, if you can get them. And I'm sure my wife would like some meat if you can procure it.'

'You know this is blackmail, don't you?' Hugo huffed.

'Not so.' Etienne slapped him on the back. 'It is just one friend helping another.'

'If you were not my friend, I would smack you square in the jaw.'

'I'd pay to see that!' Etienne laughed. 'Just a few bits – I won't tell a soul.'

Elodie soon returned with Antoine, a smear of brown on her lips. Hugo went to wipe it away for her, but she stepped back and licked her lips. 'What have you been eating?' he asked her, receiving a blank stare in reply.

He held out his hand for her to take, and bidding Etienne and the boy goodbye, made his way back to the house.

The girl sat at the table as he made her some lunch – a haphazard meal of a boiled egg and tinned peaches he found at the back of the pantry. He watched as she ate, the syrupy peaches sliding into her mouth, the juices running from her lips.

'What were you eating earlier?' he asked, knowing he would receive no reply.

A knock at the door made the girl clatter her spoon into her bowl, and he jumped up to open it. Two gendarmes stood on the doorstep, young men whom Hugo had never seen before.

'What can I do for you?' he asked.

'Pierre sent us,' the youngest one said, his feet shuffling from side to side as he spoke. 'May we come in?'

Hugo opened the door further to allow them entry and escorted them into the living room. Neither of them sat.

'Please, sit,' Hugo said.

'We're here about the radio,' the other one spoke now, his eyes darting about.

'I don't have a radio,' Hugo said. 'I handed it in a month ago as requested.'

'You see, the thing is, there was a radio transmission not

far from here last night. One of the German patrol boats picked it up and sent us word. They were going to send soldiers, you know, to see you. But Pierre said we would deal with it.'

The shuffling policeman nodded in agreement, and Hugo could see that neither of them really knew what they were doing.

'And where is Pierre?' Hugo asked.

'Busy, he says,' the shuffler replied. 'So, we are to take a look, make sure you didn't forget a radio.'

'I didn't forget, but please feel free to look around. I can assure you that you will find nothing.'

The pair looked at each other, then at Hugo, and nodded. Hugo left them to search and joined Elodie at the kitchen table. Her eyes were on the peaches in her bowl, and she sat so still that she almost looked like a statue.

'Eat, eat.' He motioned to her. 'It will be fine.'

He sat closer to her and placed his arm around her which she leaned into, her head on his shoulder. They sat like that for almost an hour, her not eating, him not talking until the two gendarmes appeared once more.

'We didn't find anything,' one said. 'But someone was transmitting.'

Hugo shrugged. 'It wasn't me.'

'That being said, they've decided to put some barbed wire up along the coast, and near you too. Stop anyone coming to shore.'

'Barbed wire? Are you serious?'

'Indeed. We are at war, or hadn't you noticed?'

'Tell Pierre I don't want it near my home.' Hugo stood. 'I'm doing nothing wrong. Why should I have that eyesore near my house?'

'It's not for Pierre to say,' the shuffler said. 'There's a new major just arrived and says we must be stricter. Pierre said to tell you to keep your blinds closed and to obey curfew. He says he won't tell you again.'

Hugo could feel anger rising but kept him calm. 'Tell Pierre thank you, and I shall heed his words of warning.'

The two nodded at him, again almost in sync as if they had practised it before coming here, and left without a word of goodbye.

'A radio?' Hugo asked himself, then suddenly thought of Kasia.

He sat at the table, his fingers dancing impatiently on the tabletop and resolved to confront her when she returned.

SEVENTEEN

KASIA

When Kasia reached Hugo's house, the light was beginning to fade and a chill in the air had arrived, making her hope that Hugo had made a warm meal again. As soon as she entered, she was surprised to see Hugo waiting for her. He snatched the suitcase out of her hand.

'What are you doing?' she asked, as he opened the case, then sat back on his haunches.

'It's a radio,' he said.

'Of course it is.'

'You should have told me,' he said. 'Why didn't you tell me?' he yelled now.

'It is safer for you if you don't know anything, Hugo. The more people that know, the more danger I put you in.'

He stood and raked his hand through his hair. 'And how would I know that? You should have told me. You and Maurice. There can be no more secrets, do you understand?'

'What's happened?' She could see the worry in his face.

'Promise me first. No more secrets.'

'It wasn't intended to be a secret...' she started.

'Promise me!' he snapped.

'I can't promise you that, Hugo.' She raised her arms in frustration. 'I will tell you what I can, but that won't be much. Can you not appreciate the work that Maurice and I are doing, how dangerous it is?'

'I can now,' he spat.

'And I can keep you safe. I will. That I can promise. If there is ever a moment when I think it is too dangerous, I will make sure that you and Elodie are safe. That, I can promise you.'

Hugo's face slackened with weary defeat. 'The gendarmes came,' he said finally. 'They picked up a radio signal last night, near here. They thought it was me.'

She suddenly felt cold all over.

'It's fine,' he said. 'They didn't find anything.'

The cold did not leave her and there was a strange buzzing in her ears.

'Did you hear me?' he asked. 'I said it was fine. You just need to be more careful and hide this. Find a place in the vineyards and bury it.'

'I, I...' she tried.

'Kasia, are you all right?' He moved to her and placed his hands on her shoulders. 'It's fine. Don't worry.' His voice softened. 'I was shocked, that's all. I didn't mean to scare you.'

'I'm not scared,' she said, finally finding her voice and pushing past him towards the sitting room.

Hugo suddenly laughed. 'See, another lie.'

She sat down and lit a cigarette, her hands trembling slightly. 'It's not a lie. I'm not scared. I was shocked myself, of course, to hear your news, but that is all.'

She could see him looking at her hands and she willed them to stay still. He turned from her and disappeared into the kitchen.

The gendarmes, so soon? She had to tell Maurice, warn him that there could be no more urgent transmissions near here, no matter what. She thought back to Warsaw when the police would turn up at Marta's door, asking questions about how all these women lived together, and how Marta talked her way out of it, plied them with money, food, drink and as soon as they left would find somewhere new to stay. Should she do the same now? Should she ask Maurice to relocate her? Before she could answer the question, Hugo returned with hot tea and biscuits.

'They are a little stale.' He indicated the biscuits.

Unsure of his sudden kindness, she did not take a biscuit, nor drink the tea and continued to smoke her cigarette.

He sat across from her, slinging one leg over the other. 'It's all right to admit it, you know.'

'Admit what?' she asked.

'That you were scared when I told you about the gendarmes.'

She forced a smile. 'Not scared, Hugo. Shocked. You do know the difference between the two words, yes?'

He sat forward as if he were going to retort, then she assumed he thought better of it and flopped back down.

'You are tiresome,' he said.

Feeling slightly better now she had bested him, she accepted his gift of tea and stale biscuits and sipped quietly at the hot drink.

'I'm sorry,' he said quietly.

'For what?'

'Shouting at you. It wasn't right. I suppose I was shocked too, about the radio, about what you and Maurice are doing.'

'You don't need to apologise. I understand. I wish I could have told you, but like I said—'

'It's safer that I don't know,' he finished for her.

'Quite.'

'What happens now?' he asked.

Kasia was wondering the same thing herself. She gave a gentle shrug of the shoulders.

'Bury that thing in the vineyards would be my first suggestion,' Hugo said.

'I will. I will speak to Maurice too. Perhaps it would be better for me to relocate.'

'Relocate?' Hugo sat up.

She placed the teacup down and smoothed down her skirt. 'Perhaps. I will ask him.'

'I don't think there is a need for that,' Hugo said quickly. 'They don't know anything. They didn't find anything. They'll assume it was someone who came ashore.'

'This is a surprising change in you,' Kasia said. 'I thought Elodie and I were in your way?'

'No. Not in my way.' Hugo stood and did not look at her and busied himself tidying the cups away. 'Not in my way. It's fine.'

She watched him walk away from her and heard him banging pots about in the kitchen. How odd. He wanted them to stay, she could tell. And yet he had been so against them just two days before. What had changed his mind? Elodie, perhaps?

She made her way upstairs to Elodie's bedroom and, not finding her there, went to the small bathroom and found the door closed. She knocked a few times, then popped her head around the door, unsure of whether it was right to go inside.

'Are you all right?' she asked, seeing Elodie's wet head peer over the side of the large tub.

A small nod was given and Kasia left her, telling her to come and find her once she was dried and dressed.

She tip-tapped back down the stairs, and after a few words with Hugo about the best place to hide the radio, made her way quickly to the vineyards, the suitcase in her hand.

Around the back of the shed, she found a spade and walked down the tenth row, counting her footsteps to fifty, then dug a hole big enough. Once she had placed the suitcase inside its hiding place, she covered it and sat for a moment, listening to the early hoot of an owl as day gave into night.

Hours later, Kasia was woken by the sound of voices, and then Elodie's face directly above hers.

'What's wrong, what's happening?' she asked.

Elodie pointed at the door.

'Downstairs?'

Elodie nodded.

She grabbed a cardigan and told Elodie to stay in the bedroom. The house was dark apart from the one light in the hallway. She stood at the top of the stairs and saw Hugo with two men – two policemen.

Hugo looked up at her and then beckoned her down.

'One minute, please,' he said to the men, who duly stepped out onto the porch to wait. Hugo turned quickly to her.

'What's happening?' she whispered.

'I don't know. They have come for me, but won't say why.'

'Hugo, I—' she started.

He shook his head. 'There is nothing to be said now. I have to go. Go to Maurice – he will know what to do. Do you know where he lives?'

She nodded, she had memorised the address Maurice had given her, even though she was unsure of how to get there.

'There is money hidden around here somewhere,' Hugo said, his eyes darting about. 'I can't remember where. Somewhere – look for it. There should be a few thousand in total. Don't stop looking until you've found it all.'

He stepped away from her and gave her a quick smile, then disappeared out into the night, towards the waiting car.

EIGHTEEN

HUGO

Hugo sat in the rear of the police car, the two young gendarmes from earlier up front, Pierre in the back seat.

'What's going on?' Hugo asked.

'It is not for me to say,' Pierre replied.

'This is no time for cryptic games. Tell me. What's happening?'

'You've been summoned,' Pierre said.

'By whom?'

'If I tell you that, what fun would that be?'

'Do you enjoy irritating me?' Hugo asked.

'Not as much as you think,' Pierre said, and stared out his window.

Hugo wanted to knock his stupid moustache off his face – indeed he would have done if it had been just the two of them – but the young pair up front made him think twice.

His fingers tapped away at his knees as if he were playing the piano, then he saw Pierre looking at him and he stopped.

'Nervous?' Pierre asked.

'Not so. Just remembering a tune I used to play when I was younger.'

'What tune was that?'

'I don't remember the name.'

'I used to play. I'm hoping to again one day. There is a nice grand piano on rue Noé, at that old hotel that closed – you know the one I mean?'

'And are you just going to take it for yourself?'

'I'm no thief, Hugo. Not at all. It will be given to me as a gift.'

'By whom?'

'You'll soon see.'

The car wove itself through the quiet cobbled streets, through the old prison gates and into the centre of town. There were no streetlights, not one person had forgotten to shutter their blinds and keep to curfew rules. Hugo had a strange urge to leap from the car and explore the ghostlike town he had known all his life.

'It's like another world,' he mumbled, as they sped past shops and restaurants.

'What did you say?'

'Nothing,' Hugo replied.

The car came to a sudden stop that made both Hugo and Pierre lurch forward in their seats.

'You need to be easier on the brakes,' Pierre barked at the driver. 'You'll ruin the damned engine.'

Despite the seriousness of the situation, Hugo wanted to laugh. As much as Pierre had tried to be threatening, menacing even, there was always something comedic about him and seeing him lurch forward in his seat as their inept driver squealed to a halt made it all the more humorous.

Hugo stepped out of the car to find himself at the entrance to the Hôtel de Ville, the town hall. 'Are we here to see the mayor?' Hugo asked, confused as to why the mayor would need to see anyone this late at night.

'In you go,' Pierre said.

Hugo, more intrigued than worried now, made his way up the stone steps of the renaissance-style building, wondering why the mayor had to have such opulent offices to mimic the hotel of the same name in Paris. Inside the foyer, lights burned low, illuminating the double marble staircase, dappling shadows on the paintings of long-dead generals and previous mayors that hung on the walls.

'Up, up,' Pierre said, his voice betraying a hint of boredom now at this task.

Hugo walked up the stairs, hearing the slap of his bare feet on the cold marble.

To the right was the mayor's office and Pierre pushed in front of him and knocked. A German soldier opened the door, nodded at them, then stepped aside for them to enter. It was then that the soldier stuck out his arm to bar Pierre's entrance.

'Just him,' he said.

Hugo saw a glimmer of irritation on Pierre's face, which he quickly composed. 'Of course, of course.'

Hugo stood in the room, the thick red and gold rug under his feet providing some warmth.

'Welcome!' a voice came from the desk at the rear, and Hugo could barely see who it was in the candlelight.

'Come, come,' the voice beckoned.

Hugo followed its sound and soon saw a short, grossly fat man sitting in the mayor's chair, his uniform straining to keep all of him enclosed.

'You were expecting the mayor?' the man asked. 'Sit. Sit.' He waved in the direction of the chair in front of him.

Hugo sat. 'I was,' he said.

'I stole his office yesterday!' The fat man laughed. 'You speak German, yes?'

Hugo nodded.

'Good, good, my French is not so bad, but it is always better to speak in our mother tongue,' he said, switching to German, the words coming thick and fast, assaulting Hugo's ears.

'I am Major König,' he said. 'I've heard a lot about you.'

'You have?' Hugo asked, his fingers tapping once more on his knees.

'Indeed. Half-German, half-French and a winemaker no less!'

'All good things then, I'm glad.' Hugo could feel his tongue sticking to the roof of his mouth as he spoke.

'Water? Something stronger? Whisky perhaps?' The major clicked his fingers at the shadow of the soldier who stood near the door.

The soldier walked to a drinks cabinet and brought two glasses of whisky. Hugo sipped at it, watching as the major knocked his back.

'You're a writer too, I hear?' The major smacked his lips together.

'I am – well, I was.'

'Am, was – which is it?'

'I suppose if one is a writer, one is always a writer?' Hugo said.

'Is that a question or a statement?'

Before Hugo could answer, the major began talking again. 'You must think it strange for me to bring you here at this time of night. And I admit, it is strange. But I am a man of whimsy – do you know that? I know if you think of our illustrious army, our Führer, you would think us all buttoned up and boring. But not me! No, not me!' He laughed.

Hugo was unsure whether to laugh along with him, and instead settled for a smile.

'So, here I am, travelling to this town, and I am thinking about writing a book about myself so that once the war is won, people can read about me. Because they will want to, won't they? Read about all the brave men of the Reich. So, here I am, on a train, and I am talking to the mayor's assistant who had accompanied me, and he starts to tell me about your wine.' The major stopped and waved his glass at the soldier. Once his glass was replenished, he continued. 'And I like wine, I do. So, I ask about you, and he tells me who you are and you are German too, as well as French, and lo and behold, a famous writer! And there it was – fate, *kismet* – you see? Do you believe in fate? I do. Always have, part of my whimsical nature, so I can understand now why I am meant to come to this tiny town – I am meant to meet you, and you're meant to write my biography. Perfect, don't you think?'

Hugo thought it was another rhetorical question, so did not answer.

'Don't you think?' Major König repeated.

'Sorry, yes, of course. But I am no biographer,' Hugo said. 'I was merely an academic of sorts. I wrote a few books that were well-received, but I am not sure that I am the man for this job.'

This made the major scrunch up his round face in such a way that it reminded Hugo of a toad.

'I think you are,' he said. 'I am sure of it.'

To make his point, the major stood and unbuttoned his jacket, allowing Hugo to see the pistol that was strapped to his belt underneath the enormous paunch of his stomach, then placed his hand over the gun. 'I think you are,' he said again.

'I am sure you're right,' Hugo said, then knocked back the whisky in one go.

Sitting down, the major heaved a sigh of what Hugo thought to be relief, his breath making the candle-flames on his desk dance, creating moving shadows on the wall. For a moment, Hugo thought that he might be dreaming – first Kasia and the girl arrive, then the police and the search for a radio, and now this.

'You are tired, I see that, so I will not keep you much longer,' the major said. 'I am delighted, *delighted*, that we will be working together!' He beamed.

Hugo tried to smile back.

'Forgive me for the way I've introduced myself. It is my whimsy, you see. I've always been full of it – my wife, if she were here, would tell you that for herself! The candles too, a part of my whimsy. I can have electric, of course I can! But the candles to me give us a sense of occasion – and what an occasion this is! Why, I've found my biographer and together we shall write my life story in all its glory!'

'We will indeed,' Hugo said.

'Good, good. Now then, those two idiots outside will take you home.'

At this, Hugo laughed a little, then stopped himself.

'No! Please do laugh! They *are* idiots. I told that Pierre as much. I hear they came to you about a radio? Ignore them, please do. Stupid boys. I said to Pierre myself, why would a writer, a winemaker, and a half-German send any message by radio?'

'Indeed, I have no idea,' Hugo said.

'Do me a favour, however, would you?' The major stood, signalling the end of their meeting.

'Of course.'

'Keep your eye out, won't you? I have some more men arriving over the coming weeks with equipment that will soon find any radio signal around these parts, but in the meantime, if you see anyone or hear anything you come straight to me, you understand?'

'Of course,' Hugo said again, feeling relief sweep through his body, leaving him exhausted.

'Wonderful!' The major held out his hand for Hugo to shake. 'What a spot of luck. Us finding each other, with you and your writing, and me and my whimsy!'

NINETEEN

KASIA

As soon as the hum of the car's engine disappeared, Kasia shut the door, and began her search. She started in Hugo's bedroom, noting how it looked as if it had already been turned over – books strewn half-open on the floor; clothes hanging off the backs of doors, chairs and in piles dotted about the room; dirty plates and glasses on the bedside tables. She checked each drawer, the pockets of trousers and jackets, even in shoes and came up with a few hundred francs. She moved then into the kitchen, then down into the cellar, which had a heady aroma of spilled wine. Behind two crates of wine, she found a small tin with another three hundred inside.

'It's not enough,' she screamed into the void.

Running up the damp cellar stairs, she was met by Elodie, who stood like a ghost in her nightdress.

'I'm looking for money,' she told the girl. 'It's a game. We have to search and find as much money as we can.'

At first, Elodie did not move, then she scampered away to the bureau at the front door and began opening all the drawers.

Together, they searched for almost an hour, and Kasia still only had just over a thousand.

'It will have to be enough,' she told Elodie. 'Perhaps he thought he had more than he has.'

Elodie was still rummaging through a drawer on the bookcase in the sitting room, then turned to Kasia. In her hand, she had money stuck between pieces of paper.

Kasia smiled and took it from her. 'Well done!'

She started to separate the money from the paper, then realised it wasn't paper but a photograph, and underneath that, a newspaper cutting from Paris – the same one she had seen in her bedroom when she first arrived.

The photo was of a young woman, a baby on her hip. It had been taken at the beach on a windy day – the woman's hair flying away, the foamy sea encroaching upon her. Then, she saw the newspaper article, seeing that it was not an article at all but an obituary – the name, Giselle Weber, wife to Hugo Weber. Another newspaper clipping accompanied it, and she was about to read it when she heard the crunch of tyres on the drive and the hum of an engine. She hastily placed the photograph and newspaper cutting into her cardigan pocket and grabbed Elodie's hand.

Before she could reach the window to see who it was, the front door swung open, then banged shut and Hugo entered.

Elodie let go of her hand and ran to Hugo, flinging her arms around him. Stunned at the display of affection, Hugo did not immediately reciprocate, then his long arms reached around the girl, holding her close.

'What happened?' Kasia asked. 'I have the money here, I think I have all of it.'

Hugo let go of Elodie and looked about him. 'I can see you searched,' he said, nodding at the open drawers, the books flung onto the floor in haste.

'You told me to,' she said huffily.

'I know. I'm sorry. I didn't mean it that way.' He walked

over to some fallen books and began to place them back on the shelves.

'What happened?' Kasia asked again.

'You won't believe me when I tell you,' he said.

'Try me.'

'Let's get Elodie to sleep first. I don't want her to worry even more.'

'She doesn't understand anyway.' Kasia was exasperated. 'Just tell me.'

'She understands more than you think,' he said, then picking up two more books, he handed them to Elodie.

She took them eagerly, then frowned.

'What have you given her?' Kasia bent down to look and saw two picture books – children's ones.

'She's too old for these,' Kasia said.

'Not so. A picture book with the word of what it is next to it. A perfect way to learn a new language, I think. I forgot I even had these.'

'Yours from when you were a boy?' she asked, to which he nodded.

Kasia took Elodie to bed, tucked her in and told her she could read the books the following day, knowing that she would probably find a shaft of light from the window and read despite being told not to.

Back downstairs, Hugo had poured her a glass of wine, his own already empty and smeared with red residue. He lay on the chaise longue with his eyes closed.

'Are you asleep?' she asked.

'Just thinking,' he said. 'Turn out the light. I've lit a few candles.'

She did as she was told and sat down. 'Feels a bit theatrical with the candles – what on earth are you going to tell me?'

'Whimsical,' Hugo said. 'The candles add to one's whimsy.'

'What are you talking about?'

Hugo opened his eyes and turned to look at her. 'The man I met this evening was our new Major. Arrived yesterday and is occupying our mayor's office. He's a strange man. Not at all what I thought a major would be like. It seems he heard I was once a writer and due to his whimsical nature – his words not mine – has decided that I will be the chosen one to write his biography.'

'Are you serious?'

'I am.' He sat, poured another glass for himself and drank it back in one gulp, then another.

Neither of them spoke for a moment, then Kasia felt a bubble of laughter overtake her. Hugo soon joined in and added to the humour by describing in detail the major, his whimsy and his own utter shock.

'He did say, though, that there will be more men, more equipment coming soon to detect radio signals, so you must be careful.'

'Why would he tell you that?' she asked. 'That's strange, don't you think? Don't you think it could be a ploy of some kind?'

'You think too much. I honestly think he's an inefficient cog in their war machine and has been shunted here because no one else knows what to do with him.'

'But still – it's unusual...'

'All of it is unusual,' Hugo said. 'I can't even think what is "usual" these days.'

She noticed that Hugo's speech was already a little slurred and watched as he poured the rest of the wine into his glass and drank it back. 'We will have to be more careful. And we will. You don't suppose he suspects me at all?'

Hugo shook his head. 'I think you should be more cautious, for certain.' He stood and fetched a bottle of whisky from the cabinet.

Kasia opened her mouth to say that perhaps he had had enough, then closed it again –it wasn't her place to say anything. Hugo lay back down and balanced the whisky bottle on his chest, now and again tipping it back into his mouth, dripping it down his chin.

She felt uncomfortable with the display and wanted to leave him and go to bed. 'Here.' She stood and handed Hugo the money from her cardigan pocket and along with it the photograph and newspaper cuttings.

At first, Hugo didn't seem to register anything other than the money and nodded his thanks, then he saw them.

'Where did you find these?' he asked.

'In the drawer on the bookshelf. They were amongst some banknotes.'

'You looked at them?' he asked, not taking his eyes from the photograph.

She was about to answer when she felt the waistband elastic of her underwear unravel a little. As she stepped forward, something small fell to the floor.

'What is this?' Hugo bent down and held up the small capsule to the light.

'Cyanide,' she said simply, trying to ignore the flame of embarrassment she felt at knowing where it had come from – she must have bust a stitch in the tiny pocket she had created for it.

'For what?'

'What do you think?'

He held the capsule between thumb and forefinger and could not take his eyes from it.

'I won't need it,' she said. 'Not ever. I don't see me going that way.'

'How can you be so sure?' he asked. 'How can any of us ever know when it is the end for us?'

Kasia shrugged. 'I just know.'

'I knew someone once who was like you. Someone who

thought she controlled her own fate,' he said, not tearing his eyes away from the pill.

She was unsure of what to say and gently took the pill from his hands.

'Do you believe in fate, Kasia? Do you believe that you were sent here for a reason?'

She shook her head.

'I do. I didn't at first. But you, the girl and now this.' He nodded at the capsule. 'It's more than a coincidence, isn't it?'

She could see his eyes were red, his lids heavy from the alcohol. 'It's been a long night, Hugo. A long couple of days. You need to rest.'

He nodded. 'Did you look at the newspaper article?' he asked.

'I did. One of them. It was an obituary of a woman with the same surname as you.'

'Has anyone close to you ever died, Kasia?' he asked, swigging once more at the whisky, then cradling it to his chest like a baby.

'Yes.'

'Who?'

'Can we talk more in the morning?' she asked, looking towards the stairs.

'Yes, yes of course. Tomorrow.'

He stood, holding the photograph and newspaper in his hands and made his way to his bedroom.

Suddenly feeling as though she had let him down in some way, she blurted, 'My sister. My sister died. She had the same eyes as Elodie. That's why I couldn't leave her in the ghetto. I had to take her with me.'

Hugo turned to look at her, an expression of sad recognition on his face, as if he were seeing her for the first time. 'My wife died,' he said quietly.

'It's hard, I know. We have all felt loss in some way.' Her words felt awkward and useless.

He shook his head. 'Do you know why I gave in to Maurice? Why I said you could stay?' He swayed as he spoke.

'No.'

'He reminded me of something – that I owed him,' he slurred.

'Owe him what?'

'A life.'

'I don't understand, Hugo. I feel like you're talking in riddles. Are you sure you're all right? I think you're in shock from this evening. I think you need to rest.'

'Indeed, I need to rest. You're right. We will talk another time. When I am rested.'

Hugo walked into his bedroom and closed the door behind him and Kasia made her own way to bed. Despite the tiredness she felt, she couldn't sleep. Hugo's ramblings had woken a memory of her sister, of her sister with one eye green and one eye brown, a sister who went missing years ago and then died.

She tossed and turned, thinking one moment of her sister and then of Hugo and the loss of his wife. Why had he said that it was fate she was there? Why had the cyanide prompted his sudden confession?

Chiding herself for not finding out more, she got up and padded down to the kitchen just as the sky began to lighten to a dull grey.

She made coffee and sat at the kitchen table, listening to the gentle coos of pigeons stirring with the dawn and the trill of sparrows as they flitted about trying out their wings for the day ahead.

'You couldn't sleep?' Hugo sat down across from her, his eyes bleary, his hair more mussed than usual.

'Not really.'

'I've been thinking,' he said. 'I didn't want to tell you about my wife—'

Kasia held up her hand. 'Then you don't have to. It's none of my business.' She could smell the residue of stale whisky on his breath.

He shook his head. 'You need to hear it from me. Everyone else knows and, sooner or later, someone will say something. Even Maurice – eventually, he will say something.'

'Why would Maurice say anything? He's your friend, he can surely keep your confidence?'

'He would, normally. But this concerns him too. You see, Maurice thinks I owe him, and I do.'

'You said you owe him a life?'

'I did. That was a lie, though. I owe two.'

'I don't understand. How can you owe Maurice two lives?'

He splayed his hands wide on the table and stared at them. 'Because I killed his daughter and his granddaughter.'

TWENTY

HUGO

'I had known Giselle all my life. The daughter of the widowed doctor Maurice, who had cared for her alone since she was a day old, was my playmate from an early age. It wasn't until the year that we both turned seventeen that I noticed my friend in a different light and she, me.

'To say that our relationship blossomed like a rose would be coarse and untrue. Rather, we were like the thorns on the stem, always pricking at each other, causing tiny scars that seared themselves into our skin. We loved as much as we fought – over small things, usually – the time of day even. She was a passionate, tempestuous woman and would blame her behaviour on the fact that she was an artist. I made the mistake once of correcting her and saying, "an *aspiring* artist", to which she grew red with rage and yelled at me, storming away in a flurry of tears.

'I was angry with her outburst, telling my parents that I was finally done with her, to which they simply nodded, and did not offer any advice or consolation. They knew, you see, what I would do as the afternoon waned and the light blue sky took on a darker hue. They knew I would go to her, crying, beseeching her to talk to me, and would sit outside her house all night until

Maurice would come tearing outside and tell me to go home. Then, at that moment, she would rush out of the house and berate her father for talking to me like that, and we would embrace, kiss, both of us happy to be together again, even though our love seemed to cause us so much pain.

'Maurice and my parents thought that eventually we would grow apart, but perhaps because they thought this, we became stubborn with our love for each other, excluded everyone and vowed to be together to prove how wrong they were.

'I think back now at our naivety. We should have parted ways, as we did not rub along well together. She loved the countryside whilst I yearned to study in Paris; she enjoyed painting and riding horses, and I preferred to drink with friends and make merry.

'When I went to university in Paris, there was a thought at the back of my mind that this may be the thing to break us. But it did not. If anything, the absence from each other made us yearn for each other more, and by the time I returned after completing my studies in philosophy, we vowed never to be apart again and decided we would marry.

'As a graduate in philosophy, I had little in the way of making a career in the town, and began to work the vineyards with my father, and wrote papers for journals into the small hours to send to Paris for publication. Giselle was occupied with her art at the time we married, but refused to study it, insisting too much knowledge would ruin her creativity.

'It was just after our marriage that Maurice gifted us a house, a house which Giselle was enamoured with and aimed to make into what she called "our magical place".

'Indeed, she did make it magical and spent hours each day painting murals on the walls, deciding that each room must feel different, like you were stepping into a new world. She even prepared a nursery, ready with anticipation of the child that she was sure we would produce.

'Those first three years of our marriage were much like the early days of our relationship. We argued, made up, cried. She was annoyed with my writing late at night and frustrated that she had not yet fallen pregnant, despite our fevered attempts.

'But then, it happened. Giselle ran to me one morning, a smile on her face – that crease that had plagued her brow for months finally smoothed. She did not have to say the words, as I knew at once what she would say. I took her into my arms, holding her tight whilst she wept with joy onto my shoulder.

'The pregnancy progressed well, and Giselle delighted each day in her swollen belly, rubbing it tenderly and singing songs to our unborn child. Our moods lessened with the thought of our baby, and I found that I started to care for my wife with more tenderness, with which she reciprocated towards me.

'This perfection lasted well after our daughter, Nanette, was born. She was a happy child, plump, with rosy cheeks and curled ringlets. Maurice was particularly besotted with her and found a reason to stop by our home each day on some pretence of checking on her health. Yet, he would reach for the child as soon as he arrived, twirling her around, making her giggle, and not caring that her chubby fists would pull at his moustache, sometimes with such force that she would remove a bristle or two.

'But like all families we were not immune to loss. My mother died when Nanette was two years old. First, she developed a cold, which then sat on her chest, making her wheeze and cough. Maurice was attentive to her and as soon as he realised that some cancer had invaded her, he told both her and me the truth.

'"I don't want a hospital," she resolutely declared. "Let me die in my home, in my bed, and that will be that."

'My father, the weaker emotionally of the two in the relationship, found some reservoir of strength for her in those last days, and I came to see how my parents still did truly love each other even after all those years, all those arguments and days when they refused to talk to each other.

'After my mother died, I threw myself into work, both at the vineyard and in my writings. I wanted to honour her in some way and made it my new goal in life to write a book about life, death and our philosophical views on God, and dedicate it to her memory. I thought that if I could achieve this, then she would live on.

'Whilst Giselle at first encouraged my writings, she soon became irritated with me and my lack of attention for her and Nanette. Our old habit of arguing and becoming friends again raised its head, yet this time I noticed that we argued more than we were friends.

'Nanette was three and a half when my book was published to critical acclaim, both commercially and in the world of academia. Where I had once been a simple man, with a family and vineyards to care for, I was now in much demand and I admit the glory, the money and the life it could offer appealed very much to me.

'The offer to move to Paris came quickly. My publisher insisted I needed to live in the capital, if only for a year, to promote the book and give talks at the university. I wanted to go, but Giselle did not.

'"This is our home!" she exclaimed upon hearing the news. "What about Nanette? This is all she knows."

'"But think of what she *could* know!" I countered. "Think of it, Giselle. An apartment in Paris, the art, the museums, the parks. She will have a year when she is filled with knowledge and wonder and beauty."

'"And what about me?" she asked. "I will know no one."

'"You will know me." I held her hand and looked deeply into her eyes. "Please, Giselle, for me. One year, that's all I ask, and then we can return home and my desire to wander the world will cease. I promise you."

'She narrowed her eyes at me. "One year. Just one."

'"I promise."

'Maurice and my father were unhappy to see us go, but to appease my father and the extra workload that my absence would bring, I hired Etienne to assist him. There was no appeasing Maurice, however. Although he finally came around to the idea, I could see the grief and worry in his eyes at not being able to see Giselle and Nanette each day.

'"It's the way of the world," he said to me one evening over a glass of brandy, the amber liquid glowing under the lights of the parlour. "People get married and make their own family. It is right and should happen."

'"We are still your family," I told him. "We will be gone just a year and then we will all be together again."

'Maurice nodded, sipped at his brandy, then placed it onto the side table and leaned forward.

'"Promise me something, Hugo," he said in earnest. "Promise me you will take care of them, no matter what. They are your priority, not the book, nor the acclaim and celebrity it may bring. They are all I have, you must keep them safe for me."

'"Of course I will." I was irked that he even had to ask this of me.

'I see now, of course, that Maurice knew me better than I knew myself. He could see in me the desire of celebrity, of being feted and praised for my brilliance. He could see I would be drawn to it much like a moth is drawn to a flame, and he was right to be worried for his daughter and grandchild.

'He was right to warn me.'

TWENTY-ONE

HUGO

'Paris was a whirlwind. I had forgotten how much I loved the city – the bars, cafés and clubs. The constant movement of people, the busyness of it all. To me, the city was always alive; even at night, nothing really stopped or could slow the city down, and it gave me energy and a feeling of importance at being a part of it. I had not felt this way when I had been at university – I had not delighted in all that the city had to offer as I was love-sick for Giselle and would return home to see her at any opportunity and when funds would allow. Indeed, I hadn't even made any friends during my academic studies – shunning the parties and music-halls to return to my lodgings and write to Giselle, to study as much as I could so I could return to see her as soon as possible.

'But this time was different. Giselle was with me, tucked away in our apartment that boasted a view of the Eiffel Tower, its floor-to-ceiling sash windows letting in the light in such a way that I refused to have any curtains drawn in the evenings.

'"Look at that light!" I told Giselle, as she looked at the view. "Think of what you can paint in here with this light streaming through."

'Giselle simply shrugged. She had lost some enthusiasm for her art after Nanette was born.

'Knowing that I would be otherwise engaged at lectures and readings I tried to cultivate some form of love for art for her once more, taking her on tours of the many galleries that Paris had to offer, walking in the sculpture gardens of Rodin, looking at the paintings of the grand masters. I bought her new canvases and paints too.

'"I like to paint directly onto the wall," she told me when I revealed yet another canvas I had had stretched onto a frame for her. "You know that."

'"But as I said, this is not our apartment; it is rented so you must find a different way."

'She looked at me then with a coldness in her eyes that made me drop the canvas onto the parquet floor and in doing so, making Nanette cry.

'After that day, things changed for us both. For me, my life became filled with a career that one could only dream of, and for Giselle, she retreated further into herself and our daughter, separating us little by little.

'Whether I did not notice this change, or whether I did and did not care, I cannot say. My mind was awash with ideas for a next book and another, and I attended every event that I was invited to. I tried to encourage Giselle to accompany me on these outings, and sometimes she did so, but most of the time she wanted to stay with our daughter, as she found fault with any nanny or sitter that we could find.

'It had been a year when Giselle asked to return home, but we could not. The next book was now being published and my star was on the rise in such a way that to leave now could spell disaster for us. I had perhaps spent more than I should have in that first year – on the expensive apartment, new clothes, restaurants – and the only way to ensure we returned home with money would be to stay another year at least.

'"I don't care about the money!" she yelled at me. "I want to go home, please! You promised just a year, that's what you said."

'"I know I said it, and I meant it when I did!" I shouted back. "But things have changed."

'"You have changed," she said, then walked away from me, to our daughter's room.

'I tried then, that year, to be a bit more present for Giselle and Nanette. I knew that Giselle would stay, I knew that she loved me too much to leave, and perhaps I took advantage of that fact despite how unhappy she was.

'I took her to restaurants I knew she liked and spent hours in the Luxembourg gardens with them both, watching them sail little boats on the lake, feeding the swans and geese on the pond. On those days we were together again, the three of us, but always I had an uneasy feeling that there was something broken now, and no matter how much we tried to mend it, we could never really knit it back together again.

'I took joy in those days with my family, especially little Nanette who was nearing five and had a whole new personality of her own. We would have our own days out together, just she and I, that would always conclude with a trip to the lake to sail a small boat that I had bought for her.

'One morning, after a night of heavy drinking at a club I had just become a member of, Nanette woke me with a kiss on the tip of my nose.

'"Papa, it's not raining," she whispered excitedly.

'I managed to peel open my eyes that still felt heavy with sleep and alcohol and looked at her smiling face above me.

'"It's not raining," she said again.

'Despite how I felt, I knew I had to get up. It had been raining solidly for two weeks, curtailing our outings to the lake and our boating adventures. I had promised that the first day it didn't rain, we would resume our escapades.

'"Papa, be quick," she admonished me, as I was slow to dress.

'"Where are you going so early?" Giselle rolled over, her eyes opening slowly.

'"Mama, it's not raining!" Nanette jumped into the bed with her mother and the two of them cuddled whilst I dressed.

'I looked at the pair – my daughter's light-brown hair, full of curls, nestled into the neck of my wife who looked at that moment, so happy, so serene that I doubt even Raphael himself could have managed to paint such a scene.

'For the past week we had not argued, and Giselle had found a friend, another artist she could spend time with. Indeed, they had gone to exhibitions together, and Giselle had bought a sketch pad and charcoals, announcing that this would be her new medium. I was glad that my wife had finally found some happiness in the city, and I ignored the voice in my mind that told me it should have not taken this long – in fact, I should have gone home with her by now.

'Nanette, impatient as always, wriggled from her mother's grasp and jumped on my back for me to carry her.

'"Come on horsey!" she yelled. "Go to the lake," and gave me a little kick.

'Giselle laughed. "Are you sure you're all right to go?"

'No doubt she had seen my tired, red eyes from hours of work the previous day, followed by too much red wine.

'"How can I say no to this little thing?" I grinned.

'"So be it." Giselle lay back in bed. "I will sleep another hour. Bring back fresh pastries on your way home."

'I promised her that I would, and with another tiny kick from Nanette, I pretended to be a horse and trotted out of the apartment.

'It was early. I hadn't even checked the time when Nanette woke me. The sun was just creeping its way up over the city, the birds just beginning their morning song as my daughter and I walked the streets of Paris hand in hand.

'My back could not take the weight of her for long, and whenever I had to give in to the pain, I felt annoyed with myself that I was ageing and there was very little that I could do about it.

'Upon reaching the gardens, the sun had risen completely, letting in that early summer warmth that I so cherished. I raised my head to the sky and closed my eyes, letting the light seep through my eyelids so that the tiny swarm of moisture from my eyes swam and danced.

'"What are you doing, Papa?" Nanette asked.

'"I'm seeing the day," I told her.

'She copied me, then scrunched up her little nose. "I can't see anything."

'I laughed and let her run a few steps ahead, the tiny white sailboat with a red sail in her hands as I strolled, marvelling at how the rain and warmth had transformed the gardens in the two weeks we had been away.

'An abundance of orange, red and purple flowers knitted together in beds, and rose bushes weighted heavily by their new blooms swayed lightly in the morning breeze. I wished I had told Giselle to come too upon seeing the flowers. She knew all the names of them, whilst I only knew that they were pretty and bright.

'"Nanette knows more about nature than you!" She would often laugh at me. And then I would give the flowers made-up names: prickly bush, spiky stem and floppy flower. She liked the game and Nanette would join in, calling the rose bushes 'clouds on sticks' and pansies, 'little faces'.

'I smiled at the memory and decided that as soon as we reached home, we would tell Giselle that we must return that afternoon and play our game.

'It was then that I realised Nanette was no longer just a few

steps ahead of me. She was completely gone. Feeling an instant
panic in my chest, I began to run, telling myself that all would
be well, she would simply be at the lake, waiting, boat in hand.
As I neared the lake, I saw a group of gentlemen, their faces
turned to the water, a shout and splashing coming from it. I ran
to them, my heart knocking against my chest, and followed their
gaze.

'In the lake was another man who had stripped off his black
jacket and top hat and was wading towards us with something
in his arms. At first, I thought it was an injured swan, its neck
lolling over his arm. But then I saw the ringlets, the hair, the
face.

'"Nanette!" I screamed. I waded out clumsily in the direction of the man, the water just covering my knees. I took my
daughter from him and to the shore where I placed her on the
ground, her eyes open, seeing nothing.

'Someone appeared – perhaps a doctor, who tried to get the
water from her lungs. More people arrived – a blur set all
around me.

'I can't remember what I said or did. Perhaps I screamed,
cried. I don't know. But soon an ambulance arrived, people in
white who lifted my daughter onto a stretcher and carried her
away.

'"It's too late," someone by my side said gently.

'I looked to the speaker, an elderly gentleman with a white
beard and startling blue eyes. I remember thinking to myself,
*why am I noticing this? Why am I thinking about this man's
face?*

'"You are in shock," he said. "Here." He took me by the
elbow and guided me to a bench.

'I shook my head; this couldn't be happening. The lake was
shallow, she was gone just a few minutes.

'"I saw her trying to reach the boat that she had set upon the
water," he said. "I was on the other side of the lake and could

see her when she fell in. I tried to get to her, I did, but I can't run fast and by the time someone else walked by, she wasn't moving."

'A gendarme came and asked me questions, but I found that I couldn't speak, I couldn't even think.

'I don't know how I reached home, but there were other people with me – perhaps the gendarme, perhaps the old man. It was a blur again. Someone told Giselle and I heard her wail – the kind of sound I had only ever heard a wild animal make.

'I tried to go to her. She had collapsed on the floor, tearing at her nightdress, pulling it over her head as if to disappear. She rocked back and forth, back and forth, the wail reaching a pitch that I was sure meant she too was dying.

'I held her to me for a moment and then she pushed me violently away. I did not try to hold her again. She had every right not to allow me into her grief – we could not grieve together – for how could we, when it was *I* who had killed our daughter?'

TWENTY-TWO

HUGO

Hugo stopped talking and looked to Kasia with scorched red eyes that were holding back tears. She too felt a lump in her throat.

'Are you all right?' She reached out to him and placed her hand on his arm.

He stared at her hand as if he had never seen a hand before and, unsure of herself, she slowly removed it.

'I just need a moment,' he said, pushing back his chair on the tiled floor. He stood at the window, staring out into the gardens, then quietly began to talk once more.

'The grief ate away at us both.

'We returned to Vannes to bury our daughter, Maurice pale, silent; my father who was ill himself, broken by watching the tiny casket being lowered into the ground. Giselle and I had barely spoken since Nanette had died, and I had assumed that we would now return home, to grieve for our girl where our families were.

'"I can't go into that house," she said, when I put it to her that we stay and send for our belongings from Paris. "It was our magical place, our home," she sobbed. "I can't bear it."

'She let me hold her then and I rocked her to sleep, just as she had done for our daughter.

'Thus, we returned to Paris, but it wasn't the same. The noise and bustle that I had once thought energetic and exciting became overwhelming. The cars, buses and trams made too much noise and ground up dust, releasing it into the air so that I thought I would choke.

'I didn't return to the lake, to the gardens. Instead, I drank my way through Paris. Giselle stayed in the apartment, taking the small attic room as her own, a place she had once promised Nanette she would make magical for her by painting the walls with fairies and birds.

'Neither of us resented the other for the way in which we grieved. I knew this was the way it had to be, I knew that the guilt that ate away at me would only subside once the burning of vodka or gin rushed down my throat. And I knew too that Giselle wanted me to feel the guilt, to live with it and let it destroy me; even though she never said it, or placed blame at my feet, I could see in her eyes what she felt.

'What Giselle did in that attic room I don't know, but as days turned to weeks, and weeks to months, I began to notice a change in her. She had stopped eating, bathing even, and had not combed her hair for such a time that it became matted at the back of her head.

'Much to the disappointment of my publisher, I stopped working altogether, allowing the bills to pile up, not caring if I were evicted from this once glorious apartment. Instead, I devoted my time to caring for Giselle. I stopped drinking and made it my goal in life to see her through this pain. I brought her sugared almonds, her favourite, and would watch as she stared glassy-eyed at the pale purple and pink candies in the silver dish, as if she didn't know what they were.

'I would place one gently into her mouth where it would loll on her tongue before slipping out and dropping to the floor. I would persist in the endeavour though, thinking that this time she would eat it, would remember how to chew.

'Soon, I realised I had to get her a doctor, who came and said that she was suffering from a madness in her mind caused by the grief of losing Nanette. I was frustrated with him.

'"Of course she is!" I yelled. "Any fool could see that! But what can I do to make her better?"

'He prescribed laudanum, which calmed her and made her sleep. Then, when she woke, she would register a little of where she was and perhaps take some broth or a small square of bread, but she would not feed herself and I had to be on hand each day to ensure she ate enough.

'I thought about calling for Maurice, thinking that perhaps his presence would bring her out of this other world where she was residing. But the guilt that I had failed him over taking care of Nanette and now his daughter was too much. I could not bear to see the grief, the disappointment on his face. Selfishly, I told him nothing – something I would regret for the rest of my life. What if it had worked? What if she had looked upon her father and woken from her grief? *What if?*

'The doctor came back and prescribed a stronger drug. "Be careful with these," he warned. "Only the prescribed dose. They are powerful and the wrong dose will stop her heart."

'I promised him I would be vigilant and hoped that this new drug would reach her somehow. "If it doesn't work," he warned, "some time in hospital will be warranted."

'I shook my head. There was no way I was going to send her away to a hospital for those with mental impairments. I knew of those places, the treatment of the patients and told him so.

'"But with your wealth we can certainly find a sanatorium for her. One where it is like home. I know of a few in Switzerland, and they have had extraordinary results for similar patients."

'In fact, I had little money left. I had wasted it on expensive rent, clothing and club memberships. I knew I could ask my father, but he was stretched thin as it was – the vineyards had done badly for two years, no doubt due to the fact that his own ill-health meant his vigilance and attentiveness to the vines had waned.

'There was Maurice, but once more I could not bear to ask, bear for him to know – *what if?*

'One glimmer of hope was that the new drug had begun to work. Over the coming days, Giselle was lucid more than she was not, and she began to dress and feed herself. I would talk constantly, trying to make her smile, and now and again she would engage with me, but I could see that talking to me pained her – it simply reminded her too much of what once was, and I reminded her of the death of her child.

'One Saturday morning, she woke and came out of the attic room, a smile on her face.

'"I feel like some fresh pastries," she said. "Can you find some?"

'I was overjoyed at hearing her voice, and seeing her stood there, alive again. I pulled her to me, promising her I would find the best pastries I could.

'As I handed over the money for the pastries at the bakery, a strange feeling overcame me. A worry that told me something was not quite right. This abrupt change in mood – this request was too unusual. Previously, she had always wanted to know where I was, even if she did not want to see me, she always wanted me nearby.

'It was then I realised I had left her medication on the counter-top in the kitchen – her morning dose that I had not yet given her; so excited was I to see her up and talking, I hadn't thought to lock it away.

'She wouldn't, would she? The doctor had warned that with her state of mind it was always a possibility that she would see the drugs as an escape, and I had heeded his words and locked them away, not really ever believing that she would do such a thing.

'Yet, stood in the bakery, the croissants still warm, a slight grease appearing on the white paper in which they were wrapped, I knew that she would.

'Dropping them onto the floor, I sprinted from the bakery. As the bells of Saint Jerome rang mournfully, I sprinted up the staircase and flung open the door to find her lying on the bed, her eyelids half-closed, the eyes underneath seeing nothing.

'The child's bed she lay on had been empty for days, weeks now, its linens washed and stored away as if they would be used again when both I and she knew they would not. Yet, she had come here to rest, clasping the teddy bear I had given to Nanette, that had once been my own, to her breast – the bear called Georges.

'I knelt beside her and whispered a prayer, not knowing whether I believed in a God any more, released the bear from her grasp and left, knowing that I would never return.'

TWENTY-THREE

KASIA

Before Kasia could say anything to Hugo, Maurice barged into the house, his cheeks pink from his bicycle ride.

'Coffee!' he demanded, not noticing the heavy atmosphere.

Hugo stood and prepared coffee for him, not speaking, not looking at either of them.

'Hungover, are we?' Maurice asked, as he took the mug from Hugo.

She saw Hugo force a tight smile. 'As always,' he said.

'Not really, are you, Hugo?' she defended him.

'I am always hungover, isn't that right, Maurice?' Hugo said in such a way that made Maurice raise his eyebrows in question.

Kasia watched the two friends stare at each other for a moment too long, then Hugo abruptly disappeared into his bedroom, slamming the door behind him.

'Always grumpy, never mind hungover,' Maurice said.

'You should go easy with him,' Kasia began, then stopped herself from saying more as Elodie appeared in the doorway.

'Ah! Little one!' Maurice opened his arms to her and Elodie went to him and allowed herself to be taken into an embrace.

Whilst Kasia busied herself with Elodie's breakfast, Maurice fussed over the girl, twitching his moustache at her, singing silly songs, all in the hope that she might say something or respond in some way.

'I thought today I had the day off,' Kasia said, as she gave Elodie a bowl of porridge that the girl looked at with distaste.

'Never a day off. Remember, you need to be seen with me, let people get used to you. I have to see Claude again, and I thought you should come.'

Kasia wanted to tell him about the police, the radio, and Hugo's revelation, but Elodie protested at the porridge and had to be coaxed to have a few small mouthfuls. When Hugo reappeared, Elodie lit up with a smile and pointed at her porridge.

'She doesn't like it,' Hugo said.

'And how do you know? Did she tell you?' Maurice asked.

'Isn't it obvious?' Hugo replied, taking the bowl away from her, beginning to prepare her something else.

Within the hour Kasia and Maurice were pedalling to Theix. The clouds hung sullenly overhead, matching Kasia's mood. Maurice slowed and came to a stop.

'What's wrong?' she asked.

'I was about to ask the same of you,' Maurice said. 'You have barely spoken, and you look as though at any moment you might burst into tears.'

She dismounted and began to walk at a slow pace that Maurice matched. 'Something happened last night,' she said. 'Actually, a few things.'

She told him about the first visit from the police and the radio signal and then about Hugo being taken to see the major.

'It isn't safe, is it?' she asked. 'I should leave.'

'Do you want to? I could understand if you did. Hugo hasn't been the most welcoming...'

She stopped then and propped her bicycle against a low stone wall, then leaned against it whilst she searched in her pocket for her cigarette case. 'That's the thing,' she said, holding a cigarette between her teeth whilst she lit it, then through a stream of smoke she added, 'I understand why.'

Whether it was the lack of sleep or the adrenaline that was now seeping away after the night's activities, she felt a lump in her throat appear again and found that she had to force the words out. 'He told me about Giselle and Nanette. He told me everything, how you blame him, how he blames himself. No wonder he felt so strongly about having a woman and a child in his house after all this time.'

Maurice's reaction to hearing his daughter's and grand-daughter's name caused him to immediately cry silent tears. He let them fall unashamedly as they disappeared into the thickness of his bushy moustache.

'I'm sorry.' Kasia went to him, but Maurice turned from her and began to climb onto his bicycle.

'Come with me,' he said gruffly.

Kasia quickly ground out her cigarette with her heel and followed Maurice who veered away from Theix. It was not long before he stopped outside wrought-iron gates, a high stone wall looping round, hiding whatever was inside from prying eyes.

'We were not far from it. Coincidence or fate? Who knows,' Maurice said.

She was about to tell him that he was talking in riddles much like Hugo had done the night before, but Maurice abandoned his bicycle and slipped between the half-open gates before she could say a thing.

She followed him, feeling the exhaustion hitting her now. Her feet were swollen, her calves ached from the cycling and her neck was stiff. Whatever Maurice wanted to show her, she hoped that he would be quick so she could perhaps get a few hours of rest at least.

But the old man seemed to have found extra energy and strode away in front of her between thick pine trees that shaded the pathway in such a way that with the low clouds, it felt like night.

Soon, the trees gave way to open space and Kasia realised where she was. In front of her, marble headstones, mausoleums and granite slabs showed her that she was in a place now reserved for the dead.

She picked her way around headstones adorned with angels, not wanting to look at the engravings to see who was buried and when they had died. When she had been younger, she would spend hours in graveyards, finding the solitude a perfect place to read undisturbed. But now, things were different, and graveyards were a reminder to her that no one was safe for long, no one was guaranteed a long life any more.

Some of the stones had half sunk into the ground, unkept for years with moss and weeds growing over them and she wondered for a moment who had forgotten these souls and if she were in the ground, would anyone remember to visit her?

Ahead, Maurice had stopped and was kneeling down in front of a headstone, the lawn freshly cut, the flowers bright against the white of the memorial.

She knelt beside him and watched as he ran his hand over the names of Giselle and Nanette.

'Buried together,' Maurice said. 'As soon as you mentioned them, I had to come to see. I don't expect you to understand, but to me it is as though in a way they are still here. You said their names and it felt strange to me that you should when you have never met them. So here you are. You can meet them now.'

Kasia nodded and said a silent prayer for them as Maurice spoke to the headstone. 'This is Kasia,' he told them. 'She's staying with Hugo. I know, I know – he can be difficult.'

The one-way conversation continued for some time with

Maurice answering unasked questions and chuckling to himself.

'I imagine their voices,' he finally said and looked to Kasia.

'I can't pretend to understand how hard it is,' she began. 'For both of you.'

'Ah, Hugo,' Maurice said, then rolled back to sit on his behind.

'Do you blame him for what happened?' she asked.

'I would like to tell you that I don't blame him, but there is a part of me, every time I see him that sort of wakes up – a part I am ashamed of – it unfurls like a ball of rage and yes, I find that I do blame him – as irrational as it is.'

'He knows you do,' she said.

Maurice nodded. 'I stupidly told him that he owed me when you arrived. I hated myself afterwards for saying it as I knew what it would do to him. The fact that he has told you everything shows that it broke him in some way – brought it all back perhaps – but then again, perhaps that is a good thing.'

'I'm not sure it is.'

Maurice shrugged. 'Who is to say what is good and bad. But Hugo and I, we have never spoken about their death. We don't talk about them at all. On the surface we are good friends, but just underneath, bubbling away are a lot of unsaid things. I want to talk to him about them, but whenever I open my mouth, the words refuse to come forth. When I met Elodie and she didn't talk, I immediately understood her. Perhaps she can speak, perhaps she chooses not to, or perhaps, like Hugo and me, the words simply will not form themselves.'

'Maybe it is time you both speak about them, about everything that happened. Don't let things fester unsaid; it changes you.'

'What have you left unsaid?' Maurice asked.

Kasia felt immediately uncomfortable and stood, smoothing down her skirt, and trained her eyes on a large mausoleum in the distance that was adorned with ornate carvings of cherubs and clouds.

'You should speak to him,' she said again.

'Maybe.'

Maurice stood, kissed his hand, then laid his palm flat on top of the headstone. 'See you soon,' he murmured.

PART TWO
THREE MONTHS LATER

1943

TWENTY-FOUR

HUGO

Vannes, March 1943

The flag of the swastika billowed out from the front of the Hôtel de Ville, causing those who entered through the main entrance to first look upwards to see if it would come free of its moorings, and then to cover their ears as the *whoomp* of the catching wind boomed around them.

Hugo stood for a moment and watched the flag, hoping that it would come free and sail away in the wind, out to sea to be lost forever. Then, readying himself for another meeting with the major, he took a deep breath and entered the building.

The major was standing at the window as Hugo entered, his hands clasped behind his back as if he were preparing himself to give orders at any moment.

'Ah the writer is here!' The major turned, his cheeks redder than usual, the spider veins that stretched over his large nose seeming more pronounced.

The major seemed to notice that Hugo was staring and took

out a handkerchief and blew his nose. 'This wind,' he said. 'It stirs up the dust in the air.'

Hugo sat and removed a fresh pad of paper from his bag, along with a pen.

'Where did we get to last time?' the major asked.

Hugo studied his notes for a moment. 'You were telling me about the military school you attended.'

'Ah yes! The first days of whimsy, if you remember!' The major sat behind his desk and rested his hands on his stomach. 'Such wonderful days – so wonderful. It was here that I met my lifelong friends – most of them dead now, so not lifelong for me, but for them, I was with them until the end.'

Hugo had not yet started writing and wasn't really paying attention. His mind continued to wander, worrying about Elodie who was being looked after by Etienne and Antoine, and then Kasia whom he had not seen in almost a week.

'Are you quite well?' the major asked.

'Yes, sorry!' Hugo began to scratch at the paper.

'So, there I was, a young man in military school and everyone had to find a speciality you see, something that only they were good at. I tried shooting, fighting, barefisted, all sorts of things, and of course I was good at all of them. Write that down – that I was good at *everything*.'

Hugo nodded, imagining the major at school, a large young man, who had few friends and was most likely bad at everything he was given to do.

'I was so good at everything that it was hard for me to decide where my career would take me. But then, my father, whose rank outstripped all of my instructors, made mention that I should be fast-tracked to become a leader of men. You see, none of this day-to-day grind for me! Oh no! I was to lead these men.'

Hugo nodded once more, feeling tired of it already.

'Now. You're probably wondering where my whimsy is at this point? I am sure you are. I mean you wouldn't think that in the army there was any room for whimsy, but there I was being trained to train others, and there and then I decided that my men, *mine*, should sing not only our country's great song each day, but they should also sing a song dedicated to me! You see, whimsy! Shall I sing it for you?'

Hugo continued to write.

'Shall I?'

Without prompting, the major burst into song, the tune so high-pitched that Hugo was sure dogs would begin to howl. The lyrics were basic – pleading allegiance to their major, thanking him for taking care of them. Once the major finished on a particularly high note that was sure to crack the windows, he let out a huge sigh and mopped his brow with his handkerchief.

'Bravo!' Hugo clapped.

'Thank you, thank you.' The major grinned at him. 'It was a shame of course, that my first and second battalions were all killed pretty sharpish. My third too, come to think of it. But that is the way with war, isn't it?'

Hugo nodded in agreement, feeling sorry for those poor boys who sang to him each day, praising him for saving their lives when they would soon die, more than likely due to his stupidity.

'I have a question for you,' the major said, leaning forward. 'You know Maurice, the doctor?'

'I do.'

'Well, I have a problem you see. In an area that is a little sensitive.' The major shuffled uncomfortably in his chair, and Hugo guessed where the area might be.

'I had a doctor, but he died in a train explosion on the way here – it seems so many of my friends are being killed,' he said mournfully.

Hugo was desperate to tell the major that it seemed that

each person that was deemed his friend was doomed to die, yet he bit his tongue.

'At any rate. I need a doctor. And a nurse. And I hear that Maurice has a pretty, young nurse, yes?'

Hugo suddenly felt cold all over. *Kasia.* What was the major playing at?

'You will ask them to come and see me. I believe they have been away quite a bit recently – you should know, of course, she is your cousin?'

'She is,' Hugo said, his mouth dry. 'They have been travelling a fair bit since Christmas – lack of doctors everywhere. They wanted to make sure they were doing all they could,' he lied.

'Admirable, very admirable.' The major nodded along. 'But perhaps you might have a word as soon they both return and let them know that perhaps treating me first would be in their best interests?'

'Of course, of course,' Hugo said.

'Good. Now. Where was I? Oh yes, everyone was dead...'

Later that afternoon, Hugo sat at the kitchen table watching as storm clouds heaved into view over the ocean, causing the sky to bruise a blue black. Elodie sat beside him, scratching a picture of Georges the bear on a piece of paper, ready to give to Kasia when she returned. She had been gone more than she had been present ever since he had told her about Giselle and Nanette, and he wondered whether his revelation had disgusted her in some way.

He had wanted to talk about it with her, but it was as though he had swallowed all the words concerning his past once more, and they went back into their hiding place, deep in his stomach.

Each week, she informed him that she would be away with Maurice under the guise of being his nurse.

'It is safer for everyone,' she had said. 'After the police coming and you being friendly with the major, it is best that I keep on the move.'

At first, he felt a little relief that she was gone, that perhaps it was safer for Elodie if she wasn't around, but soon he found that he missed her, which made him irritable and grumpy. The evening meal was not the same without her and her quips about his food – the gentle sparring between them becoming friendly almost, silly, making them both laugh. Elodie was different too and looked out of the windows more often than normal as if by doing so, she would manifest Kasia coming down the driveway, waving and smiling at her.

When she returned, everything felt a little lighter. She would regale Hugo with titbits of her journey as much as she could, giving him news of the German troops, the morale of the people in the towns and rumours of when the Allies might get to France. He marvelled at her but never praised her even though he could see that she was eager to hear him say how brave she was, how bright, how clever. Again, he wanted to say those things to her, but once more the words disappeared as soon as he thought of them.

'What am I going to do about the major?' Hugo asked Elodie.

She cocked her head to the side as if considering his question, and he was sure that she had started to understand almost everything he said yet would still not reply.

'He wants to see Kasia and Maurice. I think he has a sore backside!' He patted his behind to let her know what the new word meant and was gratified to see that she gave him a big grin.

'It isn't safe, though, is it?' he asked her.

She shrugged and went back to her drawing of the bear.

TWENTY-FIVE

KASIA

Storms had battered the coast for nearly two months, and the lodgings that Maurice had procured for her in each town and village were less than ideal in the weather. Most were small farm buildings, sometimes abandoned, that had little in the way of luxuries such as an indoor toilet; thus during cold, wet nights when the wind blew so strongly it felt as though it would lift her off the ground, she would have to run to the outhouse to squat over a hole.

Claude's attic room was her favourite place to stay. It was tiny, with a small porthole window that looked out to sea. A collection of shells lined the windowsill, ones he and his wife had collected over the years, he had said, and in each room of his house, jars were stocked full of barnacles, mollusc shells and horseshoe crabs. Not that she had had any idea what each shell was, but Claude knew and would sit with her in the evenings as she tended to the wound on his foot that refused to heal and explain each one, which animal it had come from.

It was where she lay now, on a narrow bed resting her legs after returning in the early hours from Damgan, a town further down the coast where she had been instrumental in relaying instructions for safe places for new agents from Britain to land. Not that she had met any of them – she had hardly seen anyone other than Maurice, who busied himself seeing patients wherever he went so that most of the time she had been utterly alone.

'It was meant to be this way,' Maurice had told her one evening as they sat huddled over a meagre fire, eating cold peas for dinner. 'A pianist's life is a solitary one. If it weren't for me being a doctor, then you wouldn't see me that much either. It is only that it is safer for you to pose as my nurse that you see so much of me!'

Kasia recoiled with the taste of the peas in the salt water.

'You dislike me that much?' Maurice asked.

'It's the peas. Not you,' she told him.

Maurice stopped eating and foraged about in his bag, drawing out a tin of plums in syrup. 'We have this?'

She eagerly took the can from him and wrenched the can opener around, relieved to smell the sweetness of the plums.

'You can ask for better rations next time you transmit,' he told her. 'Tell them it is getting harder and harder to get food.'

She had agreed to his suggestion and duly asked for more rations with the next drop which would not occur for another few weeks. She yearned to meet the agents that she transmitted for. There was Louis, a code name of course, but a regular contact who seemed to be invincible. One minute he was blowing up bridges, the next smuggling papers to the Allies, then he would disappear, only to turn up weeks later after a daring escape from SS guards.

Of course there were the harrowing stories too. She hated those transmissions. She would have to read that a woman, a female spy, had been captured, tortured, her fingernails pulled out, and some of her teeth, then sent to a camp. Trying not to think about it too much, with shaking fingers she would type out the message to the home office, thinking that with each tap of morse code, she was relaying the worst news possible for the woman's family.

Every evening when she would sleep, she felt relief that she had survived another day but as soon as she woke, the fear would be back, the memory of the woman and her fingernails and teeth and the anxiety would churn in her stomach once more.

Each transmission was riskier than the last. More troops had arrived and were patrolling the streets and even the rutted countryside tracks, their eyes scanning each face, their hands never letting go of the guns that they held.

She had been stopped only a few times, and each time she had been lucky to have Maurice with her. As soon as they heard he was a doctor and she a nurse, they would visibly relax and begin to show them the sores on their feet from the endless chafing of their boots, or a wound they had received elsewhere that would not heal. At first, she had hated helping them and had used all her strength to smile at them, joke and flirt with them, but soon she began to feel sorry for some of them.

She remembered now a young soldier who had stopped her and Maurice as they entered yet another new village. He was just eighteen, he told them and was eager to show them a photograph of his mother that he kept with him at all times.

'I have a problem,' he had told them, turning his head to show them his left ear that was swollen to twice its size.

Kasia winced, imagining the throbbing heat that coursed through it.

'It was just a small cut,' he told them. 'Tiny. Nothing more than a razor cut, you know. But then, I don't know what happened, but in two days it is the size of my fist!'

Maurice had instructed the boy to sit whilst he lanced the ear, Kasia talking to him all the while so he would not think about what Maurice was about to do.

'It will hurt, won't it?' he asked her.

'It will. A little.'

'I'm no good with pain. My mother said I was a sensitive baby. I was so scared when I got called up and had to fight – the thought of a bullet, or worse.' The boy scrunched his eyes up as the blade of the scalpel touched his ear. Without thinking, Kasia took his hand in hers.

'Tell me about your mother, about your home.'

With his eyes still in a tight knot, he gave a slight nod. 'It's just me and my mother. My brother, he was killed ages ago now, and mother, she cried when I left and said we should run away. But my friends, they mocked me when I said it – said I had to be a good German and we had to do what the Führer wanted. I don't care what he wants if I'm honest. I'm not meant to say that and I wouldn't normally, but I'm scared, see, the pain, my ear.'

He stopped.

'Keep going,' Kasia told him, as Maurice pressed on the abscess to drain it. 'It's nearly done.'

'I didn't want to go. Really, I didn't. Some of my friends here, they want to go home now. I want to go home,' he cried, as Maurice pressed harder.

'You will. Soon it will be all over,' she said.

'Done!' Maurice held a piece of gauze over the boy's ear. 'Tell him to keep it clean. Don't pick at the scab that will form and he will be fine.'

The boy had thanked them and given Maurice a packet of cigarettes as payment, letting them go on their way with a wave.

That evening after seeing the boy, Kasia was transmitting in a ploughed field, far from her lodgings, a short message to tell the British that their latest agent had arrived safely and would be in touch. As she began to pack the radio away, a *pop pop* of gunfire rattled in the distance.

She grabbed the handles of the suitcase and made her way

to the road when she suddenly saw headlights quickly approaching.

'Shit,' she heard herself say, her body frozen for a second whilst she tried to think of what to do. She couldn't argue her way out of this – she was out after curfew, in a field, with a suitcase. This was it. This was the moment that she had been waiting for.

Then, instinct took over and she turned and ran awkwardly over the tilled mounds of earth, twice rolling her ankle. The suitcase was getting heavy in her hands, wrenching at her shoulders, and her legs moved as if she were in a dream, too slow, too cumbersome.

She looked behind her to see the truck nearing and she quickly flattened herself against the soil, tasting the cold earth in her mouth. The rumble of the engine continued on, passing her, not seeing her, yet she did not move for a few minutes more, just to be sure.

Finally, she stood and dusted herself down, checking her ankle for anything more serious than a small sprain, then began a wobbly walk back to her lodgings.

That night she was to stay at a friend of Maurice's – another doctor who himself was ill and required Maurice's presence. As she turned into the village, the church spire leading the way in the night, she saw a bundle of clothes by the side of the road.

She did not want to stop – shouldn't in fact, yet how could she not? She moved nearer to the huddle and kicked it gently, hoping that it was simply a drunk who had fallen on their way home. There was no response. She bent down to get a closer look and in that moment the moon appeared from behind a cloud, casting light on the person's face. It was then that she saw half of the face was missing; a bullet had entered the temple and upon exiting had taken with it the rest. But she still knew the features – the ear, that still had gauze taped to it – the soldier from earlier. She did not check for a pulse, knowing that she would not find one, and ran to her lodgings, the suitcase banging against her thighs.

'He's dead!' she said, as she burst into the house. Maurice and his friend were sitting by the fire playing cards.

'Who is?' Maurice looked up.

'The boy. The soldier from earlier. The one with the ear.'

Shakily, she told them what had happened, and Maurice made her sit by the warm flames and drink a measure of brandy.

'Probably got into a fight, or maybe someone took against having a German about,' Maurice said.

Kasia shook her head – she had heard the shots, seen the truck. 'It was them – his own. Is it because we helped him?'

Maurice shook his head. 'More likely he might've said how he wanted to go home. Maybe said, too, how he didn't want to do what the Führer ordered.'

'But they can't just—' she started.

Maurice held his hand up to silence her. 'They can. They do. This is war. Don't forget that.'

'Are you awake?' Maurice's voice cut into her thoughts of the past few days, of the boy with half his face missing, of the fear she had felt, alone and cold in that field.

'Just,' she replied.

Maurice slowly opened the door.

'It's Claude,' he said. 'I'm afraid our friend has gone.'

TWENTY-SIX

KASIA

'Are you sure about this?' Kasia asked Maurice, as they walked up to Hugo's front door, Remi asleep in her arms.

'Elodie will love him,' Maurice assured her.

'And Hugo?' she asked.

Maurice did not answer.

Before they could open the door themselves, Hugo opened it, his face cleanly shaved, his clothes ironed.

'You're back!' he exclaimed.

He ushered them inside, where Elodie stood proudly holding her picture of Georges the bear.

'She made it for you,' he said.

Then, Elodie let out a squeal of delight – the first sound Kasia had ever heard from her, believing at first that the girl was simply excited to see her once more. Then, she realised. *Remi.* Elodie raced to Kasia, dropping her picture on the floor, and held out her hands to take the dog away. Remi wriggled in her grasp, then licked her face, making her squeal once more.

'I think she likes him,' Maurice said.

'Was anyone going to ask me if *I* wanted a dog?' Hugo asked.

'You can hardly deny it her now,' Kasia said and smirked. 'I'd call it a *fait accompli.*' She was gratified to see Hugo smile back at her and give a pretend roll of the eyes.

'What happened to Claude?' he asked, as he patted the dog's head.

'Gone. In his sleep,' Maurice replied.

'I was resting – I should have checked on him.' Kasia felt a pang of guilt that she had left the old man to sleep in late – why hadn't she checked on him; perhaps she could have done something.

As if reading her thoughts, Maurice said, 'There's nothing you could have done. Nothing. He had heart problems, diabetes, all sorts of things. Quite frankly I am surprised that he has lasted this long.'

Hugo nodded in the direction of the sitting room. 'There is something we must talk about,' he said.

Leaving Elodie with Remi who was now sniffing about his new surroundings, Elodie focused on watching his every step, the trio sat in comfort, Kasia feeling grateful to be back, to the feeling of a soft cushion underneath her and the sound of life around her – of Elodie and Hugo.

'Major König wants to see you,' he said bluntly.

The calm Kasia had felt left quickly. She sat straight-backed. 'Why?'

'Not just you. Maurice too. He says he has a problem, a sensitive one.'

'A ploy,' Maurice said, his moustache twitching. 'He'd have his own doctor.'

'I have to leave.' Kasia stood, her eyes darting about, the thought of the woman and her pulled teeth and fingernails at the forefront of her mind once more.

'Calm down.' Hugo placed his hands on her shoulders and eased her back into the chair. 'He says his doctor died, and I do believe he has an ailment of some kind. I don't think it is a ploy.'

'Don't be naive, Hugo,' Maurice said.

'I'm not being naive,' Hugo said.

'You are,' Maurice persisted.

'And you are being ridiculous! Do you not think I can exercise my own judgement of a person?'

'Well, it was you that didn't want to take risks, and now look—'

'Stop! Both of you. Stop!' Kasia stood. 'You are like a pair of children.'

The two of them looked at her, both with an air of kicked puppy about them.

'Thank you, Hugo, for telling me, and thank you, Maurice for outlining the danger of this. But I will make my own decision about the major. I will decide what is best. Is that clear?'

Both men nodded in agreement, and she left them staring after her as she clomped her way upstairs to lie down.

TWENTY-SEVEN

THE POLISH GIRL

One week had turned into two, then three. Then, the autumn had given way to winter and Christmas, which Hugo made them celebrate. She knew she wasn't supposed to celebrate, but she had loved it. She and Hugo had decorated a tree with paper bunting, and he had wrapped gifts for them and placed them underneath the tree.

It seemed to her that winter that everything rattled or creaked. The doors never stayed still – an invading breath of air that had sneaked through the cracks of the windows would make them open and close of their own accord, either with a forceful bang, or with a moan of a hinge. The windows too made a noise – a shushing of constant wind that crept through the tiny gaps in the sill, causing the curtains to flap and making her think a ghost had arrived.

In the new year, the winter had ramped up its campaign, bringing strong winds that knocked the electricity out in those precious few hours when it was on, bogging down the roads with icy mud and making it almost impossible to go out to meet Antoine.

Almost impossible, but not quite. Any time Hugo had to

work, she was allowed to go with Antoine to their secret hut, and each time Antoine would bring new things he had found or stolen. He had a German soldier's helmet – he said he found it outside a hotel. At least that's what she thought he had said. Her French was coming along, she understood more than she could say – if she had wanted to speak – and she would allow herself to mouth words along with Antoine who didn't seem to mind that no sound ever came out.

She missed Kasia when she was away, but Hugo always kept her entertained with visits to town to see Cécile where she would sit in the rear of the bakery and gorge herself on buttery croissants. She was almost happy, she thought. Almost.

She liked it best when Kasia was back, the suitcase that held the radio always in her hands that would then disappear into the vineyards. She knew where Kasia buried it, had watched her one evening and wondered why she would need to bury a radio. She had wanted to show Antoine the radio, but each time she saw him, Kasia had already left, taking it away and leaving a mound of fresh earth to show where it had once lived.

When Kasia was back, she noticed that Hugo was happier. He sang as he made food for them, he shaved and washed his hair. He would laugh with Kasia, and she saw how Kasia would watch Hugo when he wasn't looking, a small smile on her lips.

Yes. She was happy. Almost.

The day, only a week until spring, that Maurice brought Remi to live with them was the happiest she had ever felt, she decided. *But what about Mama and Papa? Zara and Benjamin?* her memory voice asked her. She hated her memory voice. It came to her at odd times, and usually at moments when she felt content or at least less anxious. Then, it would come, reminding her of the past, of the things she tried so hard to forget.

No. Not today. Not with Remi on her lap, gently snoring. Her memory voice had to disappear and leave her alone forever.

'*Allez,*' Hugo said to her. She stood and placed Remi down

whilst she wriggled into her coat that Maurice had brought for her and boots that were too big, but which Hugo had stuffed socks into to make them fit.

She bent down to pick Remi up.

'*Non. Partez sans lui.*'

She pouted. There was no way she was leaving Remi behind – she wanted to show him to Antoine, and Kasia was resting upstairs, so she couldn't watch him. Hugo shook his head, then opened the front door and she knew he would give in to her. At the vineyards, Hugo left with the man she now knew to be Etienne in the direction of the barn, a few crates sitting outside that were new and unopened.

Antoine was delighted to see Remi and they ran to their stone hut, Elodie holding the dog tightly to her so that he did not get cold. Inside the hut, Antoine laid out a blanket he had brought for them to sit on, and the pair fussed Remi who was glad of the constant attention.

'*J'ai de nouveau un secret,*' Antoine declared, moving to the corner of the hut, bringing out a small radio.

He began to twiddle the dial, but nothing came from the speakers. As he fiddled with it, she felt the words come into her mouth, and before she knew it, they were out, in full, in her voice.

'*Ma mère possède une radio.*'

Antoine stared at her. So, she said it again, in case she had not said it correctly. Should she have called Kasia her mother? Was that right? Kasia had said she had to pretend that was the case.

'*Mais tu sais parler!*' Antoine said, then clapped his hands together.

She smiled – she liked that her voice had made him happy. So, she tried more words, more sentences that Antoine corrected for her when she got it wrong. *My mother has a radio.*

She speaks to people on it. She buries it in the vineyard. I am Polish. I will show you the radio.

On and on she went, Antoine delighting in each mispronounced sentence, picking new words for her to say, asking her questions.

A burst of rain above pinged onto the half-fallen-down roof, and the pair conceded that it was time to leave. Gathering Remi to her, she followed him back to the vineyards, to Hugo, wondering why today her voice had finally broken free.

Remi wriggled in her arms and gave a snort as the cold rain fell onto his fur. It was the dog, she decided. It was Remi making her happy, and Hugo being funny and kind, and Kasia too. And how they all sat together in the evenings and ate dinner and then sometimes danced to music that Hugo played from the gramophone. It was all of it.

She told Antoine before they reached Hugo not to reveal that she had spoken just yet – she wanted to surprise Kasia and Hugo that evening. Antoine agreed, though he said he would find it difficult not to tell as he was so happy and proud he wanted to shout it from the ramparts in town.

Feeling a surge of happiness that her voice hadn't upset anyone, she too found it difficult to stay quiet until that evening.

As soon as Hugo placed the potato soup onto the table, she tried the words first in her head – *I'm hungry*. Then, they shot out of her mouth, causing Hugo to drop the ladle he was using, splattering soup over the tabletop.

Then, she said the word she had most wanted to say.

'*Merde.*'

TWENTY-EIGHT

HUGO

'What did you just say?' Hugo asked.

He looked to Kasia whose mouth hung open – it was she who had fallen dumb now.

'Say it again, what did you say?' he asked Elodie.

'*Merde*,' she repeated, then grinned.

Hugo began to laugh, then he danced and clapped his hands. He moved to her, picked her up and twirled her about the kitchen.

'You speak! You're speaking! Kasia, she can speak!'

Kasia still sat staring at Elodie's empty chair, so Hugo placed Elodie down, grabbed Kasia's hand and dragged her to her feet. Suddenly, Kasia laughed, then began to cry.

Elodie frowned. 'You're sad,' she said.

'No! I'm not sad! I'm happy,' Kasia said, grabbing her hand. 'These are happy tears!'

Kasia hugged Elodie, who in turn hugged Hugo and then Hugo found himself embracing Kasia who kissed him on his cheek.

'Potato soup is no food for a celebration!' he said, moving away from Kasia, even though he didn't really want to.

Rummaging in the pantry, he found the chocolates he had received that morning in the latest consignment of black-market products – they had been earmarked for Henri who said he needed them for a birthday tart he was making for Cécile – and brought them to the table.

'*Voilà*! We shall eat chocolates for dinner, and we shall drink this.' He produced a bottle of champagne for him and Kasia.

It was hard to know where to start – what questions to ask – so that they found themselves all talking at once, then laughing as no one spoke, and started again, talking over each other.

'Tell me,' Kasia said, 'What is your real name? We've been calling you Elodie.'

'It is Elodie,' she said.

'No, your *real* name,' Kasia repeated.

'Elodie. That's my name now.'

'You don't have to be called that,' Hugo said. 'You can tell us your name.'

'It is my name now.' She pouted. 'And I'm eleven now. I was eleven last month.'

'You had a birthday, and we did not even know!' Hugo said. 'We shall right that wrong tomorrow. We shall pretend it is your birthday, and you can have whatever you want.'

Elodie grinned at him and stuffed another chocolate in her mouth. 'Can Antoine come?'

'He can. And Maurice too.'

'You must be careful,' Kasia said. 'Remember that to Antoine I am your mother and Hugo is my cousin.'

'I remember,' she said. 'Can I show Antoine the radio when he comes?'

'Radio?' Hugo asked, and looked to Kasia who had lost some colour in her face. 'What radio?'

'The one in the suitcase. The one you put in the hole with

the grapes. I want to show Antoine. I told him about the radio. Can I show him?'

Hugo waited for Kasia to respond and, when she did not, he looked to Remi. 'It might be time for you to go to bed as I think Remi is getting tired.'

He saw Elodie look to the little dog who was snoring gently at her feet. 'I must tell him a story,' she said, a few of her tenses muddled. 'A story is what happened when I went to bed.'

Hugo nodded, not correcting her, letting her have free rein of the new words before she had to get bogged down with tenses. He kissed the top of her head and watched as she made her way to bed, blowing a kiss from the middle stair with one hand as she held Remi in the other.

Kasia pretended to catch the kiss and gave a little laugh.

'She told Antoine about the radio,' Kasia said in one quick breath, her eyes wide.

'It doesn't matter. He's just a child.' Hugo tried to calm her.

Kasia shook her head. 'And the major wanting to see me! Can't you see, Hugo?'

'See what?'

'What if the major knows about the radio too?'

Hugo laughed. 'How could he? She's only just told Antoine. The major asked to see you before she said anything.'

'But what if he asks her? Or Antoine?' She stood now, waving her arms about, her mind spinning wildly.

'It's nothing. It's just Antoine. I will speak to him and make sure that it goes no further. I would hazard a guess that he has already forgotten what she said. He is a child, after all.'

She shook her head again. 'It's too much of a risk. What if he tells his father?'

'Etienne? He won't say anything. Firstly, he hates the Germans, and secondly, I'm keeping him happy with extra rations and some luxuries – I doubt he would say anything.'

'You doubt, but it's not certain...'

'Kasia, you're overthinking this.' Hugo stood, grabbing her arms and held them gently against her sides. 'It's nothing. It can be fixed,' he said, yet he did not quite believe the words.

'I'm not, Hugo. I have to leave.'

'I'll speak to Etienne tomorrow, and Antoine too. You don't need to leave,' he said quickly.

'I do. You need to speak to Antoine anyway, but I still need to leave. I can't put you and Elodie in any more danger.'

Hugo shook his head, trying to find the right words that would break through her resolve.

'I have to,' she said quietly now, looking at him and placing her hand on his cheek. 'I don't want to. But I could never stay forever. Six weeks is the average life span of someone doing what I'm doing – it is a miracle that I have not been found out yet. I should have left sooner.'

'And what about Elodie? She has just started to talk. Just started to act like a normal child and then you'll drag her away?' Hugo half yelled.

'She won't be coming with me,' she said. 'I can't risk her life. I can't risk yours. I should have gone sooner,' she said again.

'But you didn't,' he said.

'I didn't because I got comfortable with you and Elodie and this place. It felt like home. It was foolish, though, it isn't my home.'

'It can be,' he said softly.

She removed her hand from his cheek and stood. 'I'm sorry. I have to. And you have to send another letter to America, to the address I gave you for Elodie. You have to get her somewhere safe.'

'...Another letter?' he asked, then stopped himself from saying anything more.

'You haven't even sent *one*?' she asked.

'I meant to!' he said. 'I truly did. I wrote it, I think. But then things just got busy, and I forgot.'

'You *forgot*?' Kasia mimicked.

'I did. I truly did. But she's happy here. There's no need—'

Kasia cut him off. 'She's not Nanette, Hugo. She's not yours.'

Hugo felt as though he had been punched in the stomach, the wind knocked clean out of him.

'I'm sorry, I'm sorry.' Suddenly, Kasia was holding his head to her, stroking his hair. 'Forgive me. I shouldn't have said that. I really shouldn't.'

He nodded gently, and she let go just enough that their eyes met for a moment too long. She shook her head and gave a little laugh, then sat down again. He followed suit, a strange bubble of excitement in his stomach from being so close to her, feeling her hand on his face, his hair.

'We can leave together,' Hugo blurted. 'The three of us. We can leave. I have money. You said your father is in America, yes? We can go there and find Elodie's family and maybe live nearby – we can build a new life,' he rambled. 'You don't need to do this job any more – you don't have to put yourself or any of us in danger.'

'No, I can't stop. Not yet,' she said.

'Why? You're going to risk everything for... what? It is too dangerous, Kasia, it is too much, please see reason. I don't want to lose you.'

She shook her head sadly. 'I have to, Hugo. I'm sorry, but I do.'

'Then tell me why. Why do you have to carry on? Why can't you leave with me?'

'I have to stay to find her,' she said quietly.

'Find who?'

'My sister.'

'You said she died.'

'I don't know if she is alive or dead. I have to know, Hugo. It has consumed me for years – it's why I wanted to come to

France in the first place, to find answers, find out what happened. I need to know.'

She stood and made her way into the sitting room and poured herself a large measure of whisky from the drinks trolley.

Exhausted, he watched as she fell into a chair and covered her face with her hands. He sat across from her and watched the candles flicker on the walls, creating shapes and shadow people.

'I can tell you what happened,' she said quietly. 'Why I have to find her, alive or dead – why it means so much. But please don't think badly of me.'

'I could never,' he replied.

With a sigh, he watched as she leaned back in her chair, clasping her hands on her lap as if in church, ready to pray.

'It began when we were young, very young...'

TWENTY-NINE

KASIA

'It began when we were young, very young. Maja came when I was three years old, a smiling child with golden hair that everyone cooed over. She was a happy child, whereas I had been sullen, I suppose. I rarely smiled and found I liked the solitude of reading and playing quietly with my doll's house.

'But Maja was different. She was loud, brash and funny. She could charm my parents with her smile and wit, and as she grew, her incredible intelligence made her a firm favourite in the house. I went from being the older, clever daughter to one who didn't quite match up to this newer model, and as much as I tried, I could never get my parents to take notice of me like they did Maja.

'Perhaps I allowed those early years where jealousy formed in the pit of my stomach to change me, to make me hate my sister in some small way, and as we grew, I found that I could not wait to leave home, to leave Maja behind and forge my own path.

'Maja was prone to fits and outbursts of anger and tantrums as a child, and it never eased as she grew up. Instead, the tantrums became more nuanced – a pout of a lip, a throwaway remark, a sudden silence from her that could only be appeased once the person she was angry with would give her whatever she wanted. And the thing is, we all, including me, gave in to her because, whilst she was difficult, she could also be extremely loving and kind.

'You once called me fearless, but it is not I who is fearless, it was Maja. She was not intimated by anything or anyone. At school she was popular whilst I had few friends, and a few times she saved me from bullies, from the girls who pulled at my pigtails or threw snowballs at me in winter. Maja would walk straight up to them and punch them in the face. She had no fear of consequence for her actions and knew that she would be able to charm her way out of any punishment, which, indeed she did.

'All at once I loved and hated my sister. I wanted to be her and yet I wanted to never see her again. Does that make sense? But deep down I knew we would be connected for ever, and I knew I would always do anything I could to protect her.

'When it was time for me to go to university, I wanted to leave home and board with two of my friends from school at their aunt's house in the centre of the city. My father thought this foolish as he worked at the university and our home was less than an hour away. But I argued my point – I could study more, I would be closer to the library, I could come home at the weekends, I would be able to attend guest lectures in the evenings. Eventually, my father, sick of my constant barrage, gave in, and I was allowed to lodge with my friends from Monday through to Friday, but I had to come home every weekend.

'Maja did not take this news well and wailed as I left that first Monday, clinging on to me as if I were going away to sea, never to return.

'"But I won't know what you're doing," she cried. "You'll be seeing and doing things without me."

'"I'll tell you about it every weekend," I promised her.

'"It's not fair," she whined. "I want to come with you."

'I kissed her on her cheek and promised I would write too, eventually seeing a flicker of a smile on her lips.

'My first years at university I came to understand who I really was. I found like-minded friends who loved science and mathematics as much as I did and we formed a little group, the leader of which was an enigmatic doctoral student named Jan.

'"You'll love Jan," my best friend Marta said. "He's dreamy."

'This was high praise from Marta, who generally thought all men to be useless and boorish. She would hold court most evenings in our small, shared bedroom, padding back and forth barefoot, smoking constantly, and telling anyone who would listen that men simply tried to control women. "We are nothing but chattels, chattels!" was her famous quote.

'"But you hate men," I said to her, when she told me about Jan.

'"Not this one." She winked at me. "He's against organised government, against our assigned roles as men and women – he's absolutely brilliant!"

'The day I met Jan was in a small coffee shop in Kazimierz – a predominantly Jewish quarter of the city, set in tiny, cobbled streets that led into a wide-open square. I loved the quarter and its many quirky bookshops, the tiny restaurants and cafés. Although I had never felt particularly "Jewish", here, I found a home and felt some of my identity that had been passed down to me through my father finally come to light.

'He sat smoking, hunched over a steaming cup of coffee, his floppy brown hair almost covering his thick, black-rimmed spectacles.

'His face was slim – chiselled, I suppose – and he had a small mouth that was set in a permanent straight line as he listened to others talk. I did not think he was dreamy, and wondered if Marta had been making a joke. But, as soon as she saw him, she wrapped her arms around him in a tight embrace, then sat next to him and waved me over.

'"Jan, Kasia, Kasia, Jan," she introduced us.

'I held out my hand for him to take, but he regarded it as if it were offensive and gave a curt nod instead.

'I remember thinking that he was rude and couldn't wait to leave with Marta to tell her all the reasons she was wrong about him. But when he spoke, my mind immediately changed.

'His voice was soft, his words measured, and he asked questions constantly. He didn't talk over anyone and would give them his whole attention as if they were the only two people in the room.

'I watched him speak to the others, feeling a strange flutter in my stomach, wishing he would turn his attention to me. But he did not. His eyes remained focused on whomever he spoke to, a slight nod of the head every few seconds as he processed what they said. I wanted to ask him a question so he would look at me, but my mouth was dry, and I felt that any question I might pose would sound childish and silly.

'In the end, on that first meeting, I didn't speak to Jan, yet all the way back to our rooms I thought of him.

'"He's got under your skin, hasn't he?" Marta asked me that evening, plopping down on my bed and grabbing my left foot to tickle the underside.

'"How does this not affect you?" she asked, as she tickled my foot, which remained still.

'I shrugged. "I like it."

'"You are worthy of a study, you know. I might do my next research project on you and your strange feet."

'I let her continue to tickle my sole, watching as she tried to figure out a way to make me want to pull away.

'"He likes *you*," she finally said, and let go of my foot and lay back, staring at the ceiling. "I knew he would. I wanted him for myself, but he wouldn't be able to handle me, I know this. So, the next best thing is that you go for him."

'"He didn't even speak to me," I told her.

'"He asked about you. Told me to bring you today – he's heard from the professor about your skills – those ciphers you cracked as a game? You are the only one who has ever completed them all. Even Jan couldn't do it in his first year. He was desperate to meet you."

'"But he didn't speak to me!" I yelled, exasperated.

'"Just means he likes you," Marta said.

'I didn't understand Marta's logic, but she seemed to be always right about men – indeed she had had her fair share, despite saying how much she hated them. "I use them, then throw them away like the garbage they are," she once said, when I challenged her on it. "Best way to treat them. Always make sure you're in control."

'But with Jan, I lost control – all of it. As the days turned into weeks, I seemed to bump into him wherever I went. Granted, I did choose the places he would most likely be – the bookshop, coffee shop, library. Each time we spoke a little and he asked me in his quiet way about my studies, always making eye contact with me as I spoke, which at first was disconcerting, but soon I found it intense in such a way that the flutter in my stomach became a huge wave.

'Our group had grown to include academic staff and recent graduates – a discussion group to begin with, one where we could share our thoughts about any subject, but one that cropped up more often than not was the political change in Germany and the rise of Hitler as Chancellor. It had precipi-tated a change in Poland, particularly amongst the Jewish community, who had started to hear of the antisemitic propa-ganda that had begun to trickle forth. Each week we met at Marta's aunt's house and would sit in her back parlour that was thick with oriental rugs, brass ornaments and paintings of half-naked people on the walls.

'We loved that room, as did Marta's aunt – a self-professed artist who was obsessed with the human form – hence the sketches and oils on every available space portraying our most intimate body parts. The first time I had seen those pictures I had recoiled in disgust, then looked to Marta, who barely noticed them. When I told her that I was a little embarrassed by them, she simply waved her hand as if swatting an annoying fly. "It's just us, Kas, just our bodies. We all have the same stuff."

'In our club we spoke of politics, of mathematics and especially ciphers. A colleague of one of the academics came from Poznań university to talk to us. His name was Aleksy and he was working with the Cypher Bureau and wanted to know about us – especially me and Jan, who had been recommended to the Bureau by one of our professors.

'Indeed, those meetings soon became much more important to us but, at the time, we were simply excited to think that we might have a career after university, that the world that awaited us was one full of opportunity and life.

'That evening, Aleksy spoke of coding machines that Captain Maksymilian Ciężki had seen and was working with the Cypher Bureau to crack codes using mathematics. It was an exciting talk, and the more Aleksy spoke of this machine, of understanding secret codes that Germany had used since the early twenties, the more I became almost irritable with anticipation that some day I too might get to work with these academics.

'I remember looking to Jan and seeing in his face the same kind of enthusiasm. It was a look that almost made him glow – his eyes brighter, his back straighter, his eyes, that normally rested on the speaker's face, flitting about.

Suddenly, our eyes locked, and we saw in each other the same thing. It was then that the other voices in the room became a distant hum in my ears, and I was acutely aware of my own heartbeat.

'Someone lit a cigarette and others followed suit, filling the small parlour with thick smoke that blurred the orange of the lamps and swirled around the naked paintings on the walls, seemingly making them shift and move.

'Whether it was the heat, the smoke, the talk of our future or the look from Jan, I don't know, but I could feel myself falling from my chair into the swirl of reds, golds and greens on the rug at my feet.

'Then, I was outside. Jan had his arms wrapped around my waist and was telling me to breathe.

'"In and out, in and out," he said calmly.

'Regaining my senses, I turned to him, and we both grinned at each other, as if seeing each other properly for the first time.

'Then, we kissed.'

THIRTY

KASIA

'Things were fine for a while – right through until my third year in 1933, when I got a surprise one late summer afternoon. I sat on the steps of our boarding house, waiting for Jan to come by and pick me up to go to an evening lecture and then on to a party held by another of our group. The evening was sticky and warm, and I wondered if a storm was going to break to ease the humidity. Just as my thoughts were wandering to whether I should return inside to fetch an umbrella, I heard someone call my name.

'"Kasia!" The voice yelled again, followed by the clitter-clatter of heels on the pavement.

'I stood and looked down the elm-lined street and there was Maja, running madly towards me, wearing a red dress and heels, a valise in her hand.

'"Maja!" I enveloped her in a hug when she reached me and could smell her fresh perfume mixed with the sweetness of the sweat on her skin.

'"This weather!" She peeled away from me. "Look at what it has done to my hair!"

'I looked and could see nothing wrong. Her hair was pinned back in a fashionable chignon, not a wisp out of place, something I would later try to emulate time and time again. I smoothed my own hair down, feeling the thick dry strands that had escaped the rough bun on the nape of my neck.

'"You're so lucky, Kas," she said, as she plopped down on the step. "You can just tie your hair any which way and it really doesn't matter to you. But me? If it's not perfect, then it bothers me all day."

'I stupidly thanked her for the backhanded compliment, then felt angry at myself for doing so.

'"Anyway, aren't you glad to see me? Come, sit." She patted the step.

'I did as she commanded and smoothed my hair once more. "What are you doing here?"

'"I've come to live with you! Isn't that great?" She slung an arm around my shoulders.

'"But you were going to go to Warsaw," I said. "In the autumn."

'"*Pah* – Warsaw. So boring. I went with Papa and didn't like it – not one bit. Then, I submitted a paper to your professor, and he was so delighted to have another sister so good at mathematics that he told me to come straight away and enrol in the summer course. Guess what?"

'"I don't know... what?" I said dumbly, not quite believing what was happening.

'"He said if I do well, I can skip first year! Isn't that amazing? And you, you're staying on to do research so we can live together."

'Her enthusiasm wasn't rubbing off on me. "I don't know what Marta would say," I said. "Or her aunt."

'She waved my worries away with a swipe of her hand. "I'm sure they'll like me."

'I wasn't so sure that Marta would agree to this, or that she would like Maja. Indeed, I was counting on Marta to put a stop to this nonsense and send her back to my parents.

"'Why didn't Papa tell me? Or Mother?" I asked.

"'They tried! I mean, you were supposed to come home every weekend, but then you got that job and more research and we never saw you."

"'I was there two weeks ago," I said, indignant.

"'Yes, but things change so quickly in two weeks. We tried telephoning, but there was never an answer. Papa tried to find you on campus but said you were like a ghost – always heard of but never seen!"

"'I'm seen! I'm always there, always!"

"'Calm down, I didn't mean it like that."

'Sure, I had spent some time with Jan going to the lakes, and camping and hopping on trains to see where they would take us, but I had been on campus, I had been studying... hadn't I?

"'Well, well, who is this?" Jan's voice broke through my thoughts, and before I could introduce him to Maja, she had already stood up and was shaking his hand.

'He looked at her and gave a tiny laugh and shook his head, then removed his hand from hers and let his arms hang limply at his sides.

"'I'm Maja, Kasia's sister. Younger of course. But just as bright."

"'Is that so?" he asked.

'I nodded. "She's smarter than me."

"'I highly doubt that," Jan said, and stepped towards me and kissed me quickly on my lips. I felt a surge of love and pride well up inside me. "Have some faith in yourself, Kasia," he told me.

'I could see Maja crinkling her brow at this affection that Jan had shown me.

'"Where have you been hiding him?" she asked.

'"I can hear you, you know," he said.

'She turned away from him. "So, where have you been hiding him? Why didn't you tell me you had a beau?"

'I shrugged.

'"Well, isn't this just fabulous?" she squealed and took me in a hug, then jumped on Jan and gave him a hug too, so forceful that it knocked his glasses askew on his face.

'"Finally, Kasia has a beau!" She childishly clapped her hands, then nodded at Jan and looked at her valise.

'He gave that short laugh again and shaking his head, picked up her case and followed her into the house.

'When Marta arrived home later that evening and found the three of us in the parlour, she wrinkled her nose at first when she saw Maja, but within the hour, Maja had worked her magic and had Marta rolling around on the floor laughing.

'"She's great, Kasia," Marta said. "You never mentioned how funny she is! Beautiful, yes, smart too, but funny – you never said. And look, look at those eyes – one brown, one green! She's like a magical little doll! I love her!"

'Maja grinned – she had got what she wanted yet again.'

'That first year with Maja was a whirlwind. She fitted into our group with ease and charmed any visiting academics so that she too was on the list to perhaps work with the Cipher Bureau once she graduated. I completed my degree and worked on a complex research paper with Jan – one that we thought would aid the Cipher Bureau and secure our futures together.

'Maja tore through the curriculum so quickly that there was talk that she would be able to complete it in just under two years and was already invited to work towards a doctoral degree.

'"That's amazing, Maja," I told her one evening. "You must accept."

'Maja sat in front of the dressing mirror, plucking at her eyebrows. "Hardly. It sounds so unbelievably dull."

'"But you love mathematics," I said. "You're a natural."

'"Says who? I've never professed any love for it. I only studied it so hard because of you."

'Confused, my mouth opened and closed like a fish gasping for air. She saw my reflection in the mirror and turned to me.

'"Didn't you know? I just wanted to be like you, Kasia. I saw how you and Papa would always talk of numbers, science, codes even. You had a secret language with him, and I wanted to be like you, to be clever and confident."

'I shook my head. She had it all wrong. "You were Papa's favourite, and Mother's. You were always everyone's favourite. And you're so much cleverer than I am – you pick everything up with ease."

'She crinkled her eyes at me. "Is that what you really think?"

'I nodded.

'"Kas. I was only everyone's favourite because I would yell, shout and stomp and make people take notice of me. And what did they take notice of? My eyes, my hair – 'she's a pretty one'. No one ever said I was interesting, or clever. You, on the other hand, Papa would tell everyone about how smart you were, how your brain worked in such a way that even he could not understand."

'"He never said that to me," I said.

'"He said it all the time, Kasia!" She raised her arms in the air. "All the time."

'She turned back to plucking at her eyebrows, and I sat and watched her for a while, feeling something shift in my thoughts towards her.

'*Was she right? Had I been Papa's favourite?*

'Yes, Papa and I had sat and read together in the evenings, but that was just because we both liked the quiet and Maja did not. Yes, he took me to the library more often than her, but again, that was because she became bored easily and would clatter about the shelves trying to find a book that had pictures of naked sculptures in them so she could embarrass the librarian when she opened the pages and asked what the man's appendage was called.

'All this time I had envied her, but here she was saying that she had envied me. I stood and wrapped my arms around her shoulders and kissed her cheek. She grinned at me in the mirror and for the first time in our lives, I truly felt like we were not just sisters, but friends.'

'Maja finished her degree in under two years and decided to stay in Kraków with me and Marta.

'We had taken over Marta's aunt's house as she had moved to be with her sister in Paris in order to experience a new type of art called Surrealism. She had given it to Marta on the condition that we did not try to redecorate, and we promised her that we would keep the house just as it was. Marta moved into her aunt's room, leaving me alone in mine, and Maja had the smallest of the bedrooms which she complained about on a daily basis.

'Marta, Jan and I still worked at the university, our research gaining momentum each day, whilst Maja took on a private tutoring position.

'"She's wasting her talents," Jan said one evening, as we lay side by side on my bed.

'I stroked his face. "It's up to her. She has to find her own way."

'Annoyed at my reply, he turned away from me, then got out of bed to dress himself.

'"Where are you going?" I asked him. We had made plans to stay in that evening, as both of us had barely spent any alone time together for months.

'"There's a meeting I want to go to," he replied.

'"What meeting?" I was unaware of anything the group had planned for the evening.

'"It's a new group," he said, not looking at me.

'"I'll come with you."

'"No. You won't like it. It's not for you. It's more cerebral, more theoretical."

'I sat confused in the bed, the sheet wrapped around me. "I don't understand."

'He sat back down on the bed to pull on his boots. "It's a speaker that has come to discuss Marxist theory. You have always said you don't agree with my politics. I know you won't like it."

'"Since when have you become involved with communism?"

'"Socialism," he turned and hissed at me. "See? You don't understand. And anyway, you always knew it was what I was truly passionate about."

'I shook my head – mathematics, our shared love of codes, ciphers, puzzles, that's what he loved. He kissed me quickly on my forehead and told me he would see me the following day, leaving me alone and completely confused.

'What had changed with Jan? He had been moody and distant lately. At first, I had thought it was because of the continued strong hold that Hitler had over Germany – there was a growing sense of unease amongst not just the Jewish community, but all Poles. I had thought, too, that our research was perhaps consuming us too much and that we both needed a break from it. But maybe it wasn't either of these things; maybe he was getting tired of me.

'I dressed in my robe and padded down the hallway in search of Maja who I knew would be home now, but her room was empty and she had left no note on the pad next to the door to say where she had gone and when she would be back – a pad that Marta insisted we had to keep us safe.

'I chewed at a ragged fingernail and searched the parlour for Marta. I found her lying on a heap of pillows on the floor, staring vacantly at the ceiling.

'"What's wrong?" I asked her.

'Upon seeing me, she sat up and smiled. "Nothing."

'Not quite believing her, I tried to probe further, but she would not budge. So, I told her my concerns about Jan, about his moods and my fear that he was pulling away from me.

'Before I knew it, I was crying. The thought of Jan leaving was torture for me. We had planned our lives out. We would work together, get married and have children. We would visit the lakes each year and buy a small cabin that would stay in our family for generations. Jan had even met my parents and I his. It was just a matter of time.

'"Hush." Marta held me close and stroked my hair.

'I waited for her soothing words that would tell me I was overthinking things and that Jan would never leave me, that we would get married. But she stayed silent.

'I looked at her with watery eyes and saw that she was chewing on her bottom lip, a habit she had when she worried about something.

'"Marta," I said. "What is it?"

'She looked at me and kissed the tip of my nose. "Nothing, Kas. Nothing. I was just thinking that you're stronger than Jan, smarter than him. If you don't end up together, it won't be the end of your life. For two years, the Bureau have wanted you to go and work with them in Warsaw, but you haven't gone because of Jan and his research."

"'That's not true—" I started.

"'It is, Kas. Aleksy has asked for you to go, how many times now? He hasn't asked Jan, though, has he?"

"'He will. He will when we finish this research."

'Marta shook her head. "But it is really your research. Jan knows it too. You are so far ahead with your calculations, he knows he isn't really adding much. That's why he's turned more to his political stuff again."

'I shook my head. Yes, Jan had recently begun to leave the group early each evening, and perhaps turned up late, but he was tired, that was all.

"'Think about it, Kasia. He knows he can't compete with you on this, so he is going somewhere where he is in the lime-light again. He can't take that you're the one people want to talk to now at our meetings. He can't take that you have better opinions on Hitler, on Germany and our politics too."

"'So what are you saying?" I asked in a small voice.

"'I'm saying to step up. Be who you are. Don't let him hold you back. Go to Warsaw. I'm going."

"'You are?" I asked, surprised. "Since when?"

'Marta lit a cigarette and blew out a thick stream in front of her. "A week ago, I was asked to go and teach – you know, all my feminist ideals? Well, it seems I have a voice people want to listen to, so I'm going to go. Come with me, Kasia. Join the Bureau. You know you want to."

'She was right. I had wanted to be part of the Bureau for years. I was desperate to know more about the machines they worked with and understand the intricacies of the ciphers. I had even learned Italian and French on top of the English and German my parents had made me learn as a child, in case other languages would come in useful.

'Instead of answering her, I started to cry again, and I let my friend hold me until I stopped.'

'Marta and I left for Warsaw in the new year of 1936, leaving Jan and Maja behind. Jan moved into the house to keep an eye on Maja, he said, and we promised to talk on the telephone as much as we could, and that we would write each day.

'The work at the bureau was taxing. Three mathematicians were the main researchers, whose minds worked in such a way that I thought I could never keep up. Marian Rejewski, Henryk Zygalski and Jerzy Różycki had already broken the Germans' codes using a machine that they called Enigma back in 1932. From then on, they were continuing to tweak the machine as the Germans changed their codes. My role was simple – equations, and more equations. To Marta, my work sounded dull, but I cannot describe the excitement in the office when one of the codes were broken and we could read exactly what the German military were planning. It was exhilarating, and I very quickly loved the job I had.

'It meant long hours, often at night, in a stuffy office where everyone smoked so that a constant cloud hung from the ceiling. Henryk and Jerzy would sometimes come into our office where there were just five other mathematicians, me and one other woman, the rest men, and make us laugh and try and relieve some of the tedium. I did not see Marian so much – he was always holed up in his office, working through equations far quicker than we could, which left us sometimes wondering why they had bothered to hire us.

'I was gone just a week when I received a letter from Jan who told me that he did not love me any more. I cannot remember everything that was written – something about changing and wanting a different life – all I remember is that it hit me in the stomach with a grief that I had never known before, with such force that I curled up into a ball on the hall floor and stayed there until Marta came home from work and peeled me off it.

'I had to take time off work, which was not ideal, but I didn't care. I wailed and howled, and then would fall silent and stare at nothing. Marta was my saviour. She lied to Marian for me and told him I was sick; she made me eat when I didn't want to, and she made me bathe when I flatly refused to do so. All the while she did this, she would keep up a stream of chatter, of anecdotes, anything that she thought would take my mind off what was really happening.

'I wanted to go back to Kraków, and was convinced that it was my leaving that had done this. "He cannot live without me!" I yelled in Marta's face one evening as I hysterically threw my clothes into a suitcase.

'It was then that Marta's gentle chivvying disappeared and what appeared in front of me was a different Marta. She slapped me.

'Stunned, I stopped screaming and crying and sat on the bed, my clothes strewn all around me.

'"Enough! Enough of this! Kasia, this has to stop! I was going to wait to tell you this, but I think you need to know. I think it will help. You have this image of Jan that isn't real – if you knew the truth, perhaps you would even hate him a little."

'"So tell me," I said quietly.

'She stared at me, then lost her nerve, her flushed cheeks slowly returning to her normal pallor.

'"Tell me!" I said more forcefully now.

'"It's not just about Jan. You won't just hate him."

'I stood then. "Tell me."

'Marta slowly nodded. "It's time, I suppose."

'She sat on my dressing chair and stared at the floor. I thought I knew what she was going to say. I remembered how she had told me some weeks ago to leave Jan; I had suspected then, of course, but now I would know for sure. But I was wrong.

'"It's Maja," she said simply.

'"Maja? What about her?"

'"She and Jan..." she began slowly.

'"No, No." I childishly covered my ears with my hands.

'Marta stood and slowly took my hands away. "You have to know, Kasia."

'I nodded, all the fight, the grief, everything was gone. I was a shell. Nothing she could say could hurt me now. She may as well say it.

'"I was worried a while back, you know," she began. "Jan was always saying he was helping Maja with her students, with her marking. At first, I thought he was being nice, but then I saw the way he looked at her, and I saw the way she looked at him. I decided to keep a closer eye on them and started to see them in the café together, in the park, and always with their heads close.

'"I never let them see me. I wanted to be sure before I said anything to you. But then I started to see how he was with you – how he would criticise you, your work, your clothes. How he and Maja would poke fun at you when we were at our meetings, and you took it all. I was waiting for you to see for yourself what was happening, and stand up for yourself, but you didn't do it.

'Then, Jan started to get more and more involved with that Marxist group and their discussions. There was talk of them moving, perhaps to France, to live in a commune that someone they knew had set up. Jan wanted to convince Maja to go with him. I don't know whether she is truly interested in their theories and way of living, but she went along with him and soon she was talking of Paris, of the life she could have there, and I could see what was going to happen."

'"It's not true," I began. "They are just friends. I would have known, would have seen—" but as soon as the words were out of my mouth, I knew I *had* seen but I had ignored it. I had put Maja's behaviour down to her just being Maja, I had excused Jan's behaviour towards me by thinking that he was just stressed. Had I not heard how he was constantly complimenting Maja on her clothes, her eyes? Had I not seen how he always accompanied her when she was lonely or bored?

"'I'm so stupid." I jumped off the bed and ran down the stairs to the communal telephone.

"'Don't—" Marta warned me.

"'I have to," I said, "I have to hear it from her."

'After three rings, I thought that no one would answer, but then there was a click and Maja's happy, singsong voice introduced herself.

"'Maja, it's me, Kasia."

'There was silence, then a loud intake of breath. "Kasia," she said. "I'm so sorry."

"'Is it true?" I asked, my voice breaking, a new onslaught of tears ready to erupt at any moment.

"'I'm sorry, Kas. I really am. I didn't mean for it to happen. It just did..."

'The tears spilled over now and my breath caught in the back of my throat. It was true. Maja and Jan.

"'Kasia, please forgive me. I love you. You're my sister, always, but I just love him too."

'Suddenly, the tears stopped, and a voice I did not recognise as my own spoke. "You are no sister of mine. I will never forgive you. Either of you. I hope I never have to lay eyes on either of you again."

"'Kasia, wait, you don't mean that!" Maja was crying now.

'I placed the telephone in the receiver and brushed past Marta to the stairs.

"'Kasia, where are you going? What are you going to do?" Marta asked.

"'I'm going to work," I said.'

.   .   .

'I threw myself into work, taking longer shifts and barely doing anything else. Marta tried to talk to me about what had happened, but I always found a way to shift the conversation to something she wanted to talk about and would sit and force a smile, listening to her as she spoke of women's rights and politics.

'It wasn't until three months later that I had to once more face the issue of Maja and Jan. It was around three o'clock in the morning, and the telephone rang just as I entered the boarding house. I had finished a twelve-hour shift and was yearning for my bed. But as anyone knows, when the telephone rings at odd hours, it is more often than not a bad sign.

'I answered it and heard my father's voice on the line.

'"Kasia? Kasia, is that you?"

'"Papa," I said, feeling guilt gnaw away at me as I had barely spoken to him or Mother for weeks, and had not yet told them that Jan and I were no longer together.

'"It's Maja," he said simply.

'I struggled to breathe, thinking that he was going to tell me what I already knew and I would have to relive the nightmare again.

'"Papa—" I began.

'"She's missing."

'"What? No, she's in Kraków with Jan," I said, feeling the hurt at finally saying those words.

'"She was," he said. "They went to Paris two weeks ago, to get married, they said. But we heard from a friend there and they never arrived."

'"Wait, to what? You knew? You knew about Maja and Jan?" I asked.

'There was silence on the other end, and I imagined Papa nodding his silvery head.

'"They'll be fine," I said, a combination of anger and hurt washing over me. Why hadn't he called to speak to me, to see if I was all right?

'"No, Kasia, you don't understand. The group they were travelling with were arrested – something to do with papers and their political leanings. No one has seen Maja or Jan, there has been no word from them. The others were released after twenty-four hours. But Maja and Jan were not, and no one knows where they are."

'It was my turn to be silent. I leaned against the wall, cradling the phone in my hands. The exhaustion from work and the emotional drain of getting through each day finally over-came me, and I wanted to sleep, sleep and wake up once every-thing was fine again.

'"Are you there?"

'I nodded and then said, "Yes."

'"Your mother is beside herself. She can't sleep or eat. Kasia, you have to find her."

'"I don't know how..."

'"Don't think I don't know what job you took. You have access to people who could find her. But perhaps you don't want to." His tone changed. "Perhaps you have not forgiven her for this whole Jan thing. I always knew he was a cad. I did – I told your mother. And now look, she comes to live with you and that Jan takes her away."

'"So this is my fault?" I shouted.

'"I'm not saying that, Kasia. I'm saying she is still your sister, my daughter. Please."

'I realised then where Maja had learned her manipulative ways. I had never thought of my father that way before, but now I could see it as clear as day – he always got what he wanted too. Where I had once thought his speeches on science, maths, poli-tics were simply academia, he had always won every argument, every discussion, and Maja had been a keen study.

'The conversation ended with me promising to try my best. And I did. For two years. As the talk of war intensified, as my work on the ciphers that we eventually gave to the British became even more overwhelming, I spent any free hours searching for her. And then Marta and some women set up a resistance group and I joined them, hoping in some small way that the contacts we had, the intelligence we may have access to might one day lead me to find out what happened to her.'

THIRTY-ONE

HUGO

Kasia fell silent and Hugo wondered if she needed more to drink, but he could see now that her eyes were filled with tears, and he watched as one escaped and tracked its way down her cheek.

He stood and went to her, taking her to him, letting her sob onto his shoulder.

'I never found her,' she sobbed. 'The more I found out, the more it seemed likely that she was dead.'

She pulled away from him and took a handkerchief from her pocket and rubbed at her eyes. Hugo took her hand and led her to the sofa where they sat together, their hands entwined with only the ticking of the clock to break the silence.

'I know you'll think I sound crazy.' She turned to him. 'All the facts point to her being dead. Jan was involved in more than a simple political ideology. The whole reason he wanted to get to France was to join an underground group that had plans to bomb government buildings. They were extremists and I never saw it, and somehow Maja had agreed to be a part of it.

'I blamed myself. My father was right. No matter what Maja did, who she was, she was still my sister, my younger sister, and I should have protected her – I should have seen the man that Jan really was.'

'You're not to blame,' Hugo said, but Kasia gave a sad shake of the head.

'My mother died from grief. That's what Papa said. She refused to eat and began to lose her mind. One night her heart simply stopped, and my father refused to believe in science this time, he saw it only through his emotions – she had died simply from missing her daughter, from thinking Maja was dead. Papa couldn't cope with it. He couldn't cope with impending talk of war, the reports of what was happening in Germany, so he left to live with a cousin in America. And I was left alone.'

'You are not alone any more, Kasia. You have me and Elodie.'

'I can't risk staying,' she said. 'You and Elodie are at risk with me here. And I have to keep looking, Hugo. It is why I came here – I have to find out what happened to Maja, and even if I can't, it is my duty, my burden, to try and help win this war in any way I can.'

'By putting yourself in danger? By risking your life? By leaving Elodie behind?' Hugo was becoming exasperated now and was trying to keep his voice low and calm.

'I don't expect you to understand, Hugo. I know it sounds mad. But I have been living with this for years. It's a part of me, it is what drives me forward. I can't rest, Hugo. I can't rest until I know the truth, and the only way for me to do that is to keep moving, keep working, make more contacts. I have to.'

Hugo let go of her hand.

'Please try to understand,' Kasia implored.

'I'm trying,' he said. 'I really am.'

'Look. We're tired, a little too drunk now perhaps, let us not quarrel. Let us talk in the morning.'

He looked at her. 'You won't leave?'

'Not right now,' she said.

Feeling tiredness creep over him, he acquiesced and watched her walk slowly up the stairs to her room, hoping that he could find the right words the next day to make her stay.

He woke to find her gone. He dressed quickly and checked each room, lingering outside her open bedroom door to see the bed freshly made, her clothes gone from their hangers, and an empty dressing table.

'Hugo.' A voice he had yet to get used to made him turn around. Elodie stood on the bottom stair, her hair tousled from sleep, her hand rubbing at her eyes, a yawn escaping. At her heels Remi sat and matched her yawn. 'Where's Kasia? I look into the room, but she is not there. Her clothes are not there,' she said, measuring out the unfamiliar words.

'She had to go on a trip,' he said, forcing a brightness into his voice.

'I find this on her bed.' She handed him a letter, then walked into the kitchen, the dog obediently following in her wake.

He knew what would be written inside and did not want to open it. He stuffed it into his trouser pocket and pretended that all was well, made breakfast for Elodie, asked her questions and genuinely delighted in her answers.

As he washed the dishes, Elodie left him to dress herself and he wondered what he was supposed to do now. Maurice! Yes, he would go and see Maurice. If anyone knew where she had gone, it would be him.

Suddenly, a cry came from above him – high-pitched and almost a wail. He dropped a plate in the sink, hearing it crack as it bounced, and raced up the stairs to Elodie.

THIRTY-TWO
THE POLISH GIRL

She had the letter in her hands. It had fallen from Hugo's pocket as he had cooked breakfast and she decided that since her name was scrawled on the front as well as Hugo's, she would try and read it.

She sat on her bed, letting Remi play with the envelope that he tore into tiny pieces and began to read the letter Kasia had left behind. She did not know many of the words, but she could understand. A shriek came from inside her -- a noise that scared Remi and sent him barking madly at her. She wailed, cried and tore at her hair.

Kasia had left. Antoine knew about the radio. It was not safe. She asked to be forgiven.

Hugo was suddenly in the room. He was holding her close and rocking her like a baby. 'My fault, my fault!' she screamed in Polish over and over again at him.

He held her until she couldn't cry any more and laid her down on her bed, placing Remi close to her.

'Tell me what's wrong?' he asked her.

She stared at him and said nothing.

'Please. You can talk. Tell me.'

She shook her head and turned away from him.

She could hear him breathing close by and wondered how long he would sit there and wait. 'I'm going to fetch Maurice,' he told her. 'Stay here. I'll be back soon.'

Remi snuggled into her back, and she felt tears starting to stream once more. This time, though, she made no noise. She simply cried silently.

Suddenly, her memory voice came back. This time it was stronger than ever, and did not simply talk to her, reminding her of her parents, her family. This time it gave her a picture, so clear in her mind that she could not escape it. She fought against the memories, but they came thick and fast, swirling in her mind, demanding to be heard.

There stood her father next to the fireplace, his violin tucked under his chin, the bow sliding across the strings with ease, his body swaying as he played.

Her older brother Benjamin and her sister, his twin, Zara sat on the floor, sewing pockets inside the linings of their coats, her mother helping them, now and again unpicking the stitches and redoing it for them.

She sat on her father's rocking chair, watching him, and wishing that he would soon teach her how to make music.

'Why isn't Eva helping?' Zara asked, sitting back on her haunches, rubbing at her fingers that she had pricked many a time over, drawing tiny droplets of blood.

Eva – her real name. It was like a sharp stab to her abdomen when she allowed herself to remember it, remember her family saying it.

Her mother looked to her, rocking back and forth and gave her a warm smile. 'She is too young.'

'She can learn,' Zara was insistent. 'She is eight now, she can learn.'

'And you're four years older,' her mother interrupted her. 'When she reaches your age, she will learn too.'

Eva saw her father's brow furrow, and then a screech of the bow – he had missed the note. He stopped and eyed Zara for a minute, and Eva wondered if he was going to scold her for interrupting. But he did not. He placed the violin on the mantelpiece and patted Zara and Benjamin on the head. 'How are my little worker bees faring?'

Benjamin grinned at his father and showed him how many secret pockets he had made.

'What will we put in the pockets, Papa?' Eva asked. 'My toys won't fit.'

He came to her and picked her up, sat down and placed her on his knee as he rocked back and forth. 'Our secrets,' he said. 'Some money, our papers, your mother's jewels.'

'Why?' she asked, twisting and turning his busy eyebrows so that they curled upwards at the end – a pastime she loved and one which her father tolerated.

'Well, soon we are going on a journey, all the way to America. And we can't take very much with us.'

'Why, Papa?' she asked again. She wanted to stay and see her friends.

'Because it will be an adventure.'

'But—'

'Don't ask why again!' Zara yelled. 'Eva, be quiet. You are never quiet. Even in your sleep you talk.'

'I don't,' she protested.

'Well, I think an adventure will be great fun.' Benjamin stood and came to her, taking her hands in his and making her dance around with him. 'Just think, Eva, all the things we will see, and all the things we will do!'

He twirled her faster and faster, and at first Eva laughed, but then she started to feel sick as her family's faces began to blur.

'Stop!' she squealed. 'Stop now!'

Benjamin ceased and she lay flat on the floor, watching the ceiling as it spun above her.

'Can I take my toys?' she panted, as her breath started to even out.

'We will get you new ones,' her father said. 'New American toys. How about that?'

That night she lay in bed and thought about the American toys that she might get soon. Were they different from Polish toys, she wondered? Did they have bears, for instance, in America? She liked teddy bears and, in fact, had five all of her own. She heard her bedroom door creak open and saw the silhouette of her father in the doorway.

'Papa?'

'You should be asleep,' he said.

'Will there be bears in America?'

He laughed a little, then came to her side. 'Indeed, there will be. Now you need to go to sleep.'

She placed her hand on his cheek. 'Why do we need to have secret pockets, Papa? Why can't I take my toys?'

He sighed heavily, then looked to the floor and she thought for a moment that he was falling asleep.

'Because things are not safe here. You know this. You don't like the bombs falling, do you? All the rubble? You don't like how my business has been taken away.'

'I don't like all of those things, but I don't mind you being home all the time,' she said.

He kissed the top of her head. 'And I like being with you. But it is time to go soon.'

'How soon?'

'I'm not sure. It could happen tomorrow. Uncle Moshe is helping us and as soon as he has our papers, then we will be leaving.'

'Uncle Moshe? You mean Aunt Anna is coming too?' She was excited now. She loved Anna and how they both had the same eyes – one green and one brown.

'Indeed, they are. But you must sleep now, little one. And tomorrow may be the beginning of our adventure.'

Despite the excitement, she slept. She remembered that. She slept. But then the memory became fractured, and she was not sure whether the next memory was from the next day or weeks later. She tried as best she could to try and piece the memories together like a jigsaw, but the edges were mishappen and refused to fit together.

Now she stood in her street, looking at her home. The roof was gone and smoke poured from the opening. Around her, neighbours screamed, and a siren wailed in the air. Her brother was next to her holding her hand, telling her to move, to walk.

She did as he told her, her feet tripping over the rubble and dust, her legs catching on debris that scratched her skin. Where was Papa in this memory? Where was Mama, and Zara? Surely they had been there too – why was it just her and Benjamin?

Benjamin was coughing a lot. He told her it was the dust in the air, but she knew it was his lungs and she knew when Mama heard him hacking, he would have to see a doctor again.

There! Up ahead, Mama, Papa and Zara.

But it was different now. They were inside Uncle Moshe and Aunt Anna's house, and she stood outside it alone. No, not alone. She had gone with Aunt Anna to get food – yes, they were all living together, her father pacing the floorboards each day waiting for papers that never arrived, Uncle Moshe drinking, her brother coughing, coughing so much that sometimes he brought up blood.

She knew this memory and scrunched her eyes up, willing it away. But her memory voice would not let it disappear.

'Here, take my hand.' It was Anna, reaching out for her.

She took her hand, and they walked along the street. Birds were singing and she could feel the sun on the back of her neck. 'We will get some bread today, I'm sure of it,' Anna was saying. 'The queue cannot be as long as it was yesterday.'

They reached the bakery, and the queue was even longer, stretching out around a corner. Finding a place in line, they waited, and Anna would not let go of her hand. There was someone behind them – a boy that Anna knew; he had been her student. Anna turned to talk to the boy and then there was another voice, a man.

Eva turned. A soldier. He was asking the boy for papers. The boy was crying – he had forgotten them. The soldier dragged the boy out of the queue and Anna cried at him to stop and followed them.

Eva was unsure of what to do. Should she follow her aunt? Or should she stay in line? *Stay in line*, she told herself. Anna would be angry if they missed their spot and came home empty-handed again. She watched as Anna spoke to the soldier, then to the boy. Suddenly, the boy started to run, and Anna started to follow him. The soldier turned and with a pepper of bullets shot both the boy and Anna.

No one in the queue moved. No one went to them. Eva wanted to, she wanted to run to her aunt who lay face down in the road, but her legs refused to move. So, she stayed. She stayed in the queue until it was her turn, then realising that Anna had the ration tickets, she left empty-handed, not looking back at the street where her aunt lay next to the boy that she used to teach.

Remi licked her ear, taking her away from the past for a moment. She turned to look at him. How long had Hugo been gone now, she wondered? Had it been days? No, hours? Her mind was a jumble of images and voices and she felt sick. She tried to concentrate on Remi, on his little nose, his brown eyes, but the final memory came for her, the one that took her voice away.

She was ten years old now, in the basement of a Catholic family who Moshe had found to take them in once the roundups started. Moshe had not stayed with them, and instead had said he would make his way to Kraków, to a man called Kasper who would be able to get them papers to leave. That had been a year ago – yes, a year – she had been nine, and Moshe still hadn't returned.

This memory was clearer than the rest. It was the smell of the basement that she could not forget – the mildew and stale air that in the summer months seemed to suffocate them all. She had a bed that she shared with Zara and Benjamin, pushed up against a wall below a tiny air vent that she would sometimes put her head close to, to breathe in some fresh air.

'We can't stay here much longer,' her mother said.

Her father was shrunken now – he never smiled, never really ate and sat smoking cigarettes, one after the other until his eyes were red with the smoke.

'He'll come back,' her father said quietly.

'He won't! For God's sake, Samuel,' her mother yelled. 'He's not coming back. He's probably dead.'

'Don't say that in front of the children,' he said.

'I don't think you can call them children after what they have seen, after what they have been through.'

Coughing came from her parents' bed and her mother bent over the figure that was bundled up with all their blankets despite the heat.

'He needs a doctor, Samuel. He can't live here. It's too damp.'

'And what would you have me do?' he asked, then laughed as if he had told a joke.

'Anything – something – please!'

The Catholic family got Benjamin a doctor after her father paid them with a string of pearls that her mother had sewn into a coat. The doctor said the same as her mother – that Benjamin would not last much longer in the damp basement and must be moved.

'To where?' her father asked.

The doctor shook his head and offered some tincture to help with the cough that did little to ease Benjamin's suffering.

Thankfully, the summer heat soon waned, and the basement became cooler. 'Is it autumn now?' Eva asked the Catholic lady who brought down their food each day.

'It is.'

'Are the leaves changing colour?'

'They are, red and orange.' She smiled at her.

'Can you take me outside to look?'

'I'm afraid not, no,' she told her.

Eva wanted to scream – she wanted to be outside, she wanted to see the leaves, to feel the clean air on her skin.

'How much longer will we stay here, Papa?' she asked.

'I don't know, Eva. Not much longer.'

That night, the night after Eva had learned it was autumn, her brother died. Her mother wailed and held his body to her, shouting at her father whenever he came close.

'It's your fault! Yours!' she screamed at him.

'It's not, it's not,' he cried. 'How can it be mine?'

Zara, Benjamin's twin, did not cry. She turned away and faced the wall and would not move, would not speak despite the amount of questions Eva threw at her.

Eva did not cry either. She pretended it wasn't real. This was all a bad dream and at any moment she would wake in her bedroom, her toys looking down at her from their shelves, her father sat on the edge of her bed, stroking her hair and telling her everything was all right now.

The Catholic family said the body could not be removed. 'Not for a few days,' the woman said. This made her mother cry more, and even when the woman brought down clean sheets to wrap him in and some incense she had brought from her church to burn to keep the stench of death away, her mother would not cease with her crying.

A few nights later, footsteps above her told her to wake. She lay still, listening to her sister's breathing.

'Shush,' her father whispered. 'There are some soldiers above us.'

This had happened a few times now, and was why they always slept in their clothes, ready to make an escape if they needed to, but each time the soldiers had left. Eva closed her eyes and drifted between sleep and wakefulness, sure that soon her father would say they had gone.

She opened her eyes and all was quiet. They had left. She stood, feeling her way along the clammy walls to her father, to tell him to light a match as she needed to go to the toilet and couldn't find where she was going despite having been multiple times already.

Suddenly, she felt something soft underfoot. She removed her foot, then moved it further upwards and again it touched something other than cold cement. Her toe felt something strange – she wiggled it – it was soft but springy – what was it? It was then she realised that it was her brother that she stood on – it was his nose that her big toe had found.

She screamed, then screamed again. 'Papa! Papa! Benjamin!'

'Hush, be quiet!' her papa said.

'Be quiet!' Zara told her.

'For God's sake, Eva, be quiet.'

But she couldn't stop. She cried for her papa, for Benjamin

and then the light came on, but as she looked upwards, it was not from the bare bulb, but from the cellar hatch, it was open and two shadowy faces looked down at her. One by one, they were dragged from the basement.

'I'm sorry, Papa, I'm sorry,' she cried, holding on to his arm. 'I thought they had gone. I didn't know.'

Her father didn't seem to hear her. She tried to speak to her mother who was half carrying a bewildered and thin Zara outside so that she was soon trailing behind them. Once outside she could see other people coming outside of their homes. Some Jewish, some not, all of them confused.

A line of trucks blocked the street, men with guns everywhere, shouting, with dogs on chain leashes barking at those who did not walk quickly enough to the waiting trucks, or at those who tried to go back into their homes. The cacophony of noise was too much for Eva and she pushed her hands against her ears to try to drown it out.

Her father was in front, trying to talk to a soldier who laughed at him, then, the soldier looked to Zara who had started to back away from the trucks. He pointed his gun at her, and her mother stood in front of Zara and started to shout.

Then her father joined her mother, creating a barricade between the soldier and Zara. The soldier laughed again and beckoned for another to join him. She couldn't hear what they were saying, she couldn't move. It was like the queue at the bakery again – her legs were like lead; her head was no longer connected to her.

She saw the soldier stub out a cigarette with his boot, then he took a step towards her family and aimed his gun at them. The other did the same. With a quick shower of *pop pops*, her family were on the ground, her mother fallen on top of Zara, her father beside them.

She tried to lick her lips, but she had no saliva. She tried to say something to the woman who had appeared next to her, but no sound came out. She tried to move and found her legs unwilling.

A soldier approached and asked her a question, but her mouth and brain no longer worked together and as much as she moved her mouth, no sound came out.

'She is deaf and dumb?' he asked the woman who was with her.

'She is just unwell,' the woman said.

'Get in.' He nodded at the truck.

The woman took her hand. 'I'm Sarah,' she said. 'If anyone asks, I am your mother.'

Sarah. The first fake mother, and then Kasia. And now Kasia was gone, and it was her fault all over again. She had spoken when she should have stayed quiet, she had felt for a moment that life was fine again and she could talk, be herself, but she had got it wrong – so utterly wrong.

THIRTY-THREE

HUGO

'She's in here,' he told Maurice, holding the bedroom door open for him. 'She won't talk. I mean again she won't... she talked before.' His words fell over themselves to be heard.

'I know, Hugo. You said on the way here that she had spoken. I know.'

Hugo followed Maurice into the room where Elodie lay, facing the window, the dog asleep in her arms. Maurice lifted her arm and checked her pulse, then took a small torch and shone it into her eyes.

'Is that necessary?' Hugo asked.

'It is. She's in shock. Trauma.'

'From Kasia leaving?'

'Probably something else,' Maurice said. 'But Kasia leaving has awoken something, I dare say.'

'So what do we do?'

'She can hear you,' Maurice said. 'Talk to her. Try and get her to talk to you.'

'And that's it? You prescribe talking?' Hugo yelled.

Maurice nodded at the door, indicating that their conversation should continue in private.

Hugo leaned down and kissed the top of her head. 'I will be back soon,' he whispered to her.

Downstairs, he found Maurice in the kitchen, pouring milk into a glass. 'Try and get her to drink this,' he said.

'I have a better idea,' Hugo countered. 'Tell me where Kasia is, and I shall fetch her and bring her back and that will solve the problem.'

'I can't,' he said.

'You can't or you won't?'

Maurice shrugged. 'What's the difference?'

'How dare you!' Hugo slammed his fist into the kitchen countertop. 'You beg me to take them in, no, you emotionally blackmail me, telling me I owe you, and then you tell me you won't help?'

'I was wrong to say that, Hugo,' Maurice said quietly. 'I was wrong. As soon as the words came out of my mouth, I could have cut my tongue out there and then.'

'You should have done.'

'I know you're angry at me, at Kasia, but to tell you anything would put you and the girl in danger. Not to mention anyone else connected to this. I cannot. I won't.'

'Then leave,' Hugo hissed.

'Hugo, come now—' Maurice began.

'I asked you to leave,' Hugo said.

Sensing Hugo's tone, Maurice simply nodded, picked up his bag and made his way to the door. 'Let me know how she is, won't you?'

Hugo opened the door for his friend, then slammed it shut in his face.

All day he tried to get Elodie to talk. He tried to encourage her with chocolates, but she would not eat; he tried to sing her songs, but she didn't smile at him like she usually did. He moved an armchair from downstairs into her room so that he could sit and sleep in the same room as her.

As she slept, he read the letter from Kasia that said as much as she had said before – she had to leave, she was sorry, but after Elodie had spoken about the radio and after the major had expressed interest in seeing her, she could not risk it.

Was that it? Did she think it was her fault Kasia had left?

He leaned towards her and gently nudged her awake. 'Elodie,' he whispered. 'It isn't your fault. Kasia did not leave because of you. I promise you. It is not your fault.'

The girl blinked back at him a few times – did she know the word *fault*? He stood and rummaged around to find the dictionary he had given her, found the word fault both in Polish and French.

'No fault,' he said simply and pointed to the words. Then, he added the hand signals that he had used with her at the start, shaking his head, then pointing to her, then at the word, fault. No, that wasn't right – did she think he was saying it *was* her fault?

Exasperated, he threw the dictionary down. How could he explain it simply? Then, an idea struck him – he would simply tell her that Kasia had gone to find someone – her sister –and that she would be back soon. Everything was good. It was fine. He said it to her slowly, focusing on each word.

'She has gone to find her sister, her sister,' he said again.

The girl did not react.

He slumped back in his chair, trying to think of what else he could do – could he draw it perhaps? Would that make her understand?

'Sister,' Elodie suddenly said, her voice low.

'Yes, yes, her sister!' He stood and stroked her hair.

'I had a sister,' she said. 'I had a brother.'

'You had... maybe you *have*?'

She shook her head; she knew this tense it seemed. 'I had.'

. . .

They spoke until dawn, Hugo piecing together her story in bits, giving her the dictionary to find the right words. Soon she understood what he was trying to say too.

'It is not my fault,' she repeated.

'No, sweet girl, it is not.'

It was then that she cried, leaning on his shoulder, crying for her parents, for her siblings, for Kasia and for herself.

THIRTY-FOUR

KASIA

Paris, Spring 1943

The streets of Paris were a welcome distraction for Kasia – she could not, and did not, have time to think of Hugo and Elodie. The streets, far from being quiet, were thick with cars, delivery trucks and armoured jeeps that seemed too big, too loud even for the roads of Paris.

A pedi-cab pulled up to the side of her as she walked, 'Where are you going?' the man asked, 'I can take you?' He waved his hand in the general direction of the small cab that was attached to his bicycle.

She knew she should walk and should not give out the address to where she was going, but the journey had been tiring – first on foot, then on two trains, followed by a short car journey with a man she did not know and who did not speak to her, who had dropped her on the outskirts of the city that morning.

She nodded her agreement and climbed in, her suitcase

with the radio and a small valise was all she had. 'Belleville,' she told him.

'Street?' he asked.

'Just get me nearby, I'll find the way when I arrive.'

He shrugged. 'Up to you.'

As he pedalled, she looked about her, trying to see the Eiffel tower or the Arc de Triomphe, but all about her were shops and cafés.

'You won't see much.' The driver turned around. 'You'll get a nice view once you're up there; go to the park – a wonderful view of the city.'

Kasia sat back, a little disappointed that her new home would be far from the sights she so longed to see. It was then that Hugo popped into her mind.

'Where is le Jardin du Luxembourg?' she asked.

'Not far from here,' he said. 'Sixth Arrondissement. I wouldn't bother going, though.'

'Why's that?'

'Bastard Germans!' He laughed. 'They're everywhere. Treat this place like they are on holiday. You should see them, eating and drinking at the cafés, walking with our women in the parks. Disgusting.' He spat the last word out.

He was not the best cyclist and wound his way in between traffic so that Kasia wondered if she would have been safer walking. She held on to a small bar that held up the cab's roof and tried not to think about either being hit by a van or toppling over around a corner.

He began talking again as the road opened up. 'When I drove, I used to hate people on bicycles – you know, always in the way, always nearly getting themselves killed. But now I've gone the other way – hate motorists. It's funny, isn't it? My wife, she says that once this is all over and we can get more fuel again, I'll be the first one out buying a car. But I wager I'll stick to this.' He patted the handlebars.

Soon, the road got steeper, and her driver had to stand to get the cab up the hill. She offered to get out and walk, but as a matter of pride, red-faced and sweating profusely, he flatly refused and told her to stay put. It certainly would have been quicker for Kasia to walk, but she did not want to offend the man and tried to make herself lighter by lifting her bum off the seat. Realising that this was foolish, she sat back down and listened to the grunting coming from her driver until he came to a very abrupt stop at the top of the hill.

'Here,' he panted. 'Here's Belleville, I can take you where you want to go, just give me a minute.'

This time Kasia insisted she would be fine to walk the rest of the way and handed him a few notes extra for the effort he put in.

'Thank you,' he said, his breath still coming in ragged gasps.

'Are you all right?' she asked.

He waved his hand at her. 'Fine, fine. Give me a moment, that's all.'

Kasia was unsure of whether to leave him at the top of the hill when he could not breathe properly, and pretended to look in her bag as his breathing calmed.

'Fine, see?' he said, then took out a cigarette from his pocket, lit it, and sped down the hill, a trail of smoke behind him.

Kasia wanted to laugh – no, she wanted to tell Hugo about him, and they would laugh together.

'Move!' a woman suddenly shouted at her as Kasia realised she was blocking the middle of the pavement.

She did as she was told, picked up her bags and began walking, hoping to find Rue de Belleville without asking for directions. It used to annoy Marta back when they were young and walking the streets of Kraków.

'Why can't you just ask where it is?' she would whine, as Kasia went down yet another street, delighting in the shops she found, the people she saw.

'Where's the fun in that?' she'd shout over her shoulder at a disgruntled Marta. 'Besides, I like to follow my nose – see where it leads me.'

On this occasion Rue de Belleville was not a hard place to find, and Kasia barely needed to sniff out a direction. The street heaved with bars, tobacco shops, nightclubs and cafés, and it seemed as though the whole of Paris had congregated in the street. Women shopped, men in suits smoked and drank coffee at pavement cafés and small motorcycles hummed through the crowds, stopping to deliver goods at shops and restaurants. She manoeuvred her way through the people, now and again getting stern looks from ladies as her cases accidentally grazed their legs.

She found number 11, a tobacconist's shop at the bottom, the second floor a hairdresser's. She looked up further and saw she would have to lug her cases to the third floor. Pressing the buzzer for a Mme Manec, she waited, hearing the chatter of people behind her.

'Did you get an extra ration ticket?'

'The neighbours disappeared – just like that—'

'I find if you bake two loaves with half the flour—'

Their voices and conversations floated over her, and she found herself imagining what their lives were like, who they were and where they lived. Then, she imagined Hugo, arm in arm with Giselle, the small Nanette at their heels as they walked.

'Come in, come in. Are you just going to stand there?'

Kasia saw that someone had opened the door, a slight woman with long blonde hair that was free from pins and flowed over her shoulders, her eyes a hard, cold blue.

'Did you hear me?' the woman asked.

She regained herself and picked up the cases and walked into a cool tiled foyer, a wrought-iron staircase spiralling upwards.

'Delphine, I expect?' the woman asked.

She nodded.

'I'm Édith,' she said, and held out her hand for Kasia to shake.

Her hand was cold and dry and Kasia could see her look to her hand that was warm and clammy from the walk and holding the suitcases. She then let go and wiped her hand on her beige trousers that seemed far too big for her frame.

'Come on, it's quite a climb.'

Édith did not offer to help Kasia with her luggage as she began to walk up the stairs.

'My name, well you know, not my real name, but Édith, I chose it because of Édith Piaf. I love her, don't you?' Before Kasia could answer, Édith continued. 'She lived here, you know? She sings at Aux Folies across from here. I've seen her, so tiny and yet such a big voice!'

They reached the top apartment, and Kasia could feel her breath coming in quick gasps and she knew now how her driver had felt getting up that hill. Édith closed the door behind them and led her into a small sitting room, barely furnished with just two chairs, a low table and an old, chipped sideboard that held a gramophone.

'My only luxury.' She pointed at it. 'I have to have music, you know?' She instantly picked up the needle and set it down, letting the soft voice of Piaf float across the space.

Kasia soon realised that Édith had a habit of asking questions at the end of a sentence but never gave her a chance to reply; in fact, she did not seem that interested in what Kasia thought about anything.

'Two bedrooms, mine is bigger, but you'll be all right, won't you, with a single?' Édith said, as they toured the rest of the apartment. 'Kitchen, not much there. I don't eat much, do you?'

Kasia opened her mouth to answer, but Édith had already moved on. 'I'm a student, at least in name and papers.' She flopped into one of the armchairs and dangled her legs over the side of the armrest.

'I thought I would be living alone,' Kasia said, and sat in the chair opposite. 'That's usually protocol, no?'

Édith didn't answer straight away, and Kasia wondered if she should repeat herself.

'Needs must,' Édith finally said. 'Lack of space and such. Besides, we'll be fine. I'm the courier and you're the pianist, so it's all right we are together. You couldn't be with any of the agents in the field and you won't meet any of the resistance groups. You'll only know me and that's all.'

Kasia wasn't so sure. The stoat had been insistent on sticking to protocol when Maurice had finally managed to get hold of him to tell him that Kasia had to leave Vannes. 'I knew this would happen,' the stoat had lamented. He had arrived late the day after Kasia left Hugo's, meeting them at the beach house. 'Too many people involved, too many people know who she is. I knew it would happen.'

'She can still work, still wants to,' Maurice had said.

The stoat had not been too sure on taking another risk with Kasia, but as her skills with the radio were near perfect, he agreed that she was still an asset.

'This time, you meet no one. You get the messages, you transmit twice a week, always at night so you will be breaking curfew. You have a Wednesday and Sunday slot at eleven p.m. to get your messages to home base. But this is Paris. There are ears everywhere, so you have to be more careful than ever.'

'How will she move about during curfew?' Maurice had asked.

'Not your problem. She'll find a way. Take your nursing papers with you. Say you have an emergency. We will place you in a safe house, somewhere pretty busy and lively so you will blend in a little more. Your contact in Paris, the courier, will have some ideas of where best to transmit. She's a true Parisian, works with a group there, one of the best couriers we have; I'm sure you two will get along swimmingly,' the stoat said, then gave Kasia a smile in such a way that she wasn't sure whether he was teasing her.

Now, Kasia looked at Édith who seemed enamoured with her toenails – she had painted them a bright red and was wiggling them and smiling – and realised that the stoat had known that they would not become the best of friends.

'I think I'll go and unpack and get settled.' Kasia stood.

'Don't unpack much,' Édith said. 'Always keep your bags ready as if you have to leave, because we do, quite a lot.'

'And what if someone checks on us here, isn't then obvious that we don't actually live here?'

'You ask a lot of questions, Delphine. It's quite irritating. You need to stop thinking so much. We are usually gone by the time anyone knocks on the door.'

'Usually?' Kasia asked.

Édith shrugged. 'There's a few who aren't quick enough. But you don't have to worry about them. I'm quick, I know things.' She tapped the side of her nose. 'I know everything there is to know, so you're fine with me.'

Exasperated with Édith's lack of concern, she stalked to her bedroom – a single bed, small chest of drawers and a view out of the sliver of the window that looked out onto the street below.

It was then she missed Hugo's house and her room with the view of the sea, the pitter patter of Elodie's feet as she ran up and down the stairs, the scent of Hugo's cooking in the kitchen wafting through the floorboards.

It was then that she wept for what she had left behind.

THIRTY-FIVE

THE POLISH GIRL

Watching the day expand and unfurl itself from sleep, Elodie wondered where Kasia might be. She looked out to the sea, imagining Kasia out there, on a boat rocking against the waves, the slap, slap of the water hitting the hull. Then, she imagined she had gone to America and was in California where they made movies – where all those pretty people lived.

Bored with her daydreams, she sat on the floor and fussed at Remi who eagerly rolled onto his belly, revealing pink skin that was in need of a scratch. Hugo had left her a note saying that he had gone to see Major König and she was to stay at home and not leave until he returned. She felt annoyed at having to stay at home yet again – it had been a month since Kasia had left, and he had told her she could only leave the house if he was with her.

'What if I go to see Maurice?' she had asked. 'I could spend time with him?'

'We don't see Maurice any more,' he had told her.

'Why not?'

'Sometimes, I think I liked it better when you didn't talk,' he had said, then grinned at her; their inside joke that Hugo found hilarious and one which she tolerated. In fact, she liked his stupid jokes. It reminded her of her father, the way he would say silly things to get a smile from one of them. She liked how her memories could now be looked upon with happiness – something which Hugo had taught her.

'We have to remember the happy times,' he said. 'If we don't, then we do their lives a disservice.'

He had taken her to his wife's and daughter's graves, telling her what happened to them and how he was trying to think of them more often, of the good times not just the bad.

'We are helping each other to be happy, aren't we?' she asked, as she ran her fingers over the engravings of Giselle and Nanette.

'We are,' he said.

She sat at the kitchen table and looked at the latest book Hugo had left for her – a story about a fairy and a small child. She started the first page and soon became bored; she would have to tell him that these books were too young, too easy for her now.

She looked up and screamed. There at the window was a person. She ducked down beneath the table, then her brain caught up with what her eyes had seen – Antoine.

'Did I scare you?' he asked, as she opened the patio door for him.

'No.'

'Then why did you hide?'

'I hide because I can,' she said.

'That doesn't make sense – say it again.'

'No. It makes sense to me,' she retorted, getting sick of being corrected by Antoine and Hugo, being constantly asked to repeat herself.

'Why so grumpy this morning?' he asked, plopping down at the table, picking up Remi and giving him a cuddle.

'I'm not grumpy,' she said. 'Just bored.'

'I know what you mean. I wish we could go to our secret place. I have some new things to show you.'

'Like what?' she asked excitedly.

'I'm not telling. You have to wait. It will be a surprise.'

'Let's go today, I need to get out of the house, please?'

Antoine shook his head. 'You know what Hugo said. I cannot repeat what you tell me. I cannot take you anywhere. I'm allowed to come to the house, but only if I help you with your French.'

'He won't know...' she tried.

'He will, and I'm scared of him, so we'll stay here for now.'

'Do you think Kasia will come back?' she asked him. She asked him this every day, hoping that his answer would be different.

'I don't know. Maybe not yet.'

'But it's safe now. You haven't told anyone about the radio, and you won't, so why can't she come back?'

'Perhaps she doesn't know?' he said.

'Will Maurice know where she is? Maybe we could write to her?'

'I think you should ask Hugo first,' Antoine said, not looking directly at her.

'Because you were scared of him,' she said.

'Because I *am* scared of him. Come on Elodie, tenses, remember?'

They spent the morning going through the children's book, Antoine trying to teach her the tenses that seemed never-ending to her.

'Tell me what you have found,' she demanded, throwing the book on the floor.

'I can't,' he said. 'I'm not being difficult. I just really can't –

you have to see it. I'll show you as soon as Hugo says you can leave the house with me – when your French is perfect.'

'I don't see why it needs to be perfect,' she said. 'It's not like the Germans speak perfect French.'

'I agree. But what if we find one who does, and what if they notice your accent and that you sometimes mix up words? They'll know. Trust me, they will.'

The front door opened and closed, alerting them to Hugo's return.

'Look what we have here!' he cried as he entered. 'The student and the teacher. How goes the learning?'

'Pretty good,' Antoine said. 'She'll be word-perfect soon enough.'

She did not answer and sat with her arms folded across her chest.

'Ah, come now.' Hugo kissed the top of her head. 'Soon enough.'

'When is soon?' she asked. 'I'm bored here all day.'

'Soon is soon,' Hugo replied.

That afternoon after Antoine left, Hugo beckoned her into the sitting room and patted the sofa for her to sit next to him.

'More lessons.' She sighed.

'No. Not today. There's something I want to talk to you about.'

'Is it about Kasia?' she asked, her heart lifting at the thought that she might be returning.

He shook his head. 'It's about a letter that I wrote a few weeks ago. A letter to America.'

'Who is in America?' she asked.

'That's what I wanted to ask you!' He laughed. 'When Kasia took you from the ghetto, the woman there gave her an address of a Mr and Mrs Goldman in California. Do you know who they are?'

She paused a moment before answering, searching her memories for any mention of Goldman, America or California. 'No,' she said.

'Well, your parents knew them, and I think you were to be sent there if anything happened. So, I sent them a letter.'

'Have they replied?'

'Not yet. But I'm sure they will. I wanted to tell you straight away, but with everything that happened I thought it best to wait a while.'

'What will happen when they reply?'

'We will have to see. They may want you to go and live with them. Is that something you would like?'

'Will you come with me?'

'No. It would just be you.'

'Then no. I don't want to go.'

Hugo smiled at her.

'What are you smiling about?' she asked.

'Nothing. I was just hoping that you would say that.'

THIRTY-SIX

KASIA

Kasia's friendship with Édith did not improve.

She tried over the following days to engage her in conversation – Édith, as she found out, was twenty-three, and her only concerns were herself, Édith Piaf, and a boy she had met in one of the resistance groups who she knew loved her with all his heart and would any day now profess it to her. Kasia had tried to counsel the girl about men like him, about how the idealism of their fight and the politics they were engaged in, and even the romanticism of working in jobs such as they did, meant that after the war, things would change, they would change.

'Hardly,' Édith had said. 'Don't you understand love, Delphine? It transcends *everything*.'

'Why not listen to your Piaf – her words – she sings of heartbreak, of lost love,' Kasia said.

'You misunderstand what she sings about – and besides, wouldn't you rather love that strongly, then lose it and know the pain, the heartbreak, because then you know it was worth it?'

Kasia thought of her own heartbreak with Jan, and now, a strange, different heartbreak over Hugo. She had been devastated when Jan had broken it off with her, but it was a different, more yearning feeling when she thought of Hugo – almost like a limb had been removed, like she was not fully herself.

She didn't divulge any of this to Édith, and barely admitted it to herself, as she did not want to encourage the girl with her flights of fancy and love and, instead, tried to take on a motherly role – making sure she ate, tidying the apartment and buying small things such as fresh flowers and cheap pictures to make it feel more homely.

'Wasting your time,' was all Édith said when she saw the touches to their home.

Despite Édith's manner, Kasia had to admit that the stoat had been right about her. As a courier she was excellent. She nipped about, getting messages from all over Paris and never complained of tiredness or long days. She was wily and had even convinced the owners of a few nightclubs and bars to allow them access to their cellars.

'For transmissions,' Édith told Kasia one evening, as she plaited her hair.

'But isn't that more dangerous, after curfew and in a bar where German soldiers sit just above us?'

Édith laughed. 'You think they bring their work to a bar with them? You think they are sat there over cheap glasses of wine, trying to listen in to transmissions? What is it that someone said – better to be in the belly of the beast or right under their noses, or something like that?'

'I just think it's too much of a risk,' Kasia said. 'Surely there are safer places?'

'None that I've found yet,' Édith said confidently. 'You are just going to have to trust me on this one.'

'And what do we say if we are caught, after curfew, going into a bar or nightclub and me with a suitcase in tow?'

Édith rolled her eyes at her. 'Look at me, and look at you. I mean, more me, but you're not bad for an older woman—'

'Excuse me?'

'Don't get all offended.' Édith waved her palms at her. 'What I'm saying is, when those *Boche* see me, and what I wear in the evening, and they have had a few to drink, they soon forget to ask questions. You need to use it to your advantage, you know?'

Unconvinced, Kasia asked for a list of other places she could easily get to in the evenings. Édith suggested the grave-yard, and another a basement in a house four streets away.

'But I'm telling you, the bar thing works. We go in before curfew, put the suitcase in the cellar, have a few drinks and a flirt, then, we pretend to leave, but we don't. We go to the cellar and wait until your transmission time, then we leave as quickly as we can. Worst case, we leave the radio and get it the next day.'

'But wouldn't that put the bar owners in danger?'

'We hide it, silly.' Édith stood and foraged about on the table to find her cigarette case. 'Haven't you learned anything?'

After two failed attempts to get to the graveyard after curfew, and one where she arrived at 6 p.m. and sat next to the tomb of a man who had died in the 1700s, waiting in the rain and wind until her transmission time, she decided to risk Édith's plan.

The bars Édith had found were all sympathetic to the cause and no matter how much Kasia pressed Édith to reveal if they were part of a network, she would not budge.

'You don't need to know,' Édith said, as they gathered their things for the first run. 'Half the time I don't even know. It's better that way. You ask too many questions, have I told you that? It's irritating.'

Édith was right about how she looked when she frequented the bars. A pretty young woman during the day in her oversized men's shirts and trousers, at night she sparkled. Her hair brushed to a gleam and pinned back loosely at the nape of her neck, low-cut dresses that showed just enough to keep a man interested without offering too much more, the hem cut just under the knee, showing shapely calves.

In comparison, Kasia felt frumpy and old and no matter how many times she brushed her hair, she could never get the same sheen as Édith.

'You're either born with it, or you're not,' Édith said, as they left the apartment. 'But you're pretty, beautiful even, when you smile.'

Kasia was unsure of whether to thank her or not so instead smiled at Édith, who grinned back.

'Good! See, beautiful!'

Despite the danger of the evening, Kasia couldn't help but feel light-footed as they walked arm in arm to the bar where a local singer would be performing that evening. It remined her of the early days in Kraków with Marta, and even her sister, that excitement of being out, of not knowing what the night would bring and of laughing and spending time with your friends.

'Now,' Édith said, as they approached the bar. 'There's an alleyway that runs at the back of this place and you are to go down it, then turn left and you will see the back of the bar and a small door behind some crates that leads to the cellar. Pop down there, stash the radio, then come up and join me.'

'You're not coming?' Kasia asked.

'Not my job. Do it quickly and I'll have us some drinks waiting.'

Édith let go of Kasia's arm and flounced away to the entrance where a few Germans were already taking note of her. Kasia slipped down the alleyway, and turned left as advised, found the small door and made her way into a dank cellar.

The smell of beer, mould and wine assaulted her as she entered. A small bare bulb hung from the ceiling, giving out little light and creating giant shadows on the brick walls as Kasia moved about. She found some empty bottles and arranged them over the case in the corner of the cellar, then dusting herself off, made her way out and to the entrance.

'Easy, right?' Édith asked as she sat next to her, perched on a bar stool. 'You just have to be confident, like you're just going about your business. The pianist I knew before was useless. Too scared all the time at seeing so many Germans. I kept telling her, walk tall, look like you have nothing to hide and you will be fine. But she was always scurrying about, always looking at the ground – it was a giveaway.'

'What happened to her?' Kasia asked, taking a sip of the cheap red that had appeared on the bar for her.

Édith shrugged. 'Just moved somewhere else. I didn't ask.'

'Don't you care?'

Édith played with the stem of her wine glass, twisting and turning it around. 'It's not that I don't care, it's just that if you care for everyone in this job, you'd be constantly worried, you know?'

Kasia nodded, even though she knew that no particular answer was required from her. They sat in companionable silence for a while, and listened to the singer, a large woman who wore so much red – red lipstick, dress, shoes – that soon Édith began to say that she reminded her of a tomato.

'See, look, when she sings, her face goes the same colour as her dress!' Édith laughed and clapped her hands together.

'Don't be mean,' Kasia said. 'I think you should slow down, your cheeks are turning red too.'

Indeed, Édith had received a fair few drinks from her German admirers and accepted them graciously, with a smile and a few kind words.

'No need to tease them too much,' she said, as she accepted yet another drink.

Just before curfew began at nine, as patrons started to leave, Kasia made her way to the toilet where a portly gentleman met her. 'Bernard,' he said, shaking her hand. 'Come with me.'

He led her to a small office and then to the door into the cellar. 'No need to go back out and then in again. Just always come and see me. Édith is such a good girl.' He grinned.

Kasia nodded in agreement – Bernard had too fallen under Édith's spell.

She sat in the dank cellar until just before eleven and then placed the headset on and signed in.

She used the same poem as she had in Vannes, even though the stoat had mentioned some new way to be introduced – talk of silk with one-time codes written on them. She was sure that this proposed new way would be much safer and would aid in fewer mistakes being made if agents forgot their poem or misremembered a word, but she so liked the poem she had been given – it made her laugh no matter how many times she repeated it to herself.

Tapping away at the transmitter, she signed on – Delphine – and then gave the key codes.

'Received,' came the reply.

Then, she tapped out the newest message:

Bridges to the south have been identified and Felix to leave within the week. Immediate request for supplies, including dynamite and more coils. Secure drop site yet to be identified after last failing. End of message.

'Message received', then static in her ears.

Happy with how quickly she was able to send the message and convinced she had made no mistakes, she packed the radio away quickly and left through the rear cellar door.

Outside, the quiet was disconcerting. The daily busyness of the streets seemingly evaporated into thin air as soon as curfew began and she hated that she could hear her own footsteps as she walked, making her think that they were not her own, but that someone was following her.

She stayed in the shadows, doorways and alleyways and tried to remember what Édith had said – look confident, look as though you're doing nothing wrong. Soon, she was relieved to see her apartment just a few feet in front of her and quickened her pace, opening the door and taking the stairs two at a time.

'Good?' Édith asked, as she sat across from her.

'It went perfectly,' Kasia told her.

'I told you it would.' Édith grinned smugly. 'You have to trust me, Delphine. I know what I'm doing. I know everything.'

Kasia stood, ready to go to bed, when Édith waved at her to sit.

'Look what I have,' she said and produced a bottle of red. 'Bernard gave it to me. Let's drink.'

It wasn't a question as much as a demand, and before Kasia could protest, Édith had found two clean mugs and slopped the wine into them.

'It's a shit wine,' Édith said. 'But what can you do? I'd rather drink shit wine than no wine at all!'

Kasia could see that Édith was merry and for the first time in a month, wanted to talk properly.

'Tell me about yourself, Delphine. I mean I know that's not your name and you can't really tell me your real name or any of that, but tell me something. I need a story before I go to sleep.'

Kasia racked her brains, trying to think of a story she could tell her that would not give too much away.

'Here, I'll make it easy for you. Have you got brothers or sisters? Me, I don't. Tell me about them if you have them – you know, what it was like having someone to talk to when you were young.'

'I have a sister,' she began. 'Well, had – maybe still have...'

Intrigued, Édith stared at her. 'What does that mean – had, have – tell me?'

Despite knowing she shouldn't reveal anything about herself, the wine or the success of the transmission made Kasia want to keep the evening going, and she told Édith about Maja, in a roundabout way.

When she had finished, Édith had uncurled herself from the armchair and sat ramrod straight.

'You said one brown eye and one green?' Édith asked.

Kasia nodded.

'And she is beautiful, clever, funny?'

Again, she nodded.

'Does she have a scar on her arm, on her right arm, like a burn mark; it looks strange, like a misshapen circle, but also a bit like a country on a map?'

Suddenly, Kasia felt like all the air in the room had been sucked out.

'She did it when she was little. She tried to make soup for me when I was sick and she burned her arm so badly, Papa was never sure it would heal, but when it did, it was ugly and puckered. She cried over it for weeks until I told her it made her completely unique and then we would look at it for hours and try and decide what it might be.'

'I know her,' Édith said.

Kasia was crying now. 'You can't, it can't be true...'

Édith came to her and took her in her arms, a gesture so unlike her that Kasia suddenly felt like laughing.

'I know her. I can find out where she lives. You can see your sister again.'

THIRTY-SEVEN

HUGO

Vannes, August 1943

The spring soon turned into a hot summer that raged about the town, scorching the once green grass to brown stubble, wilting the flowers in window boxes and putting the Germans in a bad mood.

Hugo continued to ply them with wine where he could, and began to seek more and more from the black market, not just for Etienne and Henri, but for others in town who were suffering.

He knew it was risky to take on more – only a matter of time before he was found out – but he reasoned that if Kasia could be brave, could take risks, then so could he. He even had an escape plan ready should anything happen – he would travel down the coast with Elodie until he reached his friend in La Rochelle, a friend who had promised him that he could get him to England with little fuss. He doubted it would be without a 'fuss' and was prepared for it to be dangerous, but it was necessary – he had to know that he had a way out.

Hugo cycled one August morning to Major König's head-quarters in the Hôtel de Ville, the manuscript he had been working on with the major tucked into his pannier.

At the prison gate that gave entrance from the fortified walls into the town centre, Hugo was stopped and asked for his papers – a routine that now no longer scared him. One of the soldiers recognised him from his meetings with the major and let him pass without another word.

The town was silent – whether from the heat or the occupation or both, Hugo did not know. His bicycle bumped over cobbles, and he looked about him to see which shops were newly closed, newspaper covering their windows. The shoe-makers was shut, as was the dress shop. He understood why of course – who had the money to mend shoes or buy new dresses when most days it was hard to get a loaf of bread?

Three people he knew had been arrested too. Not many, but enough to stir the tide of fear through the townsfolk, and Hugo wondered whether that was why the men had been arrested in the first place – not for breaking curfew but as an excuse to browbeat the town into submission.

Since the major had arrived, things had changed and, in a way, Hugo was glad that Kasia had left when she had. Two radio operators, both British, had been caught not far out of town by the vans that scoured the countryside day and night, the electronics in the back ready to pick up any signal that was not known to them. He wished in a way that he still spoke to Maurice so he could ask him what became of the operators. But then again, perhaps it was better that he didn't know.

He stopped briefly outside the doctor's surgery and pushed an envelope under the door. Despite his anger at Maurice, he still got him supplies and would leave him a note to let him know where to find them – to deliver them to him would be too dangerous now.

He pulled to a stop outside the Hôtel de Ville, the red and

black flag of the Reich covering half of the building, hanging from the roof, making its way down, obscuring the top windows. He often wondered what it was like for those people who worked in the top offices – was their room continually aglow with red? Did they mind it? He was sure he would go mad.

The major welcomed him into his office with a languid wave of the hand. In front of him, he had two electric fans whirring at full capacity, fluttering the papers on his desk, and yet Hugo could see that the major was still bright red and sweating.

'This heat!' the major whined. 'I cannot bear it. I cannot. All my creativity has disappeared, Hugo. I doubt we will ever finish my story if this heat continues.'

'We could leave it for today?' Hugo suggested.

The major stuck his head close to the fan, and Hugo wished the blades would escape their casing and strike his face. 'No. No. We must continue. But before we do, any word on your cousin? You told me she had left to tend to her mother, and she is still not back – leaving you with the child?'

Hugo sat and crossed his legs as if considering the serious-ness of his situation – a cousin looking after her mother who was dying, and him, a bachelor taking care of her child. 'It is hard without her here,' he said. 'But I manage.'

'A shame. Such a shame. I was so looking forward to meeting her, you know. A few of the men had seen her about and said how striking she was.'

'I suppose she is,' Hugo admitted.

'Not that I would do anything. I have a wife, waiting for me back at home.' The major laughed. 'Waiting, day in day out. A striking woman herself – no not striking,' the major thought for a second – 'handsome. Yes. She is a handsome woman.'

Hugo watched as the major twisted in his chair a few times, trying to get comfortable.

'Did you see Maurice again?' Hugo asked. He knew he had,

everyone in town was laughing about the major's piles, but he couldn't help himself – he wanted him to feel embarrassed.

'I have,' the major said shortly. 'Where were we up to last time we spoke?'

Hugo checked his notes. 'We were up to 1939 – September 1939, to be exact.'

'Ah yes! The glory days. Those were the days that my whimsy knew no bounds, Hugo. I was one of the first into Poland with my battalion – have I told you this already? Probably not. There we were, entering Poland, and we saw the Polish forces, a pitiful bunch who quickly laid down their arms at the sight of the majesty of our power. Can you write that, word for word, "majesty of our power"?' he asked.

'I can,' Hugo scribbled it down.

'Good. So, there we were, fighting now and again, but nothing much considering the air force we had, bombing a straight line all the way to Warsaw!'

'Warsaw...' Hugo said. 'You were in Warsaw?'

'I was. Did I not tell you this? Before my promotion, I was there until 1941, or 42 – doesn't matter which; what matters is my whimsy, Hugo.'

Hugo nodded. *His whimsy*. He was sick of the word.

'Warsaw was pretty much gone by the time we got there – bombed buildings and the like and everyone wondering what to do next. Seeing as how I had been injured on our journey, I was given a desk job for a while in the new government.'

'You were injured? You didn't mention that.'

'I was. Almost. It was a battle in which there was fierce fighting – fierce, Hugo – and I stepped out of my car and would you believe it, some Polish bastard had dug a trench nearby and into it I went, breaking my foot! Of course, when you write it, you will see to it that you mention that I killed four Poles who were waiting in the trench, won't you?'

'Did you?'

'Did I what?

'Kill four men?'

The major waved his question away. 'So, there I am, a broken foot and a desk job and there were all these meetings all the time, Hugo. Boring things. I couldn't bear them. But then one day, there was talk of what to do with the Jews. Of course we were going to segregate them as we had in Germany, but there were so many Jews this time, refugees from other towns that had spilled into the city, so everyone was talking of building five or more smaller ghettos in which to segregate them. But here comes my whimsy, Hugo, I suggested one large ghetto, one that we cut off from the rest of the city – almost like a city in itself but just for the Jews! And you know what, they loved it!'

Hugo had stopped writing now. His hand would not obey his brain and the pen sat still above the paper. Warsaw. The ghetto that Elodie was found in, the ghetto that her parents died trying to avoid.

'Is something the matter?' the major asked.

Hugo swallowed back his anger. 'Just the heat, Major. The heat.'

'Indeed!' The major stood up quickly, his stomach wobbling with force. 'You must go home now, rest. I cannot have you getting heatstroke. Who else would write my whimsies?'

Hugo stood and thanked the major and made his way home at twice the speed, the notes in his panniers, he imagined burning a hole in the material.

At home he raced into his bedroom with the awful words of the major and threw the pages onto his bed. He knew what he was going to do with this, with the man himself, but he had to be patient.

'Hugo?' Elodie's voice sang out to him. He quickly splashed cold water on his face and went to find her.

'Etienne brought these.' She sat at the kitchen table and waved three envelopes in her hand. 'He collected the mail for you.'

'Did you thank him?'

'I did. Don't you want to look at them?'

'In a moment,' he said, filling a glass with water and drinking it straight back.

'I think this one you might want to see.'

He went to her and took the one envelope she now held in her hand.

'Look at the postmark,' she said.

America. California.

'You didn't open it?' he said.

'I don't know English. You said you would teach it to me.'

He ripped open the envelope and drew out the letter – one page on thin paper. Scanning the words, he felt his heart thumping in his chest and his mouth dry even though he had just drunk.

'What does it say?' she asked.

He pulled a chair out from the table and sat down heavily.

'They want me to go, don't they? I have to leave?'

Hugo shook his head. 'No. The opposite, in fact.'

'They don't want me?'

'They say that they knew your parents through a group they belonged to in Poland. They were sponsoring them. The address you have is one which was given to your father should they reach America, and they would then have someone they knew to help them get settled. They say that they can't take a child as they are elderly, but I should write again if I would like them to help find a family for you.'

'They don't want me,' she said quietly.

Hugo put his hand on hers. 'But *I* do. If you want to stay with me?'

She looked up at him, grinning from ear to ear. 'They don't want me!' she cried, then wrapped her arms around Hugo's neck. 'I knew you were to be my papa. I just knew it.'

Fighting back tears, Hugo held on to her, wishing that Kasia were there, wishing that she wanted to be with him too.

THIRTY-EIGHT

KASIA

Paris, September 1943

The problem with Édith's promise to find Maja was that she could not remember the name that she now went by.

'It's French of course,' Édith said, pacing the apartment, a newly acquired pipe sticking from her mouth that she never lit.

'You look like Sherlock Holmes with that thing in your mouth,' Kasia told her.

'Do I?' Édith turned to her with a grin. 'That's exactly what I was hoping for.'

'Where on earth did you get it?'

'Stole it,' Édith said, and resumed her pacing. 'A corporal took a fancy to me and wouldn't understand the word no. So when he went to the bathroom, I took it.'

'You really shouldn't do that,' Kasia chided. 'What if he saw you? What if he called the police?'

'What if, what if?' Édith repeated. 'Anyway, let's think of names. Say some names and it will come to me, I'm sure.'

For the first two weeks, they played this game daily and Édith was no closer to remembering the name. Soon, Kasia began to think that Édith did not know her at all.

'But the scar!' Édith said, 'How could I have known that?'

'Perhaps it is a coincidence,' Kasia said, not quite believing the words.

'Ah yes, a woman with one brown eye and one green with a scar on her arm. Yes, I'm sure that there are lots of women like that roaming the streets of Paris!'

They had to put the name game to one side once Édith got word that their radio signals had been picked up and they were to move house quickly.

Kasia was sad to leave Belleville; she had got used to its ways, the people, the chatter.

'It'll be just the same where we are going next,' Édith said, as they lugged their belongings in the dead of night. 'It will be fine.'

The next safe house was a basement that had been converted into a small bedroom with a double bed, a tiny kitchenette and a sink.

'Where are we to bathe?' Édith had cried upon seeing it. 'You know I have to wash my hair every other day.'

Kasia had pointed to the sink, to which Édith had let out a moan of despair and thrown herself childishly upon the bed. 'And we have to sleep together!'

It was getting harder and harder to find places to transmit from, and Kasia had to make her transmissions shorter and shorter, travelling all around Paris and its suburbs to get the messages out. A nearby church was used sometimes, and other basements belonging to people Kasia did not know and would never know. The rear of a bakery, a slaughterhouse that reeked of flesh and blood, and chilled Kasia to the bone.

'They'll move you on again soon – out of the city,' Édith told her one afternoon as they lay on the double bed in their underwear, both exhausted from the previous day of traipsing around Paris, the suffocating heat of the summer wearing down their patience and their moods.

'Not soon enough,' Kasia moaned. 'There's no air in this room!'

'Stop squirming about!' Édith yelled. 'You move all the warm air. Stay still.'

Kasia did as she was told, then felt Édith's fingers touch hers. 'I don't want you to go. But that's not why I said it, so that I could tell you I wanted you to stay.'

'You could come with me?'

'Paris is mine.' Édith sighed. 'I couldn't leave it, and I couldn't leave Marcel.'

'Marcel still won't profess his love for you; when are you going to give it up?'

'Never.' Édith turned to her. 'Listen, we haven't much time, have we, to find your sister? The average life span of people in our job is six weeks, did you know that? Marcel told me. And how long have you been doing this? How long have I? They'll move you on before you're caught, so we have to find her quickly.'

Kasia stared at the spider-cracked plaster ceiling above her. 'I don't think I was meant to find her. You can't remember her name, you can't remember who she said she was, or what she did. How are we going to find her?'

'I remembered something,' Édith said.

Kasia turned her head to look at her, the halo of blonde hair on the pillow, those eyes that she had once thought cold and hard were light and mischievous.

'I remembered that where I met her was a meeting, of sorts. It was some communist shit, you know? But at the time Marcel was interested in it, so I thought I'd give it a go. But they had their own ways and own groups, and Marcel didn't go again.'

'How did you not remember this before?'

'I don't know. I go to so many stupid meetings and things that they all blend into one. Anyway, I'll ask Marcel tonight. He'll remember where it was, perhaps who she was.'

'You're seeing Marcel?' Kasia asked. 'But it's Thursday – you only go out on Fridays.'

'Different kind of meet this time.' She grinned. 'A party of sorts, someone died, was found out, so we have a little celebration of their life. Sounds weird, but it's what we do.'

Kasia wanted to go with her, but Édith reminded her that the group would be put at risk if she knew any of them.

That evening she sat in the basement on the bed, nerves fluttering in her stomach. Had Édith spoken to Marcel yet? Had he said who her sister was now, where she might be?

Frustrated, she paced the room and wished Hugo were there to calm her nerves. She thought back to her time with him, how even though he annoyed her, even goaded her into pointless arguments, he had a quiet way about him, almost as though he could sense when she was unhappy or worried.

She tore at the skin at the side of her thumb with her teeth. The warm pain took her thoughts away from Hugo. Good. Don't think about him. Don't think about Elodie. She concentrated on the pain in her thumb, on her steps as she paced until she heard the gentle thud of Édith's footsteps on the basement stair.

'Vivienne!' Édith exclaimed upon flinging open the door. 'How did we not say that name?'

'Vivienne who?' Kasia asked.

'Toussaint. I didn't remember it, but Marcel did. He knows of the husband, Albert. The one in the wheelchair.'

'Wheelchair? You didn't mention a husband or that he was in a wheelchair.'

'Because I didn't remember, but then when Marcel said it tonight, *voilà*, I could see them both. Albert Toussaint, the worst of the worst of men.'

'Why do you say that?' Kasia wondered if Albert was Jan, or if her sister had a new husband.

'Self-righteous, thinks all women love him. You can see that he is all show, all mouth, thinks he is more intelligent and more good-looking than he is. Threatened by women. Looking at you when you talk and all that rubbish – I saw him for what he was.'

Upon hearing Édith's description of Albert, Kasia began to laugh.

'What's so funny?' Édith asked.

'I didn't see it, but now I do! You are so right. He is such a joke of a man – how could I not have seen it?'

She soon felt the laughter turn to sobs and let her body ease into it.

'Are you all right?' Édith sat next to her.

'I'm fine.' Kasia lifted her head and smiled. 'It's a relief – all those years I still had him on this pedestal, not seeing him for real, but now I look back and I can see that's exactly the man he was – always putting himself first, only really listening to my thoughts so he would then argue that I was wrong. Getting jealous over job opportunities. No wonder he went to Maja – he wanted someone younger, who would look at him as I had done in the beginning.'

'You mean you were with your sister's husband first?' Édith asked, her eyes wide. 'How did you not tell me that part of the story? It's the best part!'

'It was a long time ago,' Kasia said. 'Now it feels like a life-time ago – almost like another world.'

'I understand. It's like there was a world, a life before the war, and then this. Then, there'll be a different life after it,' Édith said.

'Why Édith, you're growing into quite a philosopher!'

Édith blushed. 'You know what I mean. The Allies are making progress. It won't be long until all this is over and then you can have any life you want. But first, first you have to see your sister and I have her address right here.'

Édith handed her a scrap of paper, the address of one Albert Toussaint scribbled onto it. She held it in her hand, memorising the address long after Édith fell asleep, curled into a ball like a puppy beside her, thinking not of her sister or Jan and the past, but of what Édith had said: soon she could have any life she wanted, and the two faces that imprinted themselves onto this dream were Hugo and Elodie.

THIRTY-NINE

KASIA

The following morning, Kasia woke as the birds began their morning song. She looked to Édith who had not moved in her sleep and was still curled tightly in a ball.

She eased herself out of bed, careful not to wake her and dressed quickly, scrunching her hair back in a rough bun. She took her time with her make-up, though. As much as she did not care what Jan thought of her after all these years, she wanted to make him realise who she was now, how confident she was. The red lipstick, almost worn down to the nub was her last effort and looking at herself, she realised she liked what she saw: she was beautiful, confident, strong – this was Kasia now and it would be in the future too.

Eager to see her sister, to put the past to bed, she did not wake Édith to tell her where she was going and left the basement with hurried steps.

The western suburbs of Paris took some time to reach, mostly on foot. She scoured the streets for the man who had given her the pedi-cycle ride when she first arrived, but not recognising any faces, she continued walking.

What would she say when Maja opened the door? Would

she shut it in her face? Could she ask why Jan was in a wheel-chair? Should she say sorry or wait for Maja to say it first?

Nerves fought with excitement in her stomach, making it growl. She stopped at a small bakery and bought a two-day-old croissant, tearing into it quickly, not caring about the stale hard ends. By eleven she had reached the street where her sister now lived – a quiet, leafy suburban scene that did not suit Maja or Jan – why were they not closer to the city? She found their house, number 23, and noted how half the steps had been concreted over to make a ramp.

Breathing in and out, two, three times, she steadied herself and rapped at the door, thinking deep down somewhere that she hoped no one would answer. But behind the green and red stained glass she saw a figure approaching and then the door was opened.

'Yes?' a woman stood in front of her, and it took Kasia a moment to realise that it was Maja. Her face was rounder, her body filled out, making her look short. Her hair, once a source of pride, was bluntly cut short at the chin, but underneath the heavily mascaraed eyelashes, she saw the eyes – one green, one brown.

'Maja?' Kasia said.

At first, the woman shook her head, and then with a flash of recognition whispered, '*Kasia?*'

'It's me,' she said.

'It is.'

Unsure of what to say, Kasia nodded towards the hallway.

Understanding the gesture, Maja stepped aside. 'Yes, yes, of course come in.'

Once inside she stood in front of her sister – her sister who she had thought was dead, her sister whom no one had heard from in years and all she could say was, 'How are you?'

Suddenly, Maja began to laugh and took her in an embrace, wrapping her arms around her tightly. '*How am I? How am I?*'

she asked, sobbing onto her shoulder. 'Oh, Kasia. I'm fine now that you are here.'

A loud thud behind Kasia made Maja suddenly let go. She wiped her eyes with the back of her hand. 'Come, come with me.'

She led Kasia into the sitting room and told her to wait, and within a minute she wheeled Jan into the room.

'Albert, I presume,' Kasia said, then looked to her sister who was biting her bottom lip, remembering that she had always done that as a child to stop herself from crying.

'You found us, then,' Jan said, then pointed at the wide windows for Maja to wheel him towards.

'You look well,' Kasia said, feeling the awkwardness of the words in her mouth.

'Do I?' He laughed, then looked at his legs. 'I highly doubt that, but then you were never that astute, were you, Kasia?'

His voice was laced with scorn, and Kasia was unsure of how to respond.

'Ignore him!' Maja trilled. 'He's always in a mood.'

'I'm in a mood because my legs don't work, you fat bitch,' he spat.

Kasia was about to say something, but Maja held up her hand to silence her, a fixed smile on her face.

'Just grumpy today,' Maja said. 'I'll get us some coffee, yes?'

Without waiting for an answer, she left the two of them together. Kasia was unsure of whether to follow her sister or stay where she was.

'You've changed,' she said, deciding to deal with Jan first, and sat down on the couch. 'Although, maybe you haven't. I mean, you were always demanding, and I never thought of you as nasty... but then again, leaving me for my sister, I suppose that was a pretty nasty thing to do.'

Jan laughed. 'Bringing that up again, are we? I knew you would. I knew as soon as I saw you, you'd want to talk about that again. But it was your fault that it happened, Kasia – yours.'

'And how was it my fault?' Kasia felt her voice rising, a ball of hot anger in her stomach.

'Always working, always thinking you could outsmart everyone, right? But I outsmarted you. You had no idea, did you, about me and Maja? Right under your nose and the clever little thing that everyone wanted to work for them didn't know a thing about it!'

'So that's it? You spited me because I was offered a job and not you? You petty little bastard!'

Kasia stood and stalked out of the room, finding her sister in the kitchen laying out biscuits as if the world were rosy and sweet.

'Just ignore him,' Maja said, not looking up from her task. 'He doesn't mean it, he's just in pain and bitter that he can't walk. Before the accident he was fine, just fine, but now...' She shrugged.

'But the way he spoke to you – the name he called you,' Kasia persisted.

Again, a shrug. 'He's right, though, isn't he? I am fat.'

Kasia sat heavily on a chair and placed her elbows on the table, cradling her head in her hands. This wasn't what she thought it would be like. She had thought Jan would be contrite, Maja her usual bubbly self. Maja would cry, apologise, and Kasia could move on – move away from what happened.

She heard a scrape of chair legs and looked up to see Maja sat across from her, her eyes full of tears. She reached across the void of the wooden table and held out her hand for Kasia to take it.

Kasia hesitated a fraction too long, and Maja slowly withdrew her hand. 'It's all right, I understand. Too soon?'

'I just don't know what to say, Maja. I've been worried about you all these years. Constantly trying to find out what happened and now I'm here and you are sat there, I just don't know what to say.'

'You searched for me?' Maja asked.

'Of course I did. Did you not think to write, to let me and Mother and Papa know you were well?'

Maja shook her head. 'I thought you all hated me. I thought it for the best. Jan, he said that you would never forgive me and there was no point in trying, so I didn't.'

'But Mother,' Kasia said. 'Did you not think of her? She died, you know. Died wondering where you were, if you were even alive!'

'I know, I know, I'm sorry Kasia, really I am.' Maja began to cry now, heavy ugly sobs. 'I hated myself for what I had done to you – but at the time I thought I was in love, I really did. And the groups that Jan and I went to – the communist groups – I really believed in them too, I really believed I was fighting for a cause.'

'Do you still?'

'No. I stopped a while back. Jan, he was a big voice here, you know. People wanted to listen to him, to let him lead them, and I stood back and let him. But with the war it's too dangerous and I stopped taking him to meetings, stopped indulging him. That makes him bitter too, you know – I decide where he goes, what he does and he hates it.'

It was then that Kasia saw a small smile creep onto Maja's face. 'He hates it. Hates it when I won't take him somewhere. A part of me feels guilty, but then he calls me a fat bitch and I don't care that much any more.'

Kasia smiled too. 'I can't believe how I ever fell for him. I have a friend who told me her impression of him, how she thought he was controlling, and it wasn't until she said it that I could look back and see all the times that he wasn't as perfect as I thought he was.'

'Like a mirror,' Maja said. 'Someone held up a mirror and

you could finally see the true reflection.'

'You see it too?'

'I do, but you know there are times, in the evening when we sit together and talk, just like the old times, and we laugh too. And then I see the man I fell in love with, and I do still think he is in there somewhere.'

'I'm not sure he is, Maja,' Kasia said gently.

Maja brushed the tears from her face and asked, 'How is Papa?'

'He's in America, left after Mother died. I think he is fine, though I haven't heard from him in over a year now.'

Maja nodded. 'I had heard he left.'

'From who?'

'Jan still has a few friends in Kraków. They told us about Mama, about Papa, but no one knew where you were.'

'What happened to Jan – his legs, I mean?' Kasia asked.

'An accident. We were stopped on the way here, a few were arrested, us too, something about the group we were travelling with had plans to bomb some buildings, all rubbish of course.' Maja heaved herself from her seat and poured boiling water onto the few coffee granules in the cups. 'We got away and we stayed in Belgium for a while and got fake documents – became French – then made our way here. It was fine for a year or so – Jan was busy with his meetings and talks of changing the world and its politics and I made friends with some women who were bored with the groups, and we set up our own little club for a while – reading, writing, discussions – not just about politics but about everything. Then, Jan was walking home one evening and was hit by a van delivering bread – can you imagine?'

Despite herself, Kasia let out a little laugh.

'It's the fact that it was a bread van that makes it funny, isn't it?' Maja asked. 'I know, I find myself trying not to laugh when Jan tells the story to people. Of course, when he tells it, it is very dramatic and not at all like it was. He broke both legs, got an infection and the muscles wasted so he finds it too painful to walk. But when he tells the story, you would think he were on the battlefield!'

'Still, I shouldn't laugh, so awful.'

Maja nodded. 'A bread van.'

Then the two, despite the inappropriateness, began to laugh, belly-full laughs that had Kasia doubled over at the table and slapping her hand on the wood.

'A van! A bread van!' Maja would say and the two would double down once more.

'What are you cackling about?' Jan had wheeled himself to the door.

Maja abruptly stopped. 'Nothing. Just a joke.'

'Tell it to me,' he said.

'I can't remember it.'

'You can't remember a joke you were just laughing about?' Then, Jan began to laugh. 'And you were so smart once, weren't you? So pretty and smart and now look at you.'

'That's enough!' Kasia sprang from her chair and leaned down so that her face was inches from Jan's. She could smell his breath, a sweet, stale odour, his skin oily. 'Speak that way to my sister again—'

'And you'll do what?' he sneered.

'You have no idea what I'm capable of, the people I know,' she whispered, and was glad to see that his mouth closed, his pupils dilated. 'You don't know me any more, Jan. You don't know what I could do.'

She stepped away from him.

'Get out of my house,' he said quietly.

'No, no, she just got here!' Maja yelled.

'Get out of my house!' he screamed now, his face red.

'Fine.' Kasia gathered her things, then felt Maja tugging at her arm.

'Don't go, please. Just ignore him, please, Kasia.'

'I'll come back, I promise. I think things just need to settle for a while.' She drew her sister to her and heard her whisper, 'I'm so sorry, Kasia.'

She kissed her sister's cheek. 'I'll be back, I promise.'

Jan had to wheel himself backwards so that Kasia could squeeze past him, and as she opened the front door, she heard him yell, 'Don't come back!'

She turned and smiled at him, telling him, 'See you soon', then blew him a kiss.

On the walk home, Kasia did not notice her surroundings. Her mind was a whirl of anger, of relief, of sadness and she tried to separate out the feelings much like sorting her laundry – sadness for Maja, for lost years; relief she was alive; anger – well that was for Jan. Then, she realised the anger was not solely for him – it was for herself too.

She thought back to all the times that a niggling feeling in her stomach had told her that something was not quite right with Jan, but she had ignored it, pushed it aside because of her love for him – how stupid could she have been?

The memories came thick and fast now – the time that he had refused to talk to her for two days because she had disagreed with him at one of their meetings, telling her that she had embarrassed him and herself. The time she was offered a job – no, twice when she was offered to go to Warsaw and Poznań and work with like-minded academics – and he had told her it was a waste of time, that she wouldn't be able to do the work, that she would make a fool of herself.

Another time in a café, when a mutual friend, David had stopped to talk to her and Jan had been in a fury that she had spoken to David and not to him. 'You're embarrassing yourself, throwing yourself at him,' he had said. And then the time he had understood and calculated an equation before she had, and had lorded it over her for months, making her tell the story to anyone who would listen about the time that Jan had beaten her to it, making her squirm in her seat.

The memories stacked one on top of the other as she walked, her hands curling themselves into fists at each fresh humiliation.

'Stop!'

She wondered if she had said the words and turned to check. It was then she saw a man running towards her.

'Stop, for God's sake, stop!'

As the figure came near, she saw it was Alain, the man who owned the building and the basement in which Kasia and Édith lived.

'What's wrong?' She stopped walking and waited for him to reach her.

'It's Édith, they came for her,' he panted.

'Who came for her?' she asked stupidly.

'Gestapo.' He shook his head. 'They know about you, about both of you, they said. They found a radio. They thought I would know something, I said I didn't – I thought you were both students. They don't believe me, they'll come back, I'm sure. Don't go to the house.' His words came fast. 'I have already left. Just now. My brother has a car and I saw you as we drove past. You must disappear now.'

'But, Édith...' she started.

'Don't go back, don't go. She's gone.'

A car horn alerted Alain to his brother who was waiting impatiently, waving his arm out of the window at him.

'I have to go. I'd say come with us, but that might not be safe...'

'No, no, it's not,' she said, seeing relief on his face.

'You'll be fine?' he asked, then not waiting for an answer, ran to his brother's car and got in.

Kasia watched the car disappear down the road, hearing the

sound of traffic, of people talking, as if everything were far away. She couldn't believe it had happened. She always knew it was a possibility – a rather likely one – but, somehow, she just had flatly refused to believe it.

Would Édith give her up? They had the radio, but Édith did not know her poem so could be of little use to them. But then, would they simply kill her or would they let her go?

She should have stuck to the protocol. She and Édith should never have lived together, why hadn't she insisted upon it? Why had she let Édith decide? If they hadn't been together, Édith would be safe.

She tried to think of what the stoat had told her to do – send a message to home base and alert them to the fact she had been compromised. But she had no radio, no way of procuring one.

She knew only Édith in Paris and wished she had at least met Marcel once so she could get word to him. It was then she realised someone did know Marcel – Jan and Maja.

Turning on her heel, she half ran back towards Maja's house, feeling the sweat drip down her legs chafing her thighs.

'Kasia!' Maja opened the door to her and ushered her inside. 'Are you all right? You're all red and sweating, did you run here?'

'I did,' Kasia's voice was hoarse.

Maja quickly fetched her a glass of water, and they sat in the sitting room together.

'Where's Jan?'

'He sleeps in the afternoon,' she said. 'His bedroom is downstairs.'

'And yours?' Kasia asked.

'Upstairs. Gives us both a bit of space.'

'Will he be awake soon? Can you wake him?'

Maja crinkled her brow. 'Why would you want me to wake him – he'll just start shouting again.'

'I need his help, Maja. Maybe yours too – please, wake him.'

FORTY

KASIA

That evening, Kasia and Maja lay in bed next to each other, their faces so close their noses almost touched.

'Do you think he will help?' Kasia asked.

'He said to let him think about it,' Maja said. 'He'll do the right thing, I'm sure of it.'

Kasia wasn't so sure. When she had told Jan and Maja that she needed to get in touch with Marcel, Jan had smirked at her. 'So now you need me? Not clever enough to sort out your own mess?'

Kasia had bitten her tongue and kept the words back that she wanted to spit at Jan. 'Please. It's important.'

Now Kasia wondered if she had done the right thing. Was Jan spiteful enough to tell the Gestapo where she was and who she was? She couldn't ignore the possibility.

'At least I get to see you,' Maja said, then yawned. 'We get to spend some time together.'

'I fear I have put you in danger, though,' Kasia said. 'Édith knows your address, she might tell them to look for me here. I can't stay long, I can't put you in danger like that.'

'Stay as long as you can, Kasia, please.'

'Why don't you leave with me?' Kasia blurted. 'Why don't you leave him and come with me? I can get you work, I'm sure of it. You were always smarter than me by far anyway!'

'Me? Hardly, Kas. I studied twice as hard to keep up with you.'

'No, you didn't. You skipped a year in university.'

'That wasn't because of my brains, Kas. That was because of my looks.'

'No, it wasn't—'

'It was,' Maja cut her off. 'The professor had a thing for me. I used it to my advantage. I wanted you to be proud of me. To think that I was as clever as you and maybe we would be closer.'

Kasia closed her eyes.

'Are you sleeping?' Maja asked.

'Just thinking. Just thinking how I had everything wrong.'

'What do you mean?'

Kasia opened her eyes and looked at her sister – the sister she had been jealous of, the sister who she thought was better than her in every way, actually felt the same about her.

'We wasted so much time, Maja,' Kasia said. 'Why didn't we just talk honestly with each other? Why didn't we tell each other how we felt?'

'We were young and stupid.'

'But we have time now, Maja. We could leave, us two. I know of this place, a house on the beach, so wonderful and strange that it feels almost magical. We could go there. I have friends, Hugo and a little girl, Elodie.'

'I couldn't leave Jan,' Maja said.

'Why not? He's horrible to you. Think of what he did, Maja, to both of us.'

'I was a part of it, Kas. You can't blame him for everything. I knew what I was doing. I knew it would hurt you and I did it anyway. And I know he is horrid sometimes, but I do love him, Kasia, I do. I can't leave him, I won't.'

'I don't care about what you did, Maja, I don't. You were young, and I know what Jan could be like. He charmed you, of course he did. And the truth was maybe I didn't love Jan like I thought I did. Maybe I was infatuated with him, and maybe you still are – it's not the same as love.'

'How do you know?'

'I just do,' Kasia said. 'I know that love can grow and get bigger over time. I know that you have to see someone's flaws as well as their good points and love them all. I know that as much as you try not to think about them, they are always there in your mind, as you sip a coffee, as you hear a song, you turn and look for them because you want to share it with them.'

'Who is he?' Maja asked. 'Tell me.'

'Who is who?'

'The man that you love like this.'

'I don't love anyone.' Kasia turned away from her sister and lay on her back.

'I still know when you're lying, Kasia. I know there's someone.'

Kasia expected her sister to nudge her and ask more questions until she got the truth from her, but she stayed quiet, allowing Kasia to think of Hugo and to wonder whether he was the one she spoke of when she talked about love.

An air raid siren woke Kasia from a dream where she was running after Édith, Hugo and Elodie down narrow alleyways, never quite reaching them.

'Maja!' Kasia nudged her sister awake. 'Do you have a cellar?'

Maja opened her eyes, then closed them again.

'Maja!'

Suddenly, her eyes flew open at the same moment a roar from overhead shook the house.

'It can't be,' Maja murmured.

The siren keened in a pitch that made Kasia's ears ring. 'Do you have a cellar?'

Maja, still in shock, stared at the window. 'It's been so safe, so safe,' Maja mumbled. 'I don't understand.'

'Maja! Do you have a cellar?' Kasia shouted at her.

Her sister stared back dumbly, then shook her head.

'What about your neighbours?'

'I don't know...'

Kasia held on to her sister's shoulders, forcing her to look her in the eye. 'Maja, stay calm. Tell me, where is the nearest shelter? You know this. You would have been told.'

'I, I...' Maja repeated, her face like that of a fish gasping for its last breaths.

Kasia left her sister and raced down the stairs, flung open the front door and looked about the street, hoping to see others making their way somewhere. But it was eerily quiet – the calm before the storm.

Another roar of a plane's engine rumbled above her, and she looked skywards, only seeing the nighttime purple of clouds against a lightening sky.

'What's happening?' Jan's voice carried through his closed bedroom door to her.

She shut the front door and opened his. 'Air raid,' she said. 'Where's the nearest shelter?'

'Two doors down, they have a basement. We can go there,' Jan said hurriedly, as he tried to manoeuvre himself off his bed and into his chair.

'I'll help.' Kasia moved to him.

'No. Get Maja,' he said. 'Don't worry about me. Get Maja, for God's sake! She hates the siren – it paralyses her. Go get her!'

It was then that Kasia saw through the bitter shell that Jan had erected over himself and could see Jan, husband to Maja, who loved her and was afraid for her. She went back to Maja who stood at an open window, her white nightdress glowing in the darkness.

'Maja, we have to—'

Kasia did not finish her words. All she saw was Maja's face turned towards her, her eyes wide, her hair blowing in the breeze as suddenly yellow and orange merged together in hot flames, engulfing them all.

PART THREE

EIGHT MONTHS LATER

1944

FORTY-ONE

THE POLISH GIRL

Vannes, May 1944

'Elodie, where is the bread?' Hugo yelled up to her.

She threw her book to one side and made her way downstairs. 'Where it always is, in the pantry.'

Hugo mumbled his thanks and disappeared for a moment, coming back with the loaf in his hands, his eyes red and bleary, the stubble on his face more than a week old and growing thicker each day.

'You need to sleep,' she told him.

'I need to finish this damned book,' he replied. 'Our Major is getting irritable and wants the draft by June.'

'That's next month. How will you finish in time?'

'It is May already?' he asked.

'It is. It has been for a few weeks now. You need to rest.'

'I can't! The major must get what he wants.'

'I don't know why you're bothering,' she said. 'Antoine says that a huge armada is coming from England, the British and the Americans and the war will be over soon.'

'I've heard the rumours, Elodie, but until I see a boat on that horizon, I have to continue with this mad man.'

'Can I see Antoine today?' she asked. 'I promise I won't go far. I'm twelve now and Antoine is two years older. We are grown-up enough.'

'That's what I worry about,' he said.

'What does that mean?' she asked.

'Nothing. Don't go into the town – don't go near the coast. Stay in the vineyards, somewhere we can find you.'

'You just don't want me to go into town because of the woman.'

'Please don't mention her again.'

'I still say she isn't real.'

'I've seen her five times, Elodie. A woman, dressed in mourning black, but not old, and when I get close to her, she disappears down alleyways as if she never existed. It's death, I tell you it is. My grandfather once told me that death is a woman and not a man, always dressed in black.'

'At first, I thought you were saying it to scare me, but now I'm starting to think that you think it is true.'

'It's more that it's an omen of sorts,' he argued. 'It's probably some widow, but when I'm tired and out of sorts, it chills me when I see her.'

Elodie went to him and wrapped her arms around his waist, her head now reaching just below his chin.

'You're growing too fast,' he said, resting his head on top of hers. 'When you first arrived, you were so tiny that I thought you were younger than ten. But then, you started to eat and then you grew and grew and wouldn't stop growing.'

'And now I can go out and play with Antoine?' she asked.

'You can. Two hours maximum. And don't think I'll fall

asleep and you'll get more time – you can rest assured that I shall not be resting. See? A word pun.' He laughed.

For his sake she laughed along with him, then let him go and picked up Remi to go and find Antoine.

The air was heavily scented with the promise of summer – the slight tanginess of lemons that hung ready to ripen on their branches, the salty breeze that came from the ocean and the woody scent of the soil. Elodie felt that in this air nothing bad could happen. The Germans would simply disappear, life would be 'normal' and Kasia would return. Nothing bad could happen in summer, she was sure of it.

She thought of what Hugo had said as she walked – how she had grown so much. She knew she had physically, but she also felt older, more serious. Before she started talking again, in her mind she had felt like a little child, a scared little girl, but then, as soon as she faced her past, it was like her mind grew up years overnight. She understood things she never had before and was interested in everything. If Zara could see her now, she would be proud of her, she knew she would. They would get along better now that she was not the little girl who asked too many questions. They would talk about boys, about their changing bodies and how hair seemed to be growing from places she never thought hair would grow from.

She wished for Zara, for her mother, for Kasia to be here with them. To have told her what to do when her monthly first came, just two months before, surprising her and making her think she was dying. Hugo had tried the best way he could to explain that she would not die, that the blood was normal and had come home the following day with pads from the pharmacy and a note from the kindly woman at the counter who described exactly what she needed to do.

Now, she met Antoine at their hut where she found him sat on his haunches drawing in the dirt with a stick.

'You're here!' He stood and wiped his hands on his trousers. 'I have something special for us today.'

'What did you find?' She placed Remi on the ground so he could sniff and pee.

'It's not here,' he said. 'Do you remember last year when I told you I had found something that I had to show you?'

She nodded.

'Well, I sort of forgot about it because we weren't able to meet much but then, today, I remembered, and we have to go there now.'

'Where is it?'

'At the beach.'

'Hugo says I am to stay away from the beach.'

'We won't be there long. Please, Elodie. I promise we will be quick. There's something else too. You keep saying that Hugo is seeing a woman, a widow, and he doesn't know who she is?'

'It's a figment of his imagination,' she said. 'He's tired and thinks it is death following him.'

'I think I know where she lives.'

'Are you serious?'

He nodded. 'I saw her in town, then I followed her, and she was headed for that part of the beach.'

'It could be a coincidence,' she said.

'It could be. But what if it isn't?'

Her interest piqued, she said, 'Well, he probably will fall asleep. As long as we aren't gone too long...'

'Great!' Antoine took this as her agreement to their adventure, picked up Remi and led the way to the beach.

All along the coast, barbed wire had sprung up over the months and years, some of it covered with seaweed and other debris from the sea, and some parts still new and shiny with their threat.

'How will the Americans and British get past this?' she

asked, pointing at it as they walked.

'They'll have their ways,' Antoine said confidently. 'I can't see the Americans getting caught on some wire. I saw a movie once, and there was this American man, a soldier and he was tall with big muscles and nothing stopped him, not even bullets.'

'The movies aren't real.'

'I know that. But he was a real American. They're big, you know. They won't get caught in some wire.'

Elodie was not sure that Antoine was correct, but she did not want to argue with him and decided it was best to stay quiet.

'Not far now,' Antoine said, leading them down a sand-strewn path, thick shady trees on either side of them. 'There,' he pointed.

She followed his direction and could just make out a picket fence with weeds growing above it.

'It's a house!' he exclaimed. 'Our new headquarters. No more staying in that dirty hut any more.'

He raced ahead of her, Remi's ears flapping in the wind, and she followed him, eager to see what lay behind the fence and the brambles. The house that stood before her wasn't much better than the hut. The roof seemed to be sagging on one side, the shutters all fallen away, the pathway littered with grass and weeds.

'It's not that great,' she said, taking Remi from him.

'Wait until you see inside,' he said. 'There are all these paintings on the walls – like birds and flowers and things and there is still furniture there. It can be a proper headquarters,' he insisted.

'We can't go in,' she said.

'Why not?'

'You said that you saw that widow going in here.'

'Well, not here exactly.' He grinned. 'Nearby. Not really here at all. I just said that so that you would come.'

'You're sure no one lives here?'

'I'm sure. I promise,' he said.

Despite her misgivings, she followed him inside, noting how the floorboards creaked with her weight.

'I don't think it's safe,' she said. 'The wood is rotten, it could give way.'

'Don't be such a misery,' he said. 'You're starting to sound more and more like Hugo.'

He led her into a dining room, a chandelier hanging above her, the dusty crystals still managing to catch glimpses of light, twirling rainbow colours on the walls.

'Who lived here?' she whispered.

'You don't have to whisper, we are the only ones here.'

'All right,' she said, her voice higher now. 'Who lived here?'

'No idea. But no one has for some time. Come with me – there's this room that you are going to love.'

He walked her through a sitting room and then down a corridor, opening the door with a flourish. The room she entered was pink – all of it. Roses trailed up the walls, linking their stems together like people linking arms. She felt a sense of calm in the room – one which she couldn't quite understand.

'It's amazing, isn't it?' Antoine asked. 'Like you're outdoors but indoors at the same time – the roses are so real that the first time I saw them, I almost thought one of the thorns would prick my finger if I touched them.'

A loud bang came from behind them, making Remi leap from her arms and scutter out of the room.

'It was just the wind,' Antoine said.

'There is no wind.'

'A breeze then.'

Ignoring him, she chased after Remi, finding him sat in the dining room, staring at something on the wall. As she approached, she could see what Remi was looking at – but it wasn't a 'what', it was a *who*.

FORTY-TWO

HUGO

The screams woke him. He sat up quickly, noting that he had fallen asleep with his head on his desk, the ink on a piece of paper smudged with his oily imprint.

'Elodie?' he yelled.

She raced into his room, her face milky white, followed by Antoine, his face much the same.

'What's happened?'

'There's a man!' she screamed.

'Where?' He stood looking around for something to use as a weapon.

'Not here. In the house.'

'This house?'

'No,' Antoine interrupted. 'The house on the beach. The house with all the paintings.'

'Which house with all the paintings?' Hugo asked, holding his breath, not ready for their answer.

'The one with the pink room,' Elodie said, her eyes puffy with tears now.

'What were you doing there? I told you not to go far. It was you, wasn't it, dragging her there?' He pointed at the boy.

'Please, Papa, listen.'

She rarely called him Papa and he didn't want to pressure her into using it, but when she did, he knew he could deny her nothing; the words pierced his heart and made him her slave.

'I'm listening,' he said.

'We went there to make our new headquarters. But there was someone there. A man. A man in a wheelchair.'

'You're sure? Maybe you just imagined it. No one has lived there for years.'

'I'm sure,' Elodie replied. 'Antoine saw him too.'

Hugo looked to the boy, who nodded in agreement.

'In a wheelchair, you say?'

'I swear to you. I saw him.'

Hugo sat back down, feeling the initial surge of adrenaline leave him. 'Perhaps he is a refugee with nowhere to stay. I think we should leave him be.'

'But—' Elodie said.

'There's a woman too,' Antoine said.

'A woman?'

'A woman. A widow. I saw her near the house the other day. Elodie said that you had seen a widow – I think it is her.'

Running a hand over his tired face, feeling the stubble that had grown softer as a full beard threatened to make its home, he resolved that he would go there and clear up this mystery once and for all. Hugo insisted that they stay at home, and that he would go alone.

'Why?' Elodie asked. 'It's not fair. We found him.'

Hearing her whine, he realised that for all that she had grown she was still very much a child, and he should not give in to her every desire.

'You'll stay here,' he said. 'I won't be long.'

Ignoring their protestations, he cycled away towards the house that he had once lived in with Giselle and Nanette.

There was no part of him that wanted to see the house again, and yet, the description of the widow interested him.

He knew, of course, that death was not following him. But after the tide had turned against Germany, after more bombs started to fall, thankfully missing Vannes, and more troops rumbled through their villages, he felt as though death were coming closer each day.

Hugo reached the home he had once shared with his wife and shook his head at its disrepair. He wondered if Maurice ever came here, but seeing the state of the garden, he thought that perhaps not. Maurice could not abide a messy garden.

He walked to the front door and pushed it open easily, hearing the creak of it on its hinges.

'Hello?' he called out, not expecting a reply.

He stepped into the dining room, then the living room and kitchen, and finally the pink room which had been Giselle's art room. He sat on the chaise and looked at the roses trailing up the wall and remember the day she had painted them – delighted with their realness, telling him to reach out and touch one and see if a thorn pricked his finger.

Dusting his trousers off as he stood, and wiping away the memories from his mind before he returned home, he said a final goodbye to the room and to Giselle.

Just as he reached the front door, a strange feeling overcame him. The hairs on the back of his neck stood to attention as he felt a cold shiver down his spine. He turned slowly, half expecting to see the widow woman, death herself there behind him, waiting with her scythe and laughed when he found the hallway empty.

It was then he looked to the dining room and noticed handprints on the wall where the false door was situated.

He walked up to it, noting that some of the handprints were low down and some a foot or so higher. Looking at the handprints low down, he saw that they were large, not a child's hand,

and would, in fact be the correct height for someone in a wheelchair.

He placed his hand where he knew the levers would give way once pressed, and with some force put his weight on the door, hearing the magic click as it opened.

As silly as it was to have a secret door in a house, he had actually been delighted by Giselle's suggestion of it. 'Think of it – we can have a secret passageway to different rooms in the house, maybe even a secret room so that when we have children and they are being loud and unruly, we can simply disappear for a while.'

Now, he let the door creak open.

'You don't have to do that,' a voice came from behind him.

He turned to see a man in a wheelchair, thick-rimmed glasses on his face, his hair parted down the middle, making him almost look like a child.

'There's no one in there. I'm the only one here.'

'Who are you?' Hugo asked. 'And what are you doing in my house?'

'Your house?' he asked.

'Whose house would it be – it certainly isn't yours.'

The man sneered at him. 'Well, I was under the impression that it was Maurice's house.'

'And how do you know Maurice?' Hugo was becoming impatient now. 'No matter what Maurice has told you, this is, in fact *my* house.'

'Well then, I suppose we have a problem,' the man said.

Hugo walked towards him, not sure of what he was going to do or say when he reached him.

'You can't hit a man in a wheelchair – that's not what you're thinking of doing, is it?' the man asked.

Hugo hated the way he talked – it was nasally, and every sentence seemed to be laced with bitterness. 'I wasn't going to hit you.' He smiled at him. 'I was simply going to wheel you out of my house and to the chief of police and let him know that someone had stolen my property.'

'And how have I stolen it? How can one steal a property? Think about it.' He tapped the side of his head. 'And here I was thinking you were an intelligent man, Hugo.'

Hugo opened his mouth to respond, but then shut it again.

'Yes. I know who you are.'

'Maurice told you, no doubt,' Hugo rallied.

'A good guess, but no. I heard all about you last year in Paris when someone we both know came to visit my wife.'

'Kasia,' the words left his mouth in one breath, and he leaned backwards to place his hands on a dining chair.

'That's the one.'

'Where is she?'

The man shrugged.

'Then you're Jan, I presume?' Hugo said, and was delighted to see the man's face register surprise.

'So what if I am?'

'And I also would presume that the woman that has been seen here is your wife?' Hugo said.

'My wife?' Jan laughed. 'Of course, yes, my wife.'

'Where is Kasia?' Hugo asked again. 'Is she with you and your wife?'

'In a manner of speaking, yes.'

Footsteps alerted Hugo to the fact that they were not alone.

'My dear!' Jan sang out, 'come and meet our guest.'

The widow that Hugo had seen about town walked into the room, a veil covering her face, a basket of potatoes in her hand.

'Hugo...' the voice came from under the veil.

'Kasia?' he whispered.

She lifted her veil. The right side of her face puckered red and scarred. 'It's me. Well, almost.'

FORTY-THREE

KASIA

She couldn't quite believe that Hugo was standing in front of her, and Jan at her side in his wheelchair. It seemed absurd to her, and she felt awkward with her veil lifted and her face on show.

He moved nearer to her, standing still in front of her, then lifted his arm and traced the burned skin with his fingers.

'You're alive,' he said, his voice breaking.

'I am.'

'And so am I,' Jan butted in. 'And I'm hungry. Don't you think you should continue this later and feed the disabled man instead?'

She turned to Jan, then back to Hugo. 'Come with me into the kitchen. Let me make him something. We can talk in private in there too, his wheelchair is too wide to get through all the doors.'

'I can hear you, you know,' Jan snapped.

Ignoring him, she walked to the kitchen, feeling Hugo close at her back.

'I don't even know where to start,' he said. 'When? How?'

'I came last November,' she said.

'Last November?' Hugo exclaimed. 'And you never thought to come to me, to Elodie, to tell us you were alive?'

'I wanted to, I did.' She pulled out a chair and sat down at the table, the wooden top still dusty and uncared for.

He sat too and reached across to take her hands. 'Why didn't you come to me?'

'Because of this,' she let go of his hand and pointed at her face, 'and because of him.' She nodded to the doorway and beyond.

'I wouldn't have cared about your face, Kasia! Did you really think I would?'

She shook her head. 'I wasn't sure, Hugo. I knew we became friends before I left – but to turn up at your door with an old boyfriend in a wheelchair? Do you really think you would have welcomed me with open arms?'

'I would have tried,' he said.

She smiled. 'Jan is difficult to care for. He can't walk at all, I have to help him bathe, I have to feed him. Would you have still tried if you knew that was what would have to happen each day?'

'Why on earth are you with him? Where is your sister?'

Kasia breathed out heavily, then retook his hand in hers, feeling the little callouses on his fingers, the ridges of his palm. 'She died. An allied bomb of all things. I was with her and managed to get free, but she wasn't so lucky.'

'And you wanted to come home?' he said. 'You wanted to come back to me and Elodie?'

She nodded. 'I didn't know where else to go. I contacted Maurice after I had been released from hospital and he said to come here. I had to bring Jan. He had no one else. Maja was gone, his ability to care for himself was gone. I couldn't just leave him.'

'You could,' Hugo said, making her smile once more.

'I wish I had that kind of resolve, but I don't. He loved Maja in his own way, and she him. I didn't feel I could leave him.'

'Do you still love him?' he asked.

She laughed and the strain on her skin made her wince.

'It still hurts?' he asked.

'It does. Maurice says that it is a good thing – it means that the nerves are not dead.'

'I assume that the laughter means that you don't love Jan?'

'You assume correctly.'

'Well, I think it's obvious what we have to do now.' Hugo stood, readying himself to leave.

She began to cry, the right eye not yet producing tears so that moisture only fell from her left. She knew he had to leave – of course he did – he had Elodie to think of.

'Why are you crying?' he asked.

'Because you're leaving,' she said.

'Not without you I'm not.' He held out his hand for her to take. 'And Jan.'

'And Jan? 'You're sure?'

'I've never been so sure of anything in my life. I love you, Kasia, or hadn't you realised that yet?'

She thought of what she had told Édith about love – how it was patient, how it was kind.

She took his hand and stood. 'You love me?'

'I do,' he said, grinning from ear to ear.

'And I you,' she said, leaning in to kiss him gently on the lips.

EPILOGUE

THE POLISH GIRL

September 1944

She found Maurice in the graveyard, his hand touching the grave of his daughter and granddaughter, his head bowed whilst his moustache twitched as he spoke quiet words.

He only looked up when she reached out to place her hand on his.

'Elodie.' He smiled.

'I didn't see you in town,' she said. 'I knew you would be here.'

'Too early to celebrate just yet,' he said.

'But the Americans and British are here!' she exclaimed, caught up with the excitement at seeing the soldiers march through the town where everyone had congregated, waving flags, blowing kisses at the soldiers. 'Antoine is disappointed, though,' she said.

'Why?'

'Not all the soldiers look like they do in the movies. He said that they are scrawny and too short.'

'Ah, young Antoine has a lot to learn about real life, I fear.' Maurice made to stand, pushing himself up with one hand, so that she reached out and helped him.

'My knees are not what they used to be. I can't sit for long. Need to keep the old bones moving. Will you walk with me?'

She nodded in agreement and linked her arm through his.

'How is it with Kasia being home?' he asked, after they had reached the wrought-iron gates.

She thought back over the past few months – the initial delight at seeing Kasia and then the fear when she saw the scars on her face. She had reached out to her, stroking the puckered skin on her face, crying tears of relief. But then, there was Jan.

Whilst she had once thought of Hugo as moody, Jan surpassed that with abundance. He would only eat what he liked and did not care when Hugo or Kasia told him they could not procure the foods he wanted. He would shout and grumble if he wasn't taken out once a day, precisely at 2 p.m., never seemingly caring about the rumble of planes overhead or the *pip pip* of gunfire that rattled through the air.

Yet, she had warmed to him, and he to her. He read to her and taught her about geography and history and would have moments when he would smile, laugh even and tell her silly made-up stories. Not that he would do that with Hugo or Kasia though and that bothered her – why couldn't he see how much they cared for him, with no thanks for their efforts?

'It's fine.' She settled for this as her answer.

'Just fine?'

'Why do you and Hugo not speak any more?' she asked. Maurice had been coming to the house regularly to tend to Jan, and Hugo had always made excuses to leave, to go back to the magical house on the beach that he was preparing for them to move into.

'The past,' Maurice said. 'So many things were unsaid for so long, and then, when a small disagreement emerged, I suppose it seemed easier to keep it going. Otherwise, we would have to speak a lot – not just the pleasantries but about everything – about the unsaid things.'

'Just say them,' she said. 'The unsaid things. Just say them.'

'It's not that simple...' Maurice started.

'It is. I didn't speak for so long. I was scared of my voice, what it would say. It is because I spoke that my family died.'

Maurice placed both his hands on her shoulders. 'That is simply not true,' he said. 'The war killed them. Not you.'

She nodded, even though she did not agree with him – she thought she would never agree with anyone telling her it was not her fault. The guilt was something she would have to live with, would have to become used to and maybe one day it would ease a little.

'Did Hugo kill your daughter and granddaughter?' she asked, already knowing the rumours that flew about like swarms of wasps in the summer air from Antoine – that Maurice blamed Hugo.

'No. No, he did not.'

'But you blame him?'

Maurice shrugged. 'These are the unsaid things that I talked about.'

'But, if I am not to blame for my family, then how can you blame Hugo? How can you tell me I am innocent and not Hugo? I don't understand.'

'Maybe you are too young to understand,' Maurice said, turning away from her to get his bicycle.

'Maybe I do understand,' she said to his back, as he pedalled away from her. 'Maybe I understand it all.'

. . .

That evening Hugo was in a jubilant mood and even with Jan's grumblings, his joy could not be contained.

'He's gone! Arrested! I saw it all with my own eyes!' He twirled in the middle of the kitchen, a spattering of red wine leaping over the rim of his glass, finding its way to the floor. 'And guess what? Guess? Guess what happened?'

Elodie looked to Kasia to see if she would guess, but she simply shook her head.

'Who cares?' Jan said.

'I do!' Hugo exclaimed. 'Go on, guess.'

Elodie was the only one who wanted to play the game and guessed that he had cried for his mama, or that he had tried to run away and got caught by an old lady with a rolling pin. Soon though, she tired of the game and begged Hugo to tell her.

'Caught with his trousers around his ankles!' Hugo cackled. 'Applying his ointment to his piles when they charged in and took him outside, not even giving him a chance to pull them up!'

Elodie laughed at the thought, as did Kasia, even Jan had a smirk on his face.

'And it was all down to me!' Hugo pronounced. 'I vowed I'd get him and his whimsy one day and I did. I told him to stay in his offices, even when the others were fleeing. I told him I would vouch for him, keep him safe – and then *voilà* – I told the Americans where he was and who he was!'

'Bravo!' Kasia clapped her hands at him and Elodie watched as he bent down to kiss her.

She squirmed at the display of affection between them, and as much as she was happy that they were together, she could not ever get used to them kissing each other.

Jan pulled a sickly face at her, and she laughed – at least he was sick of it too.

'What will you do with his manuscript?' Kasia asked.

'Print it,' Hugo said, slopping more wine into his glass.

'Why would you do that? You're giving him what he wants,' Jan chimed in.

'Not so, not so my friend. You see, I will print it exactly as he said it – the lies, half-truths and ridiculous tales he wove. And then, I shall get a cartoonist to draw a picture of him for the very final page with his trousers around his ankles, his piles on show for all to see!'

'I think it will be a bestseller,' Kasia said, and Hugo moved towards her once more to kiss her.

Thankfully, there was a knock on the door, stopping Hugo from displaying his affection and Elodie ran to the door to welcome anyone who would disturb it.

On the doorstep stood Maurice, his hat in his hands as if he were paying respects at a funeral.

'Who is it?' Hugo called out, then stuck his head around to see. 'Oh.'

'May I come in?' Maurice asked.

Hugo nodded. 'Jan's in here,' he said, then disappeared back into the sitting room.

'I'm not here for Jan.' Maurice followed him and Elodie trailed behind.

'Oh,' Hugo said again.

'I think it's time we talk, Hugo.'

'Is it indeed,' Hugo said.

Kasia went to welcome Maurice, but Hugo stepped forward, blocking her path. Elodie held her breath and she imagined that Kasia and Jan were doing the same – what was he going to say?

It felt like a minute or more passed before Hugo gave a slight nod of the head at his study and the pair disappeared behind the door.

Elodie raced to it and set her ear against it, desperate to hear of the unsaid things, desperate to know what had happened all those years before.

'Leave them,' Jan said quietly. 'Leave them.'

'Will they become friends again?' she asked, looking to both Kasia and Jan.

'I don't know,' Kasia said. 'But at least they have finally found their voices.'

A LETTER FROM CARLY

Thank you so much for reading *All the Courage We Have Found*. If you'd like to keep up to date with all my latest releases, you can sign up at the following link. Your email address will never be shared, and you can unsubscribe at any time.

www.bookouture.com/carly-schabowski

This book was not only interesting to write, but I felt that there was a need to do so – to shed light on the many women who worked tirelessly during WWII in a multitude of roles. One such role was that of the resistance and the Special Operations Executive which relied on women to spy behind enemy lines, to operate radios and relay signals, espionage, and much, much more.

Indeed, it was the secrets that these women kept that made me think of our everyday lives and the secrets we keep from others. This theme became interwoven through the lives of Hugo, Kasia, and the Polish girl, hopefully showing their bravery in the face of differing adversities.

Lastly, those women in Poland who set up their own resistance groups in order to help those in the ghettos, whilst risking their lives, touched me deeply. And this book is a compilation of so many stories of female spies and resistance members rolled into the character of Kasia, to hopefully shed some light on their courage and sacrifices.

KEEP IN TOUCH WITH CARLY

twitter.com/@carlyschab11

BIBLIOGRAPHY

Books

Alexievich, Svetlana. *Last Witnesses: An Oral History of the Children of World War II*. Translated by Richard Pevear and Larissa Volokhonsky. Penguin Random House, 2019.

Batalion, Judy. *The Light of Days: Women Fighters of the Jewish Resistance – A New York Times Bestseller*. Little, Brown Book Group. Kindle Edition.

Faulks, Sebastian. *Girl At The Lion d'Or*. Random House. Kindle Edition.

Hebditch, David. *Covert Radio Agents, 1939–1945: Signals From Behind Enemy Lines*. Pen and Sword Military, 2021.

Marks, Leo. *Between Silk and Cyanide*. The History Press. Kindle Edition.

O'Connor, Bernard. *Elzbieta Zawacka: Polish soldier and courier during World War Two*. Lulu.com

Strauss, Gwen. *The Nine*. Manilla Press, Bonnier Books UK. Kindle Edition.

National Archives

Reference: HS
Title: Records of Special Operations Executive
Date: 1936-1992
Held by: The National Archives, Kew
Legal status: Public Record(s)
Language: English
Creator: Foreign and Commonwealth Office, SOE Adviser, 1968–2002
Foreign Office, SOE Adviser, 1946–1968
Foreign Office, Special Operations Executive, 1945–1946
Ministry of Economic Warfare, Special Operations Executive, 1940–1945

Websites

1 September 1939: The Beginning of Hell, Polish History, https://polishhistory.pl/1-september-1939-the-beginning-of-hell/

90 Years of the Polish Cipher Bureau, Warsaw Institute, https://warsawinstitute.org/90-years-polish-cipher-bureau/

A Call to Spy – The Story of Vera Atkins, https://www.hhhistory.com/2022/01/vera-atkins-successful-wwii-british-spy.html

Bletchley Park remembers Polish code breakers, BBC, 14 July 2011, https://www.bbc.co.uk/news/uk-england-beds-bucks-herts-14141406

Celebrating Female Cryptologic Pioneers During National Women's History Month & All Year Long! Cyptologic Foundation, https://cryptologicfoundation.org/what-we-do/stimulate/women-in-cryptology.html

First Breaking of Enigma Code by the Team of Polish Cipher Bureau, 1932–1939, Milestones, ETHW, https://ethw.org/Milestones:First_Breaking_of_Enigma_Code_by_the_Team_of_Polish_Cipher_Bureau,_1932-1939

The Early Days of the Polish Cipher Bureau, 1919–1920, The National Museum of Computing, https://www.tnmoc.org/events/2021/3/17/the-early-days-of-the-polish-cipher-bureau-1919-1920

Journal Articles

Mostafa Said Dalia, Literary Representations of Trauma, Memory, and Identity in the Novels of Elias Khoury and Rabīʿ Jābir, Source: Journal of Arabic Literature, Vol. 40, No. 2 (2009), pp. 208–236, Published by: Brill, Stable URL: http://www.jstor.org/stable/25598005

Robben, C.G.M, Antonius, How Traumatized Societies Remember: The Aftermath of Argentina's Dirty War, , Cultural Critique, No. 59 (Winter, 2005), pp. 120–164, Published by: University of Minnesota Press, Stable URL: http://www.jstor.org/stable/4489199

Walker, Janet, The Traumatic Paradox: Documentary Films, Historical Fictions, and Cataclysmic Past Events, Source: Signs, Vol. 22, No. 4 (Summer, 1997), pp. 803–825, Published by: The University of Chicago Press, Stable URL: http://www.jstor.org/stable/3175221

ACKNOWLEDGEMENTS

I would like to thank Kathryn Taussig for her wonderful suggestions and my lovely new editor, Jess Whitlum-Cooper, who I am so excited to be working with!

A huge thanks to my agent Jo Bell for constantly talking me down when I am doubting myself and my writing, and a big thank you to Alison Boyes, an awesome friend, who still helped me with the translations despite going through so much herself.

Printed in Great Britain
by Amazon

42451267R00172